TAKEN

TAKEN

ROBERT CRAIS

First published in Great Britain in 2012 by Orion Books,
an imprint of The Orion Publishing Group Ltd
Orion House, 5 Upper Saint Martin's Lane
London WC2H 9EA

An Hachette UK Company

1 3 5 7 9 10 8 6 4 2

A CIP catalogue record for this book is
available from the British Library.

ISBN (Hardback) 978 1 4091 1603 5
ISBN (Export Trade Paperback) 978 1 4091 1604 2

Printed in Great Britain by
Clays Ltd, St Ives plc

The Orion Publishing Group's policy is to use papers that are natural,
renewable and recyclable products and made from wood grown in
sustainable forests. The logging and manufacturing processes are expected
to conform to the environmental regulations of the country of origin.

www.orionbooks.co.uk

for Aaron Priest

more than an agent
my good and trusted friend
with love

"Cut you,
 I bleed.
 Our name is love."

                                        — *Tattooed Beach Sluts*

Jiminy Cricket: Hey, where ya goin'?
Pinocchio: I'm going to find him!

PROLOGUE:
JACK AND KRISTA

Jack Berman wrapped his arms around his girlfriend, Krista Morales, and watched his breath fog in the cold desert air. Twenty minutes after midnight, fourteen miles south of Rancho Mirage in the otherwise impenetrable darkness of the Anza-Borrego Desert, Jack and Krista were lit in the harsh purple glare of the lights that blossomed from Danny Trehorn's truck, Jack so much in love with this girl his heart beat with hers.

Trehorn gunned his engine.

"You guys comin' or what?"

Krista snuggled deeper into Jack's arms.

"Let's stay a little longer. Just us. Not them. I want to tell you something."

Jack called to his friend.

"Mañana, dude. We're gonna hang."

"We roll early, bro. See you at nine."

"See us at noon."

"Pussy! We'll wake your ass up!"

Trehorn dropped back into his truck, and spun a one-eighty back toward town, *Ride of the Valkyries* blaring on his sound system. Chuck Lautner and Deli Blake tucked Chuck's ancient Land Cruiser in tight behind Trehorn, their headlamps flashing over Jack's Mustang, which was parked up the old county road where the ground was more even. They had come out to show

Krista a drug smuggler's airplane that had crashed in 1972 because Krista wanted to see it.

Jack grew colder as their tail lights receded, and the desert grew darker. A thin crescent moon and cloudy star field gave them enough light to see, but little more.

Jack said, "Dark."

She didn't answer.

Jack said, "Cold."

He snuggled closer, spooning into her back, both of them staring at nothing. Jack wondered what she was seeing.

Krista had been pensive all night even though she had pushed them to come, and now her wanting to tell him something felt ominous. Jack had the sick feeling she was pregnant or dumping him. Krista was two months from graduating *summa cum laude* at Loyola Marymount in Los Angeles, and had taken a job in D.C. Jack had dropped out of USC.

Jack nuzzled into her hair.

"Are we okay?"

She pushed away far enough to study him, then smiled.

"There have never been two people better than us. I am totally in love with you."

"You had me worried."

"Thanks for getting Danny to bring us out here. I don't think he wanted to come."

"It's a long drive if you've seen it a million times. He stopped coming out here in high school."

According to Trehorn, the twin-engine Cessna 310 had crashed while bringing in a load of coke at night during a sandstorm. A local drug dealer named Greek Cisneros cleared enough cactus and rocks to fashion a landing strip in the middle of the desert twenty miles outside Palm Springs, and used the airplane to bring cocaine and marijuana up from Mexico, almost always at night when the outline of the runway was marked by burning tubs of gasoline. On the night of the crash, the right wingtip hooked into the ground, the landing gear collapsed, and the left wing snapped off outside the left engine. Fuel pouring from the ruptured fuel tanks ignited, enveloping the airplane in flames. The engines and instruments had long ago been salvaged for parts, but the broken airframe remained where it died, rusting, corroded, and covered with generations of overlapping graffiti and spray-painted initials: LJ+DF, eat me, PSHS#1.

Krista took his hand, and tugged him toward the plane.

"Come with me. I want to show you something."

"Can't you tell me about it in the car? I'm cold."

"No, not in the car. This is important."

Jack followed her along the fuselage to the tail, wondering what she wanted to show him about this stupid airplane, but instead she led him onto the overgrown remains of the runway. She stared into the darkness that masked the desert. Her smart, black eyes shined like jewels filled with starlight. Jack touched her hair.

"Kris?"

They had known each other for one year, two months, and sixteen days. They had been head-over-heels, crazy, there-and-back, inside-out, bottom-to-top in love for five months, three weeks, and eleven days. He hadn't told her the truth about himself until after she declared her love. If he had secrets then, she had secrets now.

Krista took his hand in both of hers, giving him the serious, all-business eyes.

"This place is special to my family."

Jack had no idea what she was talking about.

"A drug runner's airstrip?"

"This place, right here between the mountains, it's a place easily found by people coming from the south, for all the same reasons the drug dealers put their landing strip here. When my mother was seven, coyotes brought her up through the desert from the south. Mom and her sister and two cousins. A man with a hearse was waiting here at this airplane to drive them into town."

Jack said, "No shit?"

Krista laughed, but her laugh was unsure.

"I never knew. She only told me a couple of weeks ago."

"I don't care."

"Hey. I'm giving you momentous family history, and you don't care?"

"I mean that she's illegal—undocumented. Who gives a shit?"

Krista tipped back to look up at him, then suddenly grabbed his ears and kissed him.

"Undocumented, but you don't have to go all PC."

Krista's mother had described a twelve-day trip on foot, in cars, and in a delivery truck where it got so hot that an old man died. The last leg of their journey had been in a covered pickup truck at night past the Salton Sea and across a sixteen-mile stretch of desert to the old crash site. The man with the hearse had driven them to a supermarket parking lot at the eastern edge of Coachella, where her uncle was waiting.

She looked south into the darkness as if she could see her mother's footsteps.

"I wouldn't be here if she hadn't come through this place. She wouldn't have met my dad. I wouldn't have met you. I wouldn't exist."

Krista looked up, and her face was all *summa-cum-laude* focused.

"Can you imagine what her journey must have been like? I'm her kid, and I can't even begin."

She was starting to say more when Jack heard a far-off squeal. He stood taller, listening, but didn't say anything until he heard it again.

"You hear it?"

Krista turned as the faint sound of a muffled engine reached them, and two lurching shapes appeared in the dim starlight. Jack studied them for a moment, and realized they were lightless trucks crawling toward them across the desert. Jack felt a stab of fear, and whispered frantically into her ear.

"This sucks, man. Let's get out of here."

"No, no, no—I want to see. Shh."

"They could be drug runners. We don't want to be here."

"Just wait!"

She pulled him to the far side of the airplane, where they settled into a low depression between the cactus.

A large box truck emerged from the dark like a ship appearing out of a fog. It rumbled onto the overgrown landing strip, and stopped less than thirty yards away. No brake lights flared when it stopped. Jack tried to make himself even smaller, and wished he had pulled Kris away.

A moment later, the cab creaked open, and two men climbed out. The driver walked a few yards in front of the truck, then studied a glowing hand-held device. This deep in the desert, Jack thought it was probably a GPS.

While the driver studied his GPS, the passenger went to the back of the truck, and pushed the box door open with a loud clatter. The man said something in Spanish, then Jack heard soft voices as silhouette people climbed from the truck.

Jack whispered, "What are they doing?"

"Shh. This is amazing."

"They gotta be illegals."

"Shh."

Krista shifted position, and Jack cringed with a fresh burst of fear. She was taking pictures with her cell phone.

"Stop. They'll see us."

"No one can see."

The people emerging stayed near the truck as if they were confused. So many people appeared Jack did not see how they had all fit inside. As many as thirty people stood uneasily in the brush, speaking in low murmurs with alien accents that Jack strained to identify.

"That isn't Spanish. What are they speaking, Chinese?"

Krista lowered her phone and strained to listen, too.

"A few Spanish speakers, but most of them sound Asian. Something else, too. Is that Arabic?"

The man who opened the truck returned to the driver, and spoke clearly in Spanish. Jack figured these two were the coyotes—guides who were hired to sneak people illegally into the U.S. He leaned closer to Krista, who was fluent in Spanish.

"What did he say?"

"'Where in hell are they? Those bastards are supposed to be here.'"

The driver mumbled something neither Jack nor Krista understood, then visibly jumped when three sets of headlights topped by roll-bar lamps snapped on a hundred yards behind the box truck, lighting the desert between in stark relief. Three off-road trucks roared forward, bouncing high on their oversized tires. The two coyotes shouted, and a scrambled chatter rose from the milling people. The driver ran into the desert, and his partner ran back to their truck. He emerged with a shotgun, and ran after his friend even as two of the incoming pickups skidded in a loose circle around the box truck, kicking up murky clouds of dust. The third chased after the fleeing men, and gunfire flashed in the dark. The crowd broke in every direction, some crying, some screaming, some scrambling back into the box truck as if they could hide.

Jack pulled Krista backward, then jumped up and ran.

"Run! C'mon, run!"

He ran hard toward his Mustang, then realized Krista wasn't with him. Men with clubs and shotguns jumped from the pickups to chase down fleeing people. Krista was still between the cactus, taking pictures.

Jack started to shout for her, but stopped himself, not wanting to draw attention. He and Krista were outside the light, and hidden by darkness. He risked a sharp hiss instead.

"Kris—"

She shook her head, telling him she was fine, and resumed taking pictures. Jack ran back to her, and grabbed her arm. Hard.

"Let's go!"

"All right. Okay—"

They started to rise as four Asian women came around the plane's tail and ran past less than ten yards away.

A man with a shotgun came around the tail after them, shouting in Spanish, and Jack wondered if these poor women could even understand what he said. Then the man stopped, and stood absolutely still as if he were a cardboard cutout against the night sky.

Jack held his breath, and prayed. He wondered why the man was standing so still, then saw the man was wearing night-vision goggles.

The man was looking at them.

There in the starlit desert landscape where no one could hear the shots, the man lifted his shotgun, and aimed at Jack Berman.

PART 1

ELVIS COLE:
six days after
they were taken

1.

When people call a private investigator because someone they love is missing, especially a child, the fear bubbles in their voice like boiling lard. When Nita Morales called that morning about her missing adult daughter, she didn't sound afraid. She was irritated. Ms. Morales phoned because the Sunday *Los Angeles Times Magazine* published a story about me eight weeks ago, rehashing a case where I cleared an innocent man who had been convicted of multiple homicides. The magazine people came to my office, took a couple of pretty good pictures, and made me sound like a cross between Philip Marlowe and Batman. If I were Nita Morales, I would have called me, too.

Her business, Hector Sports & Promotions, was on the east side of the Los Angeles River near the Sixth Street Bridge, not far from where giant radioactive ants boiled up from the sewer to be roasted by James Arness in the 1954 classic, *Them!* It was a warehouse area now, but no less dangerous. Buildings were layered with gang tags and graffiti, and signs warned employees to lock their cars. Steel bars covered windows and concertina wire lined roofs, but not to keep out the ants.

That spring morning, 8:55 A.M., a low haze filled the sky with a glare so bright I squinted behind the Wayfarers as I found the address. Hector

Sports & Promotions was in a newer building with a gated, ten-foot chain-link fence enclosing their parking lot.

A young Latin guy with thick shoulders and dull eyes came out when I stopped, as if he had been waiting.

"You the magazine guy?"

The magazine guy.

"That's right. Elvis Cole. I have a ten o'clock with Ms. Morales."

"I gotta unlock the gate. See the empty spot where it says *Delivery?* Park there. You might want to put up the top and lock it."

"Think it'll be safe?"

That would be me, flashing the ironic smile at their overkill battlestar security.

"For sure. They only steal clean cars."

That would be him, putting me in my place.

He shook his head sadly as I drove past.

"I had an old Vette like this, I'd show some love. I'd pop those dents, for sure."

That would be him, rubbing it in. My Jamaica yellow 1966 Corvette Stingray convertible is a classic. It's also dirty.

He locked the parking gate behind us, told me he was Nita Morales's assistant, and led me inside. We passed through an outer office with a counter for customers, and a man and woman at separate desks. The man and woman both looked over, and the man held up the Sunday magazine issue with my story. Embarrassing.

We passed through a door onto the shop floor where fifteen or twenty people were operating machines that sewed logos on baseball caps and photo-inked mugs. Nita Morales had a glass office on the far side of the shop where she could see the floor and everything happening there. She saw us coming, and stepped from behind her desk to greet the magazine guy when we entered. Tight smile. Dry hand. All business.

"Hi, Mr. Cole, I'm Nita. You look like your picture."

"The one where I look stupid or the one where I look confused?"

"The one where you look like a smart, determined detective who gets the job done."

I liked her immediately.

"Would you like something? Coffee or a soft drink?"

"No, thanks. I'm good."

"Jerry, where's the swag bag? You left it in here, right?"

She explained as Jerry the Assistant handed me a white plastic bag.

"We made a little gift for you this morning. Here, take a look."

A large white T-shirt and a matching baseball cap were in the bag. I smiled at the cap, then held up the T-shirt. "Elvis Cole Detective Agency" had been silk-screened onto the front in black and red letters, with "world's greatest detective" in smaller letters below it. An emblem saying the same had been sewn on the front of the cap.

"You like them?"

"I like them a lot."

I put them back in the bag.

"This is very cool, but I haven't agreed to help you. You understand that, don't you?"

"You will. You're going to find her. It won't be hard for the World's Greatest Detective."

She got that from the magazine.

"The 'world's greatest' thing was a joke, Ms. Morales. The guy who wrote the article put it in the story like I meant it. I didn't. It was a joke."

"I have some things to show you. Give me a second. I have to get them together."

She dismissed the assistant, and returned to her desk while I looked around. Shelves along the wall opposite her desk were lined with mugs, cups, bobbleheads, T-shirts, caps, giveaway toys, and dozens of other promotional items. Want team shirts for your kid's soccer club? They could do it. Want the name of your insurance agency on cheap plastic cups for the Knights of Columbus barbeque? That's what they did. Photos of youth teams dotted the walls, the kids all wearing shirts made by Hector Sports.

I said, "Who's Hector?"

"My husband. He started the company twenty-two years ago, silk-screening T-shirts. I run it now. Cancer."

"Sorry."

"Me, too. Seven years, this June."

"You must run it well. Business looks good."

"No one's getting rich, but we're doing okay. Here, let's sit."

She came around her desk so we could sit together on matching metal chairs. Nita Morales was in her mid-forties, built sturdy, and wore a conservative blue business skirt and ruffled white shirt. Her sleek black hair showed no gray, and framed her broad face well. Her nails were carefully done, and her wedding ring was still in place, seven years later, this June.

She held out a snapshot.

"This is who you're going to find. This is Krista."

"I haven't agreed yet, Ms. Morales."

"You will. Look."

"We haven't talked price."

"Look at her."

Krista Morales had a heart-shaped face, golden skin, and a smile that dimpled her right cheek. Her eyes were deep chocolate, and her hair glistened with the deep black sheen of a crow's wing in the sun. I smiled at the picture, then handed it back.

"Pretty."

"Smart. She's going to graduate *summa cum laude* in two months from Loyola Marymount. Then she's going to work in Washington as a congressional aide. After that, maybe the first Latina president, you think?"

"Wow. You must be proud."

"Beyond proud. Her father and I, we didn't graduate high school. I had no English until I was nine. This business, we built with sweat and the grace of God. Krista—"

She ticked off the points on her fingers.

"—highest GPA in her class, editor of the student newspaper, National

Honor Society, Phi Beta Kappa. This girl is making our dreams come true."

She suddenly stopped, and stared through the glass wall into the shop. Even with the angle, I saw her eyes glisten.

"They're good people, but you have to watch them."

"I understand. Take your time."

She cleared her throat as she pulled herself together, then Nita Morales's face darkened from a sunrise of pride to the iron sky of a thunderstorm. She put Krista's picture aside, and handed me a page showing a name and Palm Springs address. The name was Jack Berman.

"She went to Palm Springs seven days ago. With a boy. Her boyfriend."

She said "boyfriend" as if it were another word for "mistake."

She described the boyfriend, and didn't have anything good to say. A USC dropout without a job and little future. Just the type of boy who could derail her daughter's ambitions.

I glanced at the address.

"He lives in Palm Springs?"

"Somewhere in L.A., I think. His family has the house in Palm Springs, or it might belong to a friend, but I don't really know. Krista hasn't told me much about him."

Old story. The less Krista told her, the less she could criticize. I put the address aside.

"Okay. So how is she missing?"

"She went for the weekend. That's what she told me, and she always tells me where she's going and exactly how long she'll be gone. But she's been gone now for a week, and she won't return my calls or texts, and I know it's that boy."

That boy.

"How long have Krista and that boy been together?"

Thinking about it seemed to sicken her.

"Six or seven months. I've only met him two or three times, but I don't like him. He has this attitude."

She said "attitude" as if it was another word for "disease."

"Do they live together?"

Her face darkened even more.

"She shares an apartment near campus with a girl. She doesn't have time for that boy."

She had time to go to Palm Springs. I had seen this story five hundred times, and knew where it was going. The good-girl daughter rebelling against the dominant mother.

"Ms. Morales, twenty-one-year-old women go away with their boy-friends. Sometimes, they have such a good time, they turn off their phones and stay a few extra days. Unless you have reason to believe otherwise, that's all this is. She'll come back."

Nita Morales studied me for a moment as if she was disappointed, then picked up her smart phone and touched the screen.

"Do you speak Spanish?"

"A few words, but, no, not really."

"I'll translate. This is the second call. I recorded it—"

Nita Morales's voice came from the tiny speaker as she answered the incoming call.

"Krista, is this you? What is going on out there?"

A young woman fired off rapid-fire Spanish. Then Nita's voice inter-rupted.

"Speak English. Why are you carrying on like this?"

The young woman shifted to English with a heavy accent.

"Mama, I know you want me to practice the English, but I cannot—"

She resumed a torrent of Spanish, whereupon Nita paused the playback.

"She's pretending. This exaggerated accent, the poor English. My daugh-ter has no accent. This isn't the way she speaks."

"What is she saying?"

"She began by saying they're concerned because they didn't get the money."

"Who's they?"

She held up a finger.

"Listen—"

She resumed the playback. A young male voice took Krista's place, and also spoke Spanish. He sounded calm and reasonable, and spoke several seconds before Nita paused the recording.

"You get any of it?"

I shook my head, feeling slightly embarrassed.

"He's saying he has expenses to cover. He wants me to wire five hundred dollars, and as soon as he gets the money he'll see that Krista gets home."

I sat forward.

"What just happened here? Was Krista abducted?"

Nita rolled her eyes, and waved me off.

"Of course not. The rest is just more Spanish. I'll tell you what they said."

"No. Play it back. I want to hear the emotional content."

The playback resumed. Nita repeatedly interrupted. The man remained calm. He waited her out each time she interrupted, then resumed as if he was reading from a script.

The recording finally ended, and Nita arched her eyebrows.

"He apologized for asking for the money. He told me where to wire it, and promised to take good care of Krista while they waited. Then he thanked me for being so helpful."

She dropped the phone to her desk. Plunk.

I said, "This was a ransom demand. It sounds like she's been abducted."

Nita Morales waved me off again.

"He put her up to this so they could get married."

"You know this for a fact?"

"You don't kidnap someone for five hundred dollars. Five hundred dollars is what your stupid boyfriend tells you to ask for when he wants money. And this business with the Spanish and the bad English? This is absurd."

"Did you pay them?"

"Not the first time. I thought she was making a joke. I thought she would call back laughing."

"But she didn't call back laughing."

"You heard. I wanted to see if she would come home, so I paid. She hasn't called again, and that was four days ago. I think they used the money to get married."

All in all, Krista Morales did not sound like a person who would shake down her mother for a few hundred bucks, but you never know.

"Why would she pretend she has poor English?"

"No idea."

"But you believe she's pretending she's been abducted to swindle five hundred dollars from you?"

Her mouth dimpled as she frowned, and the dimples were hard knots. But after a moment they softened.

"Even smart girls do stupid things when they think a boy loves them. I was so upset I drove out there, but they weren't home. I waited almost four hours, but no one came, so I left a note. For all I know they went to Las Vegas."

"Did you call the police?"

She stiffened, and her face grew hard.

"Absolutely not. Krista has everything ahead of her—possibilities no one in my family would have even dreamed. I'm not going to ruin her future with nonsense like this. I'm not going to let her throw her life away by doing something stupid."

"If what you believe is true, Berman might have her involved in something more serious."

"This is why you're going to find her. The man they wrote the article about, he would save this girl's future."

"If she's married, there's nothing I can do. I can't force her back if she doesn't want to come."

"You don't have to bring her back. Just find her, and tell me what's going on. Will you help me, Mr. Cole?"

"It's what I do."

"I thought so. You aren't the World's Greatest Detective for nothing."

She burst into a wide smile, went behind her desk, and held up a green checkbook.

"I'll pay you five thousand dollars if you find her. Is that fair?"

"I'll charge you a thousand a day, and we'll start with a two-thousand-dollar retainer. Expenses are mine. You'll save money."

She smiled even wider, and opened a pen.

"I'll pay you ten thousand if you kill him."

I smiled at her, and she smiled back. Neither of us moved, and neither spoke. Outside on the floor, the big stitching machines whined like howling coyotes as they sewed patches to baseball caps.

She bent to write a check.

"I was kidding. That was a joke."

"Like me being the World's Greatest Detective."

"Exactly. When can you leave for Palm Springs?"

"I'll start at her apartment. It's closer."

"You're the detective. You know best."

She wrote the check, tore it from the checkbook, then gave me a large manila envelope.

"I put some things together you might want. Krista's address, her phone number, a picture, the receipt when I wired the money. Things like that."

"Okay. Thanks."

"Anything else?"

"This will be fine. I'll start with her roommate. Maybe you could call her, let her know I'm coming?"

"Oh, I can do better than that."

She picked up a red leather purse, and went to the door.

"I have a key. I'll let you into her apartment and introduce you."

"Sorry, Ms. Morales. I'd rather go alone."

Her eyes grew dark and hard.

"You might be the World's Greatest Detective, but I'm the World's Greatest Mother. Don't forget your swag."

She walked out without waiting.

2.

Loyola Marymount University was a Jesuit university with a tough academic reputation. Krista had a full-ride scholarship for all four years that covered her share of a two-bedroom apartment only seven blocks from the campus, which was as far from downtown L.A. as possible and still on land—a mile and a half from the beach at the edge of Marina del Rey.

The World's Greatest Mother and I took separate cars, picked up the I-10, and caravanned west across the city. Nita had phoned Krista's roommate from her car, so Mary Sue Osborne returned home early from class and was waiting when we arrived.

Mary Sue was pale and round, with a spray of freckles, blue eyes, and small, wire-framed glasses. She wore a blue top, tan cargo shorts, and flip-flops, and her light brown hair was braided.

She peered at me over the spectacles when she let us in.

"Hey."

"Hey back."

"Are you really the World's Greatest Detective?"

"That was a joke."

Nita had filled her in on the drive. Krista and Mary Sue had been roommates for two years, and had worked together on the student paper for four. This was obvious as soon as we entered. Long neat rows of front pages from the weekly student newspaper were push-pinned to the walls, along with a movie poster from *All the President's Men*.

I made a big deal out of their wall.

"Man, this is amazing. Is this your paper?"

"I'm the managing editor. Kris is editor in chief. The capo-di-tutti-capi."

This was called building rapport, but Nita steamrolled over the moment.

"He doesn't have time for this, Mary. Have you heard from her?"

"No, ma'am. Not yet."

"Tell him about that boy."

Mary Sue made a kind of fish-eyed shrug at me.

"What do you want to know?"

Nita said, "Did that boy convince Krista to marry him? Is he mixed up in some kind of crime?"

I cleared my throat.

"Remember when I said I'd rather come alone?"

"Yes."

"This is why. Maybe Mary Sue and I should talk in Krista's room. Alone."

Nita Morales fixed me with a glare as if she had second thoughts about me being the World's Greatest Detective, but she abruptly went to the kitchen.

"I'll be out here if you need me. Texting Kris, and praying she answers."

I lowered my voice as I followed Mary Sue through a short hall to Krista's room.

"She doesn't like him."

"No shit, Sherlock."

Krista's bedroom was small, but well furnished with a single bed, a chest of drawers, and a well-worn George R.R. Martin paperback faceup on her pillow. An L-shaped desk arranged with a computer, printer, jars of pens and pencils, and neat stacks of printouts filled the opposite corner. Large foam-boards on the walls above her desk were push-pinned with pictures of her friends.

Mary Sue saw me clocking the pictures.

"The Wall of Infamy. That's what we call it. This is me."

She pointed at a picture of herself wearing an enormous floppy hat.

"Is Berman here?"

"Sure. Right here—"

She pointed out a close shot of a young man with short dark hair, thin face, and gray T-shirt. He stood with his hands in his back pockets, staring at the camera as if he didn't like having his picture taken. All in all, Berman was in six pictures. In one of the shots, he was leaning against the rear of a silver, late-model Mustang. The license plate was blurry, but readable— 6KNX421. When Mary Sue confirmed this was Berman's car, I copied the plate, then took the close shot of Berman from the board.

"I'm going to borrow this."

"I'll blame Nita. Take what you want."

"You think Nita is right?"

"About what?"

"Marriage."

"No way. They're definitely into each other, but she's jazzed about moving to D.C. I've heard her talking with him about it on the phone. Lots of people do the long-distance thing."

"So why isn't she back?"

Mary Sue climbed onto Krista's bed, and crossed her legs.

"Dude. The year's essentially over. Yeah, Kris was due back Sunday, but she finished her classwork weeks ago. She was going to write a piece for the paper, but if they're having a blast in Margaritaville, why not enjoy? That's where I'd be if I had a hoochie boy to go with."

"So you aren't worried?"

She frowned as she thought about it.

"Not like Nita, but kinda. It's weird she isn't returning my texts, but they're way out in Palm Springs. Maybe she can't get a signal."

I thought about it and decided the signal business was unlikely. You didn't stay overdue and out of reach for a week because of bad cell service. I also considered telling her about the five-hundred-dollar ransom demand, but Nita had asked me to save Krista the embarrassment.

"Is Berman the kind of guy who would be involved in something sketchy?"

"I never met him. I don't know, but I doubt it."

I looked at her, surprised.

"Are you kidding?"

"If you knew Kris, you would doubt it, too. She's the straightest person on earth."

"I didn't mean that. I meant, how is it you've never met him? They've been together for over a year."

She shrugged.

"He's never been here when I've been here, and he never comes in."

"Not even when he picks her up?"

"Parking here sucks. She goes out to his car."

"He never hangs out?"

"She goes to his place. No roommates."

Nita appeared in the doorway, looking tense and irritated.

"I can't just sit out there doing nothing. I'm going to check her bathroom and closet. If she planned a longer stay, maybe I can tell by what she took."

"Good idea."

I didn't really think it was a good idea, but it would keep her busy. She disappeared into the bathroom, and I turned back to Krista's Wall of Infamy and considered the picture of Berman and his Mustang. Maybe they had returned on Sunday like she promised, only she had kept the party going by staying with him.

"You know where he lives?"

"Uh-uh. I think it's in Brentwood or one of those canyon places, but I'm not sure."

"Does Krista keep an address book?"

"Her phone, for sure. Nobody uses paper. She might have a contact list on her computer, but her computer's locked. You need a password."

"Okay. How about you help me search her stuff? An envelope saved with a birthday card might give us a home address. A handwritten note on a letterhead. Something like that."

"Okay. Sure."

Mary Sue started on the computer leg of Krista's desk, and I started on the leg scattered with papers. I fingered through the printouts and clippings, looking for anything useful about Berman or their trip to Palm Springs. Most of the printouts were articles about illegal immigration, mass graves in Mexico, and the increasing power of the Mexican cartels. Several were interviews with immigration activists and political figures. Sections of text in almost every article were highlighted in yellow, but none of the notes I found were about Jack Berman, wedding chapels, or Vegas acts. Most appeared to be about the material at hand: *who makes the money? where do they come from? who is involved?*

Mary Sue edged closer to see what I was doing.

"This is research for her editorial. You won't find anything there."

"You never know. People make notes on whatever's handy."

"Uh-huh. I guess."

"Is this the piece she was going to finish Sunday night?"

"Yeah. It's about illegal immigration and immigration policy. She got super into it a couple of weeks ago."

Nita appeared in the doorway.

"What was she doing?"

Mary Sue repeated herself.

"Writing her editorial. It's her last editorial. She's been working on it for a couple of weeks."

Nita came over and picked up the articles. Her face was lined so deeply as she read, she looked like a stack of folded towels.

I said, "Did she pack for a long trip or a weekend?"

Nita didn't answer.

"Ms. Morales?"

She looked at me, but her eyes were vacant, as if she couldn't quite see me. It took her another full second to answer.

"Everything's fine."

She backed away, blinked three times, then left. We only knew she had gone when we heard the front door.

Mary Sue said, "What's wrong?"

I considered the articles Krista had highlighted, then looked at Mary Sue.

"Would you do me a favor?"

"Sure. I live to serve."

"Keep looking. Look for something that tells us where Krista went, or why, and where and how to find her boyfriend, okay?"

"Okay. Sure."

I gave her my card, left her in Krista's room, and found Nita Morales seated behind the wheel of her car. Her sunglasses were on, but she hadn't started the engine. She was holding the wheel in the ten and two o'clock positions, and staring straight ahead.

I got into the passenger's side, and made my voice gentle.

"You okay?"

She shook her head.

"Talk to me."

Nita studied me from the far side of her car on that spring day, a distance too close to some clients and miles too far from others. She looked as if we were going a hundred miles an hour even though we weren't moving.

"I am not a legal resident of the United States. My sister and I were sent here when I was seven years old and she was nine. We came to live with an uncle who was legally here on a work visa. I have been here illegally ever since. I am here illegally now."

"May I ask why you told me?"

"What Mary Sue said. That Krista started all this two weeks ago."

"You told her two weeks ago."

"This isn't something you tell a child, but she is almost twenty-one, and now she has this job in Washington. I thought she should know. So she can protect herself."

"Did she react badly?"

"I didn't think so, but she grew worried when we discussed what would happen if this became known."

I wasn't an expert on immigration, but anyone living in Southern California becomes conversant with the issue.

"Do you have a criminal record?"

"Of course not."

"Are you involved in a criminal enterprise?"

"Please don't make fun of this."

"Nita, I'm not. I'm trying to tell you ICE isn't going to knock down your door. Are you scared Krista is doing whatever she's doing because you told her?"

"I've lied to her."

"You said it yourself. This isn't something you could have told her when she was a child."

She closed her eyes as hard as she clenched the steering wheel.

"She must be ashamed. This girl earned a job with the Congress, and now her mother is a wetback."

She tried to hold it together, but convulsed with a sob, and covered her face with her hands. I leaned across the console and held her. It was awkward to hold her like that, but I held her until she straightened herself.

"I'm sorry. This isn't how I thought it would be. I don't know what to do."

"You don't have to do anything. The World's Greatest Detective takes it from here."

A tiny smile flickered her lips.

"I thought you hated being called that."

"I made an exception so you'll feel better."

She studied me for a moment, then picked up her purse and placed it in her lap.

"I didn't hire you because of an article. I did my homework, but the picture caught my attention. I read the article because of the picture. The one with your clock."

"Pinocchio."

"The puppet who wanted to be a boy."

Two pictures illustrated the article. One was a close shot of me on the phone at my desk. The second photograph was a full-page shot of me leaning against the wall. I was wearing a shoulder holster, sunglasses, and a lovely Jams World print shirt. The shoulder holster and sunglasses were the photographer's idea. They made me look like a turd. But my Pinocchio clock was on the wall behind me, smiling at everyone who enters my office. Its eyes roll from side to side as it tocks. The photographer thought it was colorful.

Nita took something from the purse, but I could not see what she held.

"My uncle had a clock like yours. He told us about Pinocchio, the puppet who dreamed an impossible dream."

"To be a flesh-and-blood boy."

"To dream of a better life. It was why we were here."

"Your uncle sounds like a good man."

"The tocking rocked me to sleep. You know how people talk about the surf? The tocking was my surf in Boyle Heights when I was seven years old. I loved that clock. Every day and all night, Pinocchio reminded us to work for our dreams. Do you see?"

She opened her hand.

"He gave this to me when I was seven years old."

A faded plastic figure of Jiminy Cricket was in her palm, the blue paint of his top hat chipped and worn. Pinocchio's conscience.

"When I saw his clock in the picture, I thought we were not so different."

She put the figure in my hand.

"I can't take this."

"Give it back when you find my baby."

I put the cricket in my pocket, and got out of her car.

JOE PIKE:
eleven days after
they were taken

3.

Dennis Orlato

Their job was to get rid of the bodies.

Twenty-two miles west of the Salton Sea, one hundred sixty-two miles east of Los Angeles, yellow dust rooster-tailed behind them as the Escalade raced across the twilight desert. The sound system boomed so they could hear bad music over the eighty-mile-per-hour wind, what with the windows down to blow out the stink.

Dennis Orlato, who was driving, punched off the music as he checked the GPS.

Pedro Ruiz, the man in the passenger seat, shifted the 12-gauge shotgun, fingering the barrel like a second dick.

"What you doin'? Give it back."

Ruiz, who was a Colombian with a badly fixed cleft lip, liked *narcocorridos*—songs that romanticized the lives of drug dealers and Latin-American guerrillas. Orlato was a sixth-generation Mexican-American from Bakersfield, and thought the songs were stupid.

Orlato said, "I'm looking for the turn. We miss it, we'll be here all night."

In the back seat, Khalil Haddad leaned forward. Haddad was a thin,

dark Yemeni drug runner who had been hauling khat into Mexico before
the cartels shut him down. Now, he worked for the Syrian like Orlato and
Ruiz. Orlato was certain Haddad talked shit about him to the Syrian, Arab
to Arab, so Orlato hated the little bastard.

Haddad said, "A kilometer, less than two. You can't miss it."

When they reached the turn, Orlato zeroed the odometer, and drove
another two-point-six miles to the head of a narrow sandy road, then stopped
again to search the land ahead. Three crumbling rock walls sprouted from
the brush less than a mile in the distance, and were all that remained of an
abandoned supply shed built for bauxite miners before the turn of the century. Orlato and Ruiz opened their doors, and climbed onto their seats to
scan the coppery gloom with binoculars.

The surrounding desert was flat for miles, broken only by rocks and scrub
too low to conceal a vehicle. The sandy road before them showed only their
tire tracks, made three days earlier, and no footprints. Seeing this, Orlato
dropped back behind the wheel. No other cars, trucks, motorcycles, people,
or ATVs had passed on this road.

"It's good. We go."

Two minutes later, they pulled up beside the walls, and went to work. It
was a nasty and dangerous job, there at the edge of the evening hour, best
done quickly before the light was lost. They stripped off their shirts and guns,
then pulled on gloves as Haddad threw open the back door. The two women
and man were the last of a group from India, *pollos* who had been on their
way to the Pacific Northwest, brought up through Mexico from Brazil and
Central America, only to be kidnapped and held for ransom as they crossed
the border into the U.S. Each had been shot in the back of the head when
their families stopped paying ransom. The three bodies were now wrapped
in plastic, and smelled of sour gas. Orlato pulled them from beneath the
carpet remnants that covered them, and let the bodies drop. Ruiz and Haddad each dragged a body to a jagged cut in the wash behind the ruins, and
Orlato dragged the last. Counting these three, they had deposited eleven

bodies here during the past nine days. Their work here west of the Salton Sea was done.

As Orlato dragged the last body, Ruiz pointed down into the cut.

"Look at this shit. What you want to do?"

An animal had gotten down among the bodies and torn open the plastic. A man's hand now reached through the split.

Orlato said, "Get the chlorine."

"Shit, we put a hundred pounds of chlorine in there already, and it didn't help. Let's get the fuck out of here."

Powdered chlorine as fine and white as confectioners' sugar was supposed to keep the coyotes away. Everyone knew the bodies would be found, but the longer it took the better. Their operation was strictly short term. They set up fast, moved often, and kept moving until they had milked or killed the last of the *pollos*.

But coyotes would spread the bones, and if a dog brought a human bone home, the police and federal authorities would swarm over the desert.

Orlato glared at Ruiz.

"Get the chlorine, you lazy fuck. Maybe you didn't put enough last time."

When Ruiz skulked away for the chlorine, Orlato scanned the horizon for approaching vehicles. He was searching the sky for helicopters when Haddad unzipped his pants.

"What're you doing?"

"Taking a piss."

"Don't piss on them bodies. The police could get your DNA."

"What do they have now, a piss detector?"

Haddad unleashed a rope that hit the plastic as loudly as tearing cloth. Orlato wanted to shove the slack-jaw bastard into the cut with the piss-soaked bodies, but instead turned to see if Ruiz was coming. As he turned, something hit him between the eyes, and three more strikes rained after the first so quickly he threw up his arms to cover his face even as his legs were swept from beneath him. He slammed onto his back, and his solar plexus exploded as he was struck again, then struck on his left temple, snapping his head to the side.

Shock and awe. A sudden, violent attack of such furious intensity Orlato had not seen the man or men who attacked him, or even understood what was happening. Orlato's head buzzed as if swarming with wasps, and his ears screamed with a high-pitched hum. Now, drifting in a sleep-world, he felt hands on his body. Someone groped his legs, waist, and groin; rolled him over, then rolled him again. Orlato's head cleared, but he offered no resistance.

A low male voice.

"Look at me."

Orlato opened his eyes, and saw a tall, muscular Anglo, dark from the sun, wearing a sleeveless gray sweatshirt and jeans. He had short hair, dark glasses, and blurry tattoos on the outer rounds of his shoulders. Orlato squinted to clear his vision. Scarlet arrows. A black revolver floated at the man's side.

Orlato showed open palms.

"*Policia?*"

A man spoke behind him.

"You're gonna wish we were *policia*."

Orlato saw that a man with spiky blond hair had Haddad pinned to the ground. The blond man held an American M4 battle rifle. He tipped the rifle toward the bodies.

"You kill these people?"

Orlato had personally murdered four of the eleven, Ruiz two, and Haddad the rest, but now Orlato shook his head.

"We only bring the bodies. We don't kill no one."

The blond man showed teeth like a shark, then lifted Haddad's bloody head by his hair, and said something in Arabic. This surprised Orlato, who had met few people who spoke it besides Arabs. In that moment, Orlato knew these two men were not the police. He assumed they were *bajadores*—predators who preyed on other criminals.

"You want the car? The keys are in my pocket. You want money? I can get you money."

The tall man said, "Up."

Orlato struggled to his feet, careful in how he moved. He remembered being searched, but had left his pistol in the Escalade, and now could not remember if the man found the five-inch knife hidden at the small of his back.

When Orlato was standing, the tall man touched the center of his own forehead.

"Anglo. This tall. He was taken."

Orlato felt a stitch in his belly. He knew who the tall man described, but shook his head, lying as he had lied about killing the *pollos*.

"I don't know who you are talkin' about."

The man's pistol snapped up so fast Orlato did not have time to react. The gun rocked his head sideways and unhinged his knees, but the man caught him.

"Elvis Cole."

The blond man shouted from his perch on Haddad, red-faced and furious.

"Where is he? What did you do with him?"

Orlato's head cleared, but he feigned being hurt worse than he was, staggering and blinking. If he fell into the man, he might be able to draw the blade, or he might grab the gun.

"I did nothing. I don't know what you're talkin' about."

The pistol snapped again, and the blond man shouted louder.

"Lying fuck! The Escalade was at the house. You bastards know. You work for the Syrian."

He jerked Haddad's face from the dirt and pointed at Orlato. Haddad's eyes bulged like a dog being crushed, and he chattered in Arabic.

The blond man shouted to his friend.

"He knows where they took him! He knows who has him."

The tall man's pistol suddenly appeared in front of Orlato's face, locked dead center between his eyes. The flat copper snouts of its bullets slept in their cylinder crypts.

"Elvis Cole. Where is he?"

The tall man thumbed back the hammer.

"Ten seconds. Where is he?"

The blond man screamed, livid with rage.

"Think we're bluffing, you will die. What did you do with him?"

Orlato abruptly realized he had only one chance. He had something they wanted, and that gave him power. Power was time, and time was life. He showed both palms, the knife now forgotten.

"Yes! Yes, they have him."

Haddad barked in Arabic, but Orlato didn't understand and did not care. The blond man pushed Haddad's face into the dirt, and barked back. The tall man ignored them.

"Eight seconds."

"Trade, me for him. The Syrian will trade."

"I don't negotiate."

The blond man shouted.

"Tell us and live!"

"A trade! By morning he will be dead!"

"Five seconds."

Orlato screamed.

"A phone call. I talk to the Syrian, we will work out a trade, and you will have this man. I swear it. I swear!"

The tall man hesitated, and Orlato felt a whisper of hope. The man they wanted was probably already dead, but if they let him call the Syrian, these men would not survive until morning. Orlato spoke quickly, bartering for his life.

"The Syrian will trade for me. I'm married to his sister. You will get your friend. I promise."

The tall man glanced at his friend. No other part of him moved. The gun didn't move. Just the head, turning and locking in place with the precision of a machine.

The blond man lifted Haddad's head.

"He's full of shit. This bastard knows."

The tall man's head swiveled back to Orlato.

"Three seconds. Where is he?"

Orlato felt a rush of fear, but still didn't believe they would kill him. They would not risk losing their friend.

"He cannot help. None of them can. I am the only way you can get your friend back."

The tall man said, "One second."

Orlato reached for the knife, but by then it was too late.

Dennis Orlato's last thought before he reached for the knife was one of fearful admiration. He thought:

"This man means it."

Orlato registered a brilliant, blinding flash, and was dead.

4.

Joe Pike

Pike turned away from the body and walked over to Jon Stone's prisoner, there in the desert in the fading bronze light. Stone had already strapped the man's wrists behind his back and his ankles together with plasticuffs. When Pike arrived, Stone lifted the man's head and peeled back his upper lip.

"Khat runner. Check out these teeth. Fuckers get green teeth from chewing the khat. Ain't this green rotten?"

"Stop it, Jon."

Stone laughed, and dropped the man's head.

Khat was a shrub native to East Africa and the Arabian Peninsula, where people chewed the leaves as a stimulant. Poor man's speed.

Stone's prisoner was in his early thirties, with ragged black hair and big eyes crazy with fear. The light was fading and the clock was running. Every passing minute would put Cole farther away or closer to death. Time was everything, and speed was life. Pike wanted to press forward, but needed what this man could give him, and that would take time.

Pike pointed his pistol at the body.

"Do you understand what happened?"

The man spit out Arabic so fast, his voice was distorted. Pike had spent freelance time in Lebanon, Saudi, Somalia, the Sudan, and Iraq. He could get by, but wasn't fluent.

Pike said, "*Qala Inklizi.*"

Telling him to say it in English.

Stone cracked the M4 across the man's ear, shouted in Arabic, and the man settled down. Jon Stone was fluent.

Pike squatted in front of the man, and lifted his head.

"If you resist, I will kill you. If you lie, I will kill you. Do you understand?"

The man uttered a soft yes.

Pike pulled him into a sitting position.

"Name."

"I am Khalil Haddad, from Yemen. Please do not kill me. I will do anything you ask."

Stone stepped away and did a quick three-sixty of the horizon.

"We gotta roll, bro. We don't want to be here if ICE choppers in."

ICE. The U.S. Immigration and Customs Enforcement. The U.S.– Mexican border from Tijuana to Brownsville was a hot zone of DEA agents after incoming dope, ATF agents after outgoing guns, and ICE agents trying to stop illegal entry. Pike was good with the heat.

"Check the vehicle."

Stone trotted to the Escalade as Pike tipped his pistol toward the bodies in the cut.

"These people from India?"

"Yes."

"Who killed them?"

"We did. Me and Orlato and Ruiz. It is what we do when they cannot pay."

This was an honest answer. *Bajadores* were bandits who kidnapped people who were trying to enter the country illegally. The kidnappers would then demand ransom payments from their families or employers. This continued until the families could or would no longer pay, then the victims were murdered. Dead victims could not bear witness.

"Elvis Cole. You know who I'm talking about?"

"The man who came for the boy and the girl."

"A young Latina. Krista Morales. An Anglo boy named Berman."

"Yes, the boy and the girl."

"Are they alive?"

"I believe so, yes, but I cannot be sure. My job was with these Indians."

"Why were they taken?"

"They were with *pollos* a Tijuana crew brought north. No one knew they were Americans."

"Korean *pollos*?"

Haddad looked surprised.

"How do you know these things?"

Pike struck him with his open palm on the forehead before Haddad finished the sentence. This was not a two-way conversation.

"Yes! Koreans. The Sinaloas stole them from the Tijuanas. The Syrian, he stole them from the Sinaloas."

Pike felt Haddad was telling the truth. Tijuana, Sinaloa, Zeta, La Familia, on and on—if the U.S. side of the border was a hot zone of law enforcement agencies, the Mexican side was a war zone controlled by cartel factions who fought and stole from each other like rabid dogs. Pike was good with war zones, too. He felt at home.

"Is Cole alive?"

"This morning, yes. He was brought to our house for the Syrian."

"Your house?"

"Where we kept the Indians."

Pike hammered back the .357, and held it to Haddad as he had held it to Orlato.

"What happened to him?"

Haddad cringed, but Pike held him close. Haddad did not want to see what Orlato had seen. He did not want to see his death coming.

"Did the Syrian kill him?"

"I don't know! Orlato and Ruiz and I, we left with the bodies. The others, they were to hold him for the Syrian."

Pike pressed the gun hard into Haddad's forehead.

"A prisoner?"

"Yes!"

"Was the Syrian going to kill him?"

"I don't know! These men, they told me the Syrian thinks your friend is a federal agent."

"How long ago was this?"

"Three hours! Maybe four!"

"When was the Syrian coming?"

"I don't know!"

"Five minutes? Five hours?"

"I don't know! I can take you to the house! Maybe they still wait!"

Pike studied Haddad, then lowered the gun.

"Yes."

Stone returned, and shook his head.

"No IDs or credit cards on the stiffs. Thirty-two hundred in cash. I took it. Registration shows the Caddy belongs to a Joan Harrell of San Diego. None of these shitbirds looks like a Joan."

Haddad said, "Everything is stolen. He has thieves who get cars and trucks for him."

"Keys?"

Stone held up the keys.

"Yeah, man. Good to go."

"Drive."

"We're taking Mr. Green Teeth?"

"He knows the way."

Stone ran hard for the Escalade.

Pike clipped the plastic binding Haddad's ankles, but left his wrists bound. Pike pulled him to his feet.

Haddad said, "You are not killing me?"

"Not yet."

The big Escalade thundered up in a cloud of dust. Pike pushed Haddad into the back seat, and climbed in behind him.

Stone powered away even as Pike closed the door. Driving hard. Pushing. They bounced over brush and rocks, and neither of them gave a damn if they tore the Escalade apart.

Haddad said, "This is not the way."

Stone said, "Shut up."

Pike said, "Faster."

They ran hard toward the mountains, driving without lights. They had to move fast or Cole would be lost.

5.

It was full-on dark when they reached Pike's Jeep, covered by brush in a low wash, two-point-two miles away. Pike pulled Haddad from the Escalade, proned him in the dirt, and wiped their prints from the Caddy while Stone cleared the brush. They rolled on in less than three minutes, Pike driving the Jeep, Stone in back with Haddad, the Escalade abandoned. They crept across the desert by starlight and moonglow that made the brush glisten.

Thirty-eight minutes later, they approached a small ranch-style home on a street of similar homes at the outskirts of Coachella, California, the most eastern of the desert communities. Two-car garages, rock lawns, clean sidewalks, streetlights.

Haddad said, "This one. On the right."

"Cole is inside?"

"When I left."

Stone said, "You better not be lyin'."

It was nine-oh-five P.M. Early. Every house on the street showed light and life except this one. It looked like a corpse.

Stone said, "Shit, it's fucking deserted. That place is black."

"The windows are covered with dark plastic and wood."

"So every light in the house could be lit, and we wouldn't see it?"

"Yes. Or hear what goes on. The windows are all like this. We screw them shut so the *pollos* can't open them, then cover them with the plastic and wood."

Pike glanced in the rearview.

"Civilians?"

"I don't understand."

Stone jabbed him with the rifle.

"Women and children, dipshit. A family. You got innocent people living in there, or just dead men like you?"

"No one lives there. The house was empty."

Stone said, "Who pays the bills? Water? Power? This shit ain't free."

"Maybe the Syrian. He gives us the address. We come, make it ready with the boards and plastic, and bring the *pollos*."

Pollos. Spanish for "chickens." As if the people they murdered weren't human.

Pike circled, and approached the house from the opposite direction. He slowed as they passed.

"How many guards were with Cole?"

"Two. Washington and Pinetta. If the Syrian is here, one or two more."

Pike thought, five guns.

Stone said, "Were you and your turd friends supposed to come back after dropping the bodies?"

"Yes. We have to clean the house, and get our things. Washington and Pinetta were going to leave with the Syrian. Ruiz was angry we had to clean."

Stone moved the M4.

"Shut up. No one gives a shit about you having to clean."

Pike continued to the first cross street, turned around, cut the lights, and pulled to the curb with a face-front view of the house. Pike locked eyes with Stone in the rearview.

"Three-sixty."

Three-sixty meant circle the house.

Stone passed the M4 to Pike, and slipped from the Jeep. Pike watched him go, wondering if Cole was in the black house. He wondered if Cole was alive, or dead, or dying as they sat on the quiet street. He wondered if Haddad was telling the truth.

"You and your crew come back, how do you enter?"

"We park in the garage, never the street or the drive. We pull into the garage and close the door before we get out. This way the neighbors don't see. The Syrian tell us this. He say never park on the street or the driveway."

"There's a door from the garage into the house?"

"Yes. Into the kitchen."

"You need a key?"

"Orlato had it."

Pike took out the keys Stone found in the Escalade, along with a garage remote. Haddad affirmed the remote would open the garage, and told him which key would unlock the door.

Pike tucked the key and remote away, then told Haddad to describe the floor plan. The house was a cookie-cutter three-bedroom. Kitchen, dining room, living room on one side of the house; master bedroom and two smaller bedrooms on the other, the two smaller rooms sharing a bath. The *pollos* had been kept in the smaller bedrooms.

Stone returned as Haddad finished the description, and slipped into the Jeep as quietly as he left.

"They wrapped it, man. I can tell there's light inside, but I couldn't see or hear anything."

Pike broke down how he wanted to hit the house, then looked at Haddad.

"Do exactly what I said. Are we clear?"

"Yes."

Pike put the Jeep in gear, cruised lightless directly to the house and turned into the drive. He drew his .357 as he slid from the Jeep. The rising moon put more light on them than Pike liked, but no one moved on the street.

Pike took Haddad by the wrists and pushed him to the left side of the garage door. Stone went to the right, and Pike clicked the remote without hesitation. As the door rumbled up, Stone immediately slid under. Pike pushed Haddad down, and crawled under with him. By the time Pike was under, Stone was set up to the right of the kitchen door, and Pike clicked the remote again to lower the door.

Haddad stopped.

"No cars. They are not here."

Pike pressed the .357 into Haddad's ribs and pushed him to the door.

"Speak when I tell you. Open the door."

Pike held tight as the key fumbled into the lock and Haddad opened the door. Haddad was at the door because the men inside would expect him. If they saw Haddad when the door opened, Pike would have an advantage. If Pike drew fire, he would fall back to open a field of fire for Stone.

The door opened to a well-lit empty kitchen.

Pike whispered.

"Say it."

Haddad called loudly.

"It is Haddad. We are back."

Pike listened for a three-count, heard nothing, then pushed Haddad into the kitchen and immediately pulled him to the left. Stone crossed the kitchen at combat speed, gun up and good to go, cleared the entry, and disappeared into the house.

Pike tracked Stone's progress by ear, pinning Haddad to the floor until Stone called from the back.

"Clear. We're good."

Pike echoed the call.

"Clear."

Pike pulled Haddad to his feet as Stone reappeared in the entry, red-faced and furious.

"This fucker's full of shit, man. The place is empty."

Stone stalked over, and stabbed Haddad with his rifle.

"Cole wasn't here. You lied out your ass!"

Haddad's eyes rolled toward Pike, pleading.

"I have not lied! Look in the living room! I will show you!"

The living room was empty except for three cheap futons set against the walls, and two cheap table lamps set on the floor. Duffel bags and blankets were lumped on the futons. Haddad lurched toward the futons, trying to point even with his hands tied behind his back.

"You see these things? These are our things. This is why we had to come back, to get these things. I have not lied. This is where I saw your friend when we left."

The corner Haddad indicated was lit by a lamp. The opposite corner, on the far side of the living room, was dim with shadows. Pike glanced at the light corner.

"Take it easy, Jon."

Stone stalked in a tight circle, moving from shadow to light as he burned off the adrenaline from his entry.

"Easy my ass, Cole in the corner. This is fuckin' bullshit. I wanna kill somebody. You see what's back there, you're gonna wanna kill this prick, too."

Haddad blurted out the words, speaking the way you speak when you fear for your life.

"He was there in the corner, by the lamp. I swear to you this is true. I saw him when Ruiz and I carried out the bodies. His hands were behind his back, like mine. Orlato was telling Washington and Pinetta to keep him here for the Syrian."

Pike holstered his pistol and went to the corner. Even this close to the lamp, the light was meager. He studied Haddad, then considered Jon Stone. Stone looked like a blond shark adrift in the shadows.

Stone said, "We're wasting time, bro. He wasn't here. And if he was, they killed him and dumped the body."

Pike said nothing. He took a knee, putting himself at Cole's level with his back to the wall to see the room as Cole had seen it. He looked at the lamp, and that's where he found the cricket.

"Elvis."

Pike tossed it to Stone, who snatched it out of the air, and frowned.

"Jiminy effin' Cricket?"

Stone tossed it back.

"The girl's mother gave it to him."

Haddad said, "I do not lie to you. I see him where you are. They wait for the Syrian."

"Was he hurt?"

"I don't know."

"Was the Syrian going to hurt him?"

"I don't know."

Stone's voice came low from the shadows.

"See the back, man. Go see what they were doing back there."

They marched Haddad to the bedroom side of the house, Jon Stone leading the way.

The eleven Indians had been housed in the two smaller bedrooms, five in one, six in the other. Both rooms smelled of urine, human waste, and body odor. The walls along the floors held dark stains as if bare bodies had sweat into the paint, and rusty stains streaked one of the walls. Remnants of clothing and sandals were scattered on the floor, but nothing of Cole's.

Stone waited in the door while Pike checked, then stepped back to let him pass.

"The killing floor."

The bathroom joining the two rooms was where they died. An extension cord with one end cut to expose the wires was coiled on the floor. Pliers, butane lighters, kitchen matches, and a blood-smeared ball-peen hammer were on the lavatory counter. The tools of torture. Bloody towels and a blood-specked pillow were on the floor.

Stone's voice was quiet.

"We've seen places like this, bro. Somalia. Rwanda. That shithole in Honduras."

This was where the hostages were tortured to make them scream for their families, where Orlato and Haddad and Ruiz demanded money to make the screaming stop. When their families no longer answered the calls, or wired the money, one by one, they would be brought into the bathroom and killed. Then, one by one, they would be wrapped in the heavy plastic, loaded into a vehicle in the garage, and driven into the desert to be dumped into the cut.

Pike studied these things, then stepped past Stone and Haddad, and went to the master bedroom. He stopped inside the door. Stone pushed Haddad in behind him, and Haddad immediately spoke.

"They have not gone."

Stone said, "Who?"

"The men who guarded your friend. Washington and Pinetta. Orlato and Ruiz and I, we slept in the living room. Washington and Pinetta, they slept in here."

Two futons were on the floor against opposite walls. A blue nylon duffel sat on the nearest, and a black gym bag sat on the other. A clock radio flashed the time.

"You see? Their clothes? Their razors? These are their things. They will come back."

The corner of Joe Pike's mouth twitched. Elvis Cole had been here, but now wasn't, which meant he had been taken to some other place. Dead or alive, someone had taken him, and that someone knew where he was. Maybe the two men who would return for their clothes.

Pike glanced at Stone.

"We're closer."

Stone made the shark grin at Haddad, and pulled him out into the hall.

"You get to live five minutes longer."

Pike held the cricket tight, then put it away as they set up for what was to come.

JACK AND KRISTA:
taken

6.

That night crackled with chaos and noise: revving truck engines, spinning tires, flashes of gunfire, and blue-white lights sweeping the brush. The man with night goggles hit Jack across the back, driving him into Krista. Jack tried to shield her from the blows, and shoved at the man with the rifle.

"We're Americans. We're not—"

The man hit him harder.

"We were just fucking around. We don't—"

The man hit him so hard a tingling flash blew up his back to the top of his head, and Jack staggered to his knees.

Krista whispered frantically as she helped him to his feet.

"Stop it. They'll kill you."

"They think we're with these people."

"They're *bajadores*. They'll kill us."

"What?"

"Stop fighting—"

Men with baseball bats and shock prods swarmed like furious wasps, herding the growing crowd back to the box truck. Jack fell into step behind Krista, shuffling along with the crowd. Most of the people around them were Asian, though a few were Latin and Middle Eastern. Krista spoke Spanish to a frightened woman beside them as Jack caught a glimpse of men in the brush lifting a body. Then Krista leaned into him, whispering—

"This lady is from Guatemala. Most of these people are from Korea. She says we're being kidnapped."

"That's crazy. This is America."

"A man named Sanchez brought them across, but the *bajadores* just killed him. Give me your wallet."

"Why do—?"

"Shh."

She traded more Spanish with the woman before turning back.

"We have to get rid of it—anything with your name. Please, baby, trust me. Don't draw their attention."

Jack slipped her the wallet, but did not see what she did with it.

They were herded toward the box truck as if the guards were under a clock. When the bunching crowd slowed, the guards beat them harder, and cried out when they were shocked. The people around Jack pleaded in languages he did not understand, their faces lost and afraid even in the dim starlight.

As they got closer to the truck, and the crowd pressed tighter, Jack wanted to run. He wanted to push through all these crying people, and run hard out into the desert, just get gone and dodge and dart from bush to cactus, and run all the way back to Los Angeles. His heart pounded, and he felt sick, like he might throw up. He felt more scared than he had ever been, even when his parents died.

Instead, Jack slipped his arms around Krista, and whispered into her hair.

"They'll find my car out here. That's how they'll find us. They'll see my car."

The waiting cargo hold was a black cavern guarded by men with guns. The gunmen searched each person before pushing them aboard. Hands moved over Krista in ways that made Jack feel ashamed, then the same hands moved over his pockets and under his jacket. They took his cell phone and keys, then pushed him up into the truck. Hands reached from within to help, then Jack was in, too.

"Jack!"

"I'm here. Where are you?"

They were forced deeper into the cavern as more people boarded until the container was crowded with sweating bodies. Then the big sliding door rattled down to chop off the last faint shreds of light. The darkness was a deep, pure black, and the close air rich with the bad smells of body odor and urine. Jack saw nothing, not even a shape or line or shadow. He heard a lock being snapped into place, and whispered.

"They locked us in."

Krista pressed herself closer, invisible in the blackness. Outside, the cab doors slammed shut, and the engine rumbled. The big truck lurched, and moved.

Jack didn't know what to do. All around them, people wept, and others spoke in voices too low to hear. A woman on the other side of the truck wailed, then Jack decided he wasn't sure if it was a woman or not. The body odor smells were so strong, Jack tried not to breathe. He held Krista tight, and spoke into her hair.

"Anyone here know where they're taking us?"

Krista spoke more Spanish, and this time a man's voice answered. A woman joined in, but their conversation was short, and then Krista switched to English.

"They say we're going to be sold. That's what *bajadores* do, and they've heard stories about the *bajadores*."

"What does that mean, sold? Like slaves?"

"No, more like ransomed. I think he meant ransomed. They kidnap people, and try to get ransom."

"Where are they taking us?"

She spoke more Spanish, and translated as the man answered.

"A house, a camp, a barn. He doesn't know. We might even be kept in this truck. He's worried because he has no money to pay. He gave all his money to the coyote."

The truck lurched as it rolled over brush and dropped off up-thrust rocks. Five minutes ago, Jack had been freezing. Now, trapped with thirty frightened people in the black belly of the truck, he was sweating, and thought he might throw up.

Krista traded more Spanish, then switched to English.

"They'll want to know who we are. Don't tell them, baby. Lie. We can't tell them who you are."

"Maybe they'll let us go."

"Just don't. You can't."

"I can pay them."

"Don't. Promise me, Jack. Don't even try."

Jack put his arms around her, and held on as they bounced slowly across the desert. A few minutes later, they were on a road, and the truck picked up speed. Jack checked the time on his digital watch. Fifteen minutes later, the road became paved. Twenty-two minutes after they reached pavement, the truck slowed, backed up, then stopped. A drive this short meant they were still in the desert.

The lock was removed, and the door rose with a ratcheting clatter, filling the truck with grim red shadows. Jack checked the time. 2:55 A.M. The people ahead of them started to move.

Krista's whisper drifted over her shoulder.

"Don't tell them who you are."

Jack and Krista followed the others into a world the color of blood.

ELVIS COLE:
six days after
they were taken

7.

Six minutes after Nita Morales drove away with her fears on that warm morning, I got into my car, phoned the Information operator, and asked if they had a listing for Jack Berman in Brentwood, California.

"No, sir. Nothing in Brentwood for a Jack Berman."

"How about Westwood, West Hollywood, or Santa Monica?"

The communities surrounding Brentwood.

"No, sir. No Jacks there, either, nor anywhere in Los Angeles. We have several Johns, a Jason, a Jarrod, a Jonah, a lot of Jameses—"

"How many Bermans altogether?"

"Fifty or sixty, at least."

"Okay. Thanks for checking."

I killed the call, then dialed a police officer I know named Carol Starkey. Starkey works as an LAPD homicide detective in Hollywood, and likes me enough to do the occasional favor.

First thing she said was, "Weren't you going to cook dinner for me? I'm waiting."

"Soon. Can you pull a DMV registration for me?"

"That's what you said last time. I think you're scared we'll have sex."

Starkey is like that.

"Can you pull the DMV or not?"

I heard some background sounds, and she lowered her voice.

"I'm at a murder up in the Birds. The paparazzi and helicopters are all over us."

The Birds was an exclusive neighborhood above the Sunset Strip where the streets were called Mockingbird, Nightingale, Blue Jay, and other bird names. The Birds was known for spectacular views and more celebrities per square inch than Beverly Hills.

She said, "Will it keep till the end of the day?"

"If it has to. I'm looking for the registered owner and an address."

"Jesus, Cole, it has to. I'm working a murder here, for Christ's sake. What's the damned tag?"

I gave her Berman's tag, and let her get back to her crime. Mary Sue made it sound like Berman had his own place, but he might still live with his parents, who might be among the fifty or sixty Bermans listed by Information. The Mustang's registration should cut through the guesswork, and give me his or their names and address. If not, I could and would call my way through the fifty or sixty other Bermans, asking if anyone knew Jack.

The last person I phoned was Krista Morales. I didn't expect her to answer, but you never know. I looked up her number in the things her mother had given me, and dialed. Her voice mail answered immediately, which told me either the phone was turned off or she was talking to someone else.

Her recorded voice said, "Hey, this is Kris. I'll get back soon. Have a great day."

I suddenly understood what Nita had told me. Krista had no accent. She sounded nothing like the girl who had phoned her mother, speaking a mix of Spanish and heavily accented English. It was as if she was playing a role, but playing it sincerely. She did not sound as if she was joking or trying to chisel five hundred bucks with a bad joke of a scam. I hung up, called her back, and left a message.

"This is Elvis Cole. I'm coming to find you."

It was ten minutes after ten that morning when I put away my phone, found a gas station, then climbed back onto the I-10 and made the two-hour drive to Palm Springs. Driving seemed better than making sixty cold calls or waiting around all day for Starkey to clear a crime scene.

I drove east across the heart of Los Angeles, through the San Gabriel Valley, and across the Inland Empire into the desert. It was a nice drive that day. The early spring air was cool with a light haze that left the sky more blue than not.

Just past the casinos in Cabazon, the I-10 Freeway breaks to the south, veering toward the Salton Sea before curving north again to cross America. I left the 10 before it veered, and dropped south into Palm Springs, where you find streets named after dead celebrities like Bob Hope, Frank Sinatra, and Dinah Shore. North of the freeway was a different world, where celebrities rarely ventured. The people who staffed the resorts and golf courses and restaurants south of the freeway lived in the low-slung housing to the north. The way Nita Morales described Jack Berman, I expected him to live on the north side, but the GPS in my phone led south to a very nice mid-century modern home on a manicured street midway between two country clubs and a golf resort.

Berman's house was a gray post-and-beam with a white rock roof, an attached carport, and towering king palms. Two royal palms peeked over his roof from the backyard, and an enormous jelly palm stood sentry by the front door, braced by two date palms set in white rocks. Pretty much every house on the block sported the same palm landscape. They didn't call the place Palm Springs for nothing.

The carport was empty and the house appeared deserted. I parked in the drive, but walked back to the street to check the mailbox. It was stuffed with ads and flyers and a thick deck of junk mail. Everything was addressed to "resident," but whoever resided here hadn't checked the mail in more than a few days. I left it, and went to the front door. The note Nita Morales left was wedged under the doormat exactly where she had left it, unread and undisturbed. I glanced at it, put it back under the mat, and rang the bell even though no one would answer.

I followed the drive past two plastic garbage cans outside what was prob-

ably a utility door, and into the carport. A wrought-iron gate divided the
carport from a swimming pool surrounded by concrete decks, and a covered
outdoor entertainment area built around an outdoor kitchen and bar. The
gate wasn't locked.

It was a nice backyard. A sixty-inch outdoor flat screen hung behind
the bar, sort of like a tiki design gone wild. Glass sliders on the back of the
house allowed an open view of the interior. I was hoping to find Krista and
Jack making out, or Jack's mother baking an apple pie, but no one was in the
pool or inside the house. The good news was there were no bodies, and no
signs of violence.

Nita Morales had left a note under the front mat, but a second note was
stuck at eye level to the living room slider. It was stuck to the glass with a
piece of chewing gum. Handwritten in black ink on the back of an *ampm*
cash receipt: *Dude! You go without me??? Whas up?* D.T. The receipt was
for twenty dollars of gasoline. Nita had probably not left the second note.

In detective circles, this was known as a clue.

The interior was strangely austere, as if someone had begun furnishing
the house, then stopped, and left the rooms mostly empty. A black leather
couch, two red chairs, and another flat screen TV furnished the living room,
but the rugs and tables had been forgotten. Other than light switches and
an alarm panel by the front door, nothing hung on the walls, giving the
place an unfinished look. I studied the alarm panel, and was pretty sure I
made out a tiny green light. A red light would mean the alarm was armed. A
green meant it wasn't.

I returned to the utility door, bumped the deadbolt, and let myself in. A
computer-generated voice spoke from the alarm pad at the front entry, an-
nouncing that the south side door was open. I listened for movement, but
heard nothing. No living person was home.

"Hello? I think your bell is broken."

When no one answered, I stepped inside, pulled the door, and quickly
searched the house. Two of the three bedrooms were empty, so my search
was minimal.

The master bedroom clearly belonged to a single male, but a bright blue overnight bag sat on the end of the bed. The bag contained three panties, two sheer bras, two light knit tops, pink shorts, a pair of running shoes, a two-piece swimsuit, and a black hoodie—about as much as a woman would pack for a relaxed weekend with a friend in the desert. A pale gray toiletries bag contained makeup, a toothbrush, and a pink plastic box of birth control pills. The pharmacy label showed the script was filled for Krista Morales. If Krista ran off to Vegas with Berman, she had left her toiletries and birth control pills behind, which young women tend not to do.

I photographed Krista's things in place as I found them, then returned to the kitchen. A Panasonic cordless phone sat on the kitchen counter beside a blinking message machine. The message machine showed three calls. I hit the Play button, and listened.

"Dude! Don't leave me hangin'! Where are you, bro?"

The first message ended, and the same male voice left a second message.

"Hey, Berman, you turn off your cell? What's up with that? Did you guys go back to the city or what? I took the day off, bro."

"You guys" was a good sign. It implied the caller knew both Berman and Krista Morales, and had seen them together.

The third message had been left by the same voice on the following day.

"Crap, man, I hope we're cool. Your cell's giving me some shit about you not accepting calls or messages. I don't even know if you're gettin' my texts. I rolled by your house. Check in, okay?"

I picked up the cordless, and checked the incoming call list. The most recent three calls were all from the same number showing a Palm Springs area code. I dialed. Four rings later, the same voice answered, but in a hushed tone.

"Dude! What, did you drop off the fuckin' earth? Where you been?"

His Caller ID had recognized Jack Berman's number.

"This isn't Jack. I'm a friend of Krista's mother."

The caller's name was Daniel Trehorn. The D.T. who left the note.

I identified myself, explained that Krista's mother was worried, and asked when he had last seen them, together or apart.

He answered in the same hushed tone.

"That was last Friday night. It's been almost a week."

It had been six days. One day after Krista Morales left her apartment to meet Jack Berman. Two days before Nita Morales received the first ransom demand.

"Where did you last see them?"

He mumbled something to someone in the background, then returned to me.

"In the desert. Listen, can we talk in twenty minutes? I'm working. I'm a caddie at Sunblaze. You know where we are?"

"I'll find it."

"On Dinah Shore, east of Gene Autry. We're on the ninth of nine. I'll meet you outside the clubhouse."

"See you in twenty."

"We had plans the next day. We were gonna hang out. Are they okay?"

"I'll see you in twenty."

Daniel Trehorn sounded worried. I sounded worried, too.

8.

Daniel Trehorn was a skinny guy in gray shorts, a maroon Sunblaze Golf Resort polo, and pristine white sneakers. A shotgun spray of zits speckled his cheeks, and mirrored orange sunglasses wrapped his eyes as he scanned the desert ahead. We were in his big Silverado pickup, all tricked out with big tires, big shocks, and big lights for life in the desert. Trehorn was driving.

"We were going to Vegas. Krista's never been to Vegas. Blast up Saturday morning, back Sunday afternoon. Kris hadda be back at school Monday. I went by to pick'm up, that was at noon, but they weren't home. I called. Nothing. I texted. Nothing. I'm thinking, what the fuck? We don't roll this way."

"You and Jack tight?"

"He's my boy. We go back."

"You know Krista, too?"

"Sure. They've been hooked up for a long time."

Trehorn was taking me twenty-three-point-two miles south of Palm Springs to the site of an old airplane crash where he had left them that Friday night, six days ago. On that Friday, Trehorn, Jack, Krista, and another couple named Chuck Lautner and Deli Blake had built a fire, drank beer, and listened to music.

I said, "Why did they stay when the rest of you left?"

"Why do people ever want to be alone under the stars? What do you think?"

"I think no one has seen or heard from them since you drove away."

The twenty-three-mile drive south was mostly on pretty good paved roads, but the last seven miles were ranch and county roads bedded with gravel or cut through sand and rocks. Twenty miles of empty desert is a long way. I wondered if their car broke down, or they had an accident, and if we would find their car overturned on the side of the road.

"You guys came out here at night?"

"Sundown, but it was almost midnight when we went back. I've been coming out here since junior high with my brother. It's no big deal when you know the way."

I looked around at the long expanse of brush and rubble. You look up "middle of nowhere," this is the definition.

"Did Jack know the way?"

"He's been out a few times. It's pretty simple when you know it."

Ten minutes later, we bounced to a stop in a cloud of yellow dust, and Trehorn pointed.

"There you go."

A twin-engine Cessna was on her belly more than a hundred yards off the road, across a field of creosote bushes, barrel cactus, and rocky sand. Clumps of brush had grown up around her like puppies nuzzling their mother. The props and windows were missing, the left wing and tail were crumpled, and her corroded skin had been a forty-year canvas for graffiti that served as a history for pretty much every local high school class and romance for the past forty years. Even after all these years, a dim outline where the land had been scraped to create a landing strip could be seen by how the brush grew.

"This is where you left them?"

"Yeah. We were by the plane. That's where everyone hangs out, you see how it's kinda clear where the old runway was? You can build a fire, cook if you want, just kinda hang. Jack left his car out here 'cause he has that Mustang, so Chuck and I drove over, and parked by the wreck. It gets dark, bro, it is *black* out here. I turn on the floods."

Trehorn had a light bar bolted to the top of his truck.

"Where did Jack leave his car?"

"Couple of lengths behind us, I guess. Chuck went on to the plane, and Jack and Kris climbed in with me. He can't drive his Pony over that stuff."

I slid out of his truck.

"Let's take a look."

"We can drive."

"Walking is good."

A long time ago the United States Army taught me how to hunt men in wild places. People in black T-shirts with loud voices taught us how to move and hide without leaving signs of our passing, and how to find and read the signs left by others. Then they sent us to dangerous places and gave us plenty of practice. I got to be pretty good at it. Good enough to survive.

I did not go immediately to the airplane. I went behind Danny's truck to see the tracks his tires left, then walked along the road until I found the same track leaving the road for the airplane.

"This is you. See? Let's follow you."

Six days after they were here, his tire tracks were still readable. We followed the trail he had left of broken creosote and manzanita, then left his trail for the airplane. It rested twenty yards off what would have been the landing strip, where it had slid sideways to a stop. Older tracks and ruts cut across the clearing were visible, too, along with discarded water bottles and beer cans that looked as if they had been there for years.

Graffiti covered every square inch of the wreck like psychedelic urban camouflage that was alien to the desert. It was a small airplane, and now, dead on its belly with missing engines and broken windows, it didn't seem like much of a reason to drive so far.

The old airplane's carcass had long been stripped of anything valuable by scavengers and souvenir hunters. The seats were gone, and eye sockets gaped from the control panel where the instruments had been removed. In the back, where the smugglers had probably strapped down bales of weed, were more crusty cans layered with dust.

We continued past the nose to a clear area, where Trehorn pointed out the black smudge that had been their fire, then made a general wave toward a break in the brush.

"We parked there, put on some tunes, and built the fire. See the cut wood? People come out, they scrounge shit from the brush, but that stuff makes a shit fire. Chuck brought real wood. It gets cold out here."

"Was the fire still burning when you and Chuck took off?"

"Embers, maybe, but that's all. It was pretty much done."

I circled the plane, found nothing, and was thinking we had driven out for nothing when I saw a brassy glint in the dust ten feet in front of him. I walked over and picked it up.

Trehorn said, "Whatcha got?"

"A nine-millimeter shell casing."

The brass casing gleamed brightly, indicating it had not been exposed to the elements long enough to tarnish. I held it up, but he wasn't impressed.

"People shoot out here all the time. That old plane has more holes than Swiss cheese."

I found two more casings a few feet away, and then a spent 12-gauge shotgun shell so new it looked like it had just come from the box.

Trehorn wandered off, searching along with me, then called from the center of the clearing.

"Shit. That's a big sonofabitch."

"What?"

He pointed at the ground.

"Tires. I run two-fifty-five-sixteens on my Silverado. These gotta be five-seventies. That's a big honkin' truck."

I didn't know two-fifty-fives from five-seventies, but the tracks he found were from a vehicle with two large tires mounted on each side. The double-tires suggested a large, heavy truck, but a large, heavy truck would have little reason to be in the middle of nowhere.

"These here the night you guys were here?"

Trehorn made a face as he shrugged.

"I dunno. It was dark."

A confusion of footprints and smaller tire tracks crisscrossed the dirt. Some appeared fresher than others, but I couldn't tell with any precision how recently they were made.

Trehorn said, "What do you think?"

"I think a lot of people were here. Which tracks are from your Silverado?"

"Back by the plane on the other side of our fire. I didn't come out here. Neither did Chuck."

Trehorn followed the large tracks toward the road, but I went in the opposite direction past the fire to the tire tracks he had left that night. When I found a clear example, I drew a large E in the sand, then noted the location relative to their fire and the airplane. I walked past the plane to continue searching the clearing when I saw a white shape caught in a creosote bush. I reached through prickly branches and found a California driver's license. It pictured an Anglo male with short red hair, lean cheeks, and two bad pimples on his forehead. The name on the DL read M. JACK BERMAN.

I said, "Well."

Trehorn was still on the far side of the airplane, so I pushed the branches aside. Three credit cards bearing Berman's name and a worn leather wallet were caught in the lower branches. The wallet contained three hundred forty-two dollars in cash.

I glanced at Trehorn again, wondering if Jack Berman had put his wallet in the bush, and why. The discarded wallet and cash made no sense. If Krista and Jack had left voluntarily, they would not have abandoned the cash. If they were forced away at gunpoint, the person doing the forcing would still take the cash. Good, bad, or indifferent—anyone tossing the wallet would totally keep the cash.

I pushed deeper into the branches. A slip of paper with a handwritten note was caught on a twig near the bottom of the bush. The note read: Q COY SANCHEZ. A second DL was on the ground at the root of the bush, showing a pretty young woman with golden skin and raven hair named KRISTA LOUISE MORALES.

I stared at her picture, then studied the note. Q COY SANCHEZ, written in blue ink with a shaky hand that left the oversize letters uneven.

Trehorn was even farther away, searching the ground as if he hoped to find the Holy Grail. He was worried about his friend Jack Berman, but I did not tell him about the things I found in the bush. I read the note again.

Q COY SANCHEZ.

"Danny!"

He looked over as I tucked the note and the DLs away.

"Let's go. There's nothing here."

I wanted to speak with Nita Morales first, and a man named Joe Pike.

9.

Three minutes after Danny Trehorn dropped me at my car, I stepped into a cold, crisp Burger King and bought an iced tea. I wanted to think about what I had found before I called Nita Morales because I wasn't sure what it meant, or what to recommend. Also, I was hot. Palm Springs is like that.

Here is how the detective (*moi*) rehearses his report to the client: Krista Morales and Jack Berman arrived safely in Palm Springs, and were seen by others that past Friday night at a remote but well-known desert location. Krista and Jack had driven to that location in Jack's vehicle, and, at their own request, remained alone when their companions returned to the city. They were neither seen nor heard from again except for two possible extortion calls during which laughably low sums of money were demanded. Six days following that Friday night, the detective ventured (ventured is always a good word to use with clients) to said remote location where he found items belonging to both Morales and Berman, including but not limited to both driver's licenses, three hundred forty-two dollars in cash, and an incomprehensible note. Q coy Sanchez. Berman's vehicle was not at the scene, nor were there any overt signs of foul play. (Foul play is another good term.)

The person who sold me the tea was a bulky young Latino maybe nineteen or twenty years old. His name tag read JOHNNY. When he gave me the change and thanked me, I showed him the note.

"Hope you don't mind me asking, but do you read Spanish?"

"No, man. Sorry. Maybe Imelda—"

He called to a chunky young woman seated at the drive-through window.

"Imelda! You read Spanish?"

She eyed me suspiciously before she answered.

"A little."

She came over and glanced at the note.

"What's 'q coy' mean?"

"I was hoping you could translate."

"Sanchez is a name."

"Uh-huh."

She shrugged.

"I don't know 'q coy.' Maybe it's misspelled."

"Any guesses what they were trying to spell?"

"No, not really."

A drive-through customer appeared, so she returned to her station.

Other customers had lined up behind me, so I took the iced tea and set up shop in a booth as far from everyone as I could get. Two men wearing Union 76 shirts came in a few minutes later, but they couldn't translate the note, and neither could a thin woman with two round little boys.

The woman and boys took a booth near mine. The boys sat together on one side, she sat on the other, and put out cups of vanilla yogurt and French fries. Nothing like balanced nutrition. The boys pushed and pulled at each other as they shoved in the food, and laughed loud so people would look at them. When the woman told them to stop, they ignored her. She looked exhausted, but happy for the distraction when I asked if she read Spanish.

She studied the note, then handed it back.

"Sanchez is a name. I don't know these other words."

"Okay, thanks for taking a look."

"'Coy' is kinda familiar, but I don't know. I think I'm confusing it with something else."

"If it comes to you."

"I don't think it's Spanish."

"Okay."

The boys pushed and pulled, and when she again told them to stop, they laughed to drown her voice as if she didn't exist.

She stared at them with hollow eyes, then leaned toward me and lowered her voice.

"I hate them. Is that so wrong? I really do hate them."

The boys laughed even louder.

They were still laughing when my phone rang with a number I didn't recognize.

"Elvis Cole."

"Mary Sue Osborne."

I took the phone and tea to a booth farther from the laughing boys. I could see my car in the parking lot, and watching it gave me a reason not to look at the woman hating her horrible little boys.

"Hey."

"Hey back. I looked up your article online. That was a nice piece. They made you seem cool."

"Seem?"

"Check out my bad self. I cracked Krista's password. I tried all these passwords, and nothing worked, so I got stupid and typed in o-p-e-n. Shazam, and I found Jack's address."

"You made my day."

"This would be true. I should be rewarded."

"What's his address?"

She rattled off an address on Tigertail Road in Brentwood. Tigertail was in an affluent canyon in the hills west of the Sepulveda Pass. Jack's parents did pretty well.

I said, "As long as I have you, let me ask you something—do you speak Spanish?"

"*Si*, amigo. Well, *poquito*. I'm fluent in French and Italian, but I can get by in Spanish."

"I'm going to read you something. I think it's Spanish."

I read it, then spelled it. Q coy Sanchez.

She said, "It isn't Spanish."

"That's what everyone says."

"Did Kris write it?"

"Would it matter? Let's say she did."

She was silent for a moment.

"I'm guessing, but I think it says ask about a coyote named Sanchez."

"It does?"

"The Q. It's a shorthand we use at the paper. Query, question, ask. Coy—
you write fast, you abbreviate. I'm guessing 'coyote' because every article on
her desk is something about coyotes sneaking people across the border. Also,
I'm a genius."

"I loves me a smart chick."

"I knew you'd see the light. They always do."

"Okay, there's one more thing."

"I know. You want me to read all these articles to see if a coyote named
Sanchez is mentioned."

"Affirmative."

She made a big deal of sighing.

"I'm so easy. You should take advantage of me."

"Thanks, buddy. This is a big help."

"Buddy. Every girl's dream, being a hot guy's buddy."

"I'm old enough to be your father. Kinda."

"Only small minds are limited by society's conventions."

I was still smiling when I hung up and phoned Nita Morales. She was in
a meeting, but immediately came to the phone. I told her where I was,
launched into a rundown of what I had learned. I was just beginning to build
up momentum when she surprised me.

"She went to that airplane?"

"You know about it?"

"This is how I came. She wanted to know what coming north was like, so I told her. Meeting there was common then if you came up the Imperial Valley. Our guide called it the airport. It was a safe place to meet and easy to find. He would say, tomorrow we are going to land at the airport, and you will get on another airplane. I hope that pilot knows how to fly. He thought this was funny."

"What was your coyote's name?"

"We did not call them coyotes. They were our guides."

"Okay. Who was he?"

"I don't think I ever knew. I was seven."

"Have you heard of a coyote named Sanchez?"

She sounded annoyed.

"I don't know people like this. People in my situation, we're not part of some underground society. You think we get together, have margarita parties, and laugh it up about how we put one over on Uncle Sam? I was seven. It's something you try to put behind you. These things are not part of my life."

I told her about the things I found in the bush, including the handwritten note.

"Mary Sue thinks it means 'ask a coyote named Sanchez.'"

"Ask what?"

"I don't know. Maybe it has nothing to do with where she is or why she's missing, but if she wanted to ask Sanchez something, then I want to ask him, too."

"The attorney I saw knows about these things."

"The attorney you saw when you looked into changing your status?"

"Yes. He is an immigration attorney who is sympathetic in these matters. I know he represents undocumented people when they are arrested. I have his number."

"Okay."

"Thomas Locano. He was very nice. Here—"

She gave me a number with a Pasadena area code. I asked her to call him. As her attorney at that time, he would need her permission to share information.

"Mr. Cole? I will call the police if you think it is best."

"I've been involved less than five hours. Let's see what develops."

"I would give up everything for her, Mr. Cole. Without hesitation. I want you to know this."

"I know you would, but you won't have to. Nothing happening now is about you. It's about finding Krista and bringing her home. The police won't ask your status, and don't care."

"Are you sure?"

Outside, a red Jeep Cherokee pulled into the parking lot and parked beside my car. The man inside did not get out. He waited without moving, dark glasses locked forward, immobile as a statue.

I checked the time.

"Yes. I'm sure. This is why I'm the World's Greatest Detective."

"You are trying to make me smile again."

"Yep."

"It did not work."

"I know. But I had to try."

I put away my phone, and went out to the Jeep. The man behind the wheel looked at me as I climbed into the passenger seat, but said nothing. Conversation was not his strong point.

Pike, Joseph, no middle initial, learned the tracking arts as a boy who grew up at the edge of a logging town, and later refined those same arts when he hunted men first as a combat Marine, then later as an LAPD police officer and a private military contractor in Africa, Central America, and the Middle East. If I was good at hunting men, Pike was better. Pike had also been my partner in the agency since we bought it together, and my friend for even longer.

"Thanks for coming."

His head dipped once. A two-hour drive, and he had come without asking why, and without explanation.

Now, I told him about Krista Morales, her Friday night at the crash site, and what I found when I walked the scene. I gave him the nine-millimeter brass casings and the spent shotgun shell.

"I found these. Trehorn says people shoot out there, so they might not matter."

Pike sniffed the brass as if the smell would tell him something, then handed them back. Maybe he could follow their scent.

"I marked Trehorn's track with an E. The bigger truck is a quad. I want your read on what happened."

Pike nodded again.

"You want me to take you out there?"

He shook his head. I had already texted him the longitude and latitude coordinates from my iPhone.

"Want Trehorn?"

"I'm good alone."

"Okay. I'm going to see this attorney. Let me know what you find."

It was one-thirty-two that afternoon when I left Pike in the desert, and drove to see Thomas Locano.

10.

Thomas Locano had a nice suite of offices on the second floor of a two-story building overlooking Mission Street in South Pasadena. His was an older building with a red tile roof, plaster walls, and heavy wooden doors. Like the building, Locano was a gracious man in his early sixties. Two younger associates were employed in his practice, and his assistant was also his wife. Elizabeth, she told me as she led me into his office.

Locano smiled when he stood to greet me, but appeared uncomfortable.

Elizabeth Locano said, "Would you like coffee, Mr. Cole? Or something else?"

"I'm fine, ma'am. Thank you."

She did not close the door on the way out.

Mr. Locano came from behind his desk so we could sit together in comfortable, overstuffed chairs, and offered a firm, dry hand.

"Nita tells me you're working for her, and are aware of her status issue."

"Yes, sir, I am. Did she tell you why I'm here?"

"Her daughter is missing. She believes it has something to do with her status, so she asked me to speak freely with you about these things."

I passed him the note from the crash site.

"I found this twenty miles outside of Palm Springs at the crash site of an old drug smuggler's plane. I believe it was written by Nita's daughter."

He frowned at the note, then tried to pass it back, but I didn't take it.
"This isn't Spanish."

"No, sir. We believe it means 'ask a coyote named Sanchez' or 'ask about a coyote named Sanchez.' So that's what I'm doing. Do you know of a coyote named Sanchez who brings people north through the Imperial Valley?"

Mr. Locano lowered the note. His cool expression told me I had insulted him.

"My practice is immigration law. I help clients obtain visas and green cards, and fight deportation and removal orders. If you believe I'm involved in something illegal, you misunderstand the nature of my work."

"That isn't what I meant to suggest, Mr. Locano. If I sounded that way, I apologize."

He didn't look mollified.

"Nita told me you're the go-to attorney when undocumented aliens are arrested, so I'm guessing you're familiar with how your clients enter this country, and who brings them across."

"This is not something I'm going to discuss with you."

I pointed at the note.

"Ask the coyote, Sanchez. Nita Morales saw the crash site when she was seven years old, and being smuggled into this country. She says it used to be a regular transfer spot where people brought north were handed off. Krista visited that same site this past Friday night, and it was the last time anyone has seen her. Today, six days later, I found this note and her driver's license ten yards from the wreckage."

He glanced at the note again, and frowned. This time when he offered it back, I took it.

"You believe she had contact with this person, Sanchez?"

"Maybe, but I don't know. Either way, she wrote this note for a reason, so I want to ask him about it. I need a first name to find him."

Locano nodded, but more to himself than me.

"I would like to help you, Mr. Cole, but this business you speak of is not what it was."

"Are you telling me no one comes north anymore?"

"Of course people come, but the guides I knew are gone. The old guides were a cousin who had come to work the seasonal crops, or an in-law who came to visit relatives. If you gave them a few dollars they would help you, as much out of friendship as for the money, but the cartels and their hoodlums have changed this. They patrol the roads like an army to control the movement of guns and drugs, and now nothing comes north without their permission."

"Including the coyotes?"

"Transporting people is big business now. Groups from Asia, Europe, and the Middle East find passage to Central America, and are taken north through Mexico in large groups. The new coyotes don't even call them people. They are *pollos*. Chickens. Not even human."

"Coyotes eat chickens."

"Not only chickens, but each other, and each other's chickens. Do you know what a *bajadore* is?"

"A bandit?"

"A bandit who steals from other bandits. These are usually members of different cartels, a Baja stealing from a Zeta, a member of the Tijuana cartel stealing from a Sinaloa or La Familia. They steal each other's drugs, guns, and *pollos*—whatever can be sold. They even steal each other."

"Sold. As in slavery?"

"Sold as in ransom. These poor people have already paid their money to the coyote, then they are kidnapped by the *bajadores*. They have nothing, so the *bajadores* demand ransom from their families. I do not know people like this. When they are arrested, I do not represent them."

I felt my mouth dry as I took in what he told me.

"Nita received two calls from Krista and a male individual, the man demanding a fee for Krista's return. Nita transferred the money, but Krista is still missing."

Locano's eyes grew darker.

"Nita said nothing of an abduction."

"Nita believes it's a joke or a scam. They only asked for five hundred dollars."

Locano looked even more disturbed.

"This is small to you and a woman with a successful business, but it is a fortune to a family counting pennies. We are talking about poor people. A few hundred, a thousand, another five hundred. The *bajadores* know with whom they are dealing."

"It still seems so little."

"Multiply it times a thousand. Two thousand. The number of people abducted would astound you, but such abductions are rare on U.S. soil. Let's hope Nita is right."

Neither of us spoke for a moment, neither of us moved as I listened to the voices in his outer office, his wife speaking with one of the younger attorneys.

"Mr. Locano, you may not know this man, but you might know someone who does, or who can find out. Ask around. Please."

He stared at me, and I could tell he was thinking. He tapped the arm of his chair, then called to his wife.

"Liz. Would you show Mr. Cole to the restroom, please?"

He stood, and I stood with him as his wife appeared in the door.

"Take your time. Wash thoroughly. It is important to be clean, don't you agree?"

"It's important to be clean."

"Take your time."

Elizabeth Locano graciously showed me to the restroom, where I took my time. It was a nice restroom, with large framed photographs of the pre-Hispanic city of Teotihuacán in southern Mexico, what the Aztecs called the City of the Gods. It was and remains one of the most beautiful cities ever built, and one I have always wanted to see. I wondered if Mr. Locano or his wife had taken them.

I washed thoroughly, then washed a second time because cleanliness was a very good thing, and it was right to be good. Mr. Locano was on the other side of the door talking over my request with his wife, and maybe making the calls I had asked him to make. I hoped so.

I was staring at the Pyramid of the Sun when my phone buzzed.

Mary Sue Osborne said, "This is your future wife speaking."

You see how they won't quit?

"What's up?"

"Okay, I went through her research. I didn't see anything about anyone named Sanchez, coyote or otherwise. Sorry, dude."

This meant I was down to Mr. Locano. If he couldn't or wouldn't come through, Q coy Sanchez would go nowhere.

I was thanking her when my phone buzzed with an incoming call, and this time I saw it was Pike.

"Gotta go, Mary Sue. Thanks."

"No chitchat? No flirty repartee?"

I switched calls to Pike.

"Elvis Cole Detective Agency, the cleanest dick in the business."

"It's worse than you thought."

I stared at the Avenue of the Dead while Pike told me.

JOE PIKE:
six days after
they were taken

11.

Joe Pike watched his friend Elvis Cole leave the Burger King parking lot, then entered the longitude and latitude into his GPS. Pike was not using a civilian GPS. He used a military handheld known as a Defense Advanced GPS Receiver, which was also known as a dagger. The DAGR was missile-guidance precise, could not be jammed, and contained the cryptography to use the Army and Air Force GPS satellite system. The DAGR was illegal for civilians to own, but Pike had used it in remote locations throughout Africa, the Middle East, and parts of Central and South America. These were military contract jobs for multinational corporations, mostly, but also the United States government. The government gave the DAGR to him even though it was a crime for him to own it. Governments do that.

Thirty-two minutes later, Pike slid from his Jeep onto a dirt road a hundred yards from the broken airplane and the overgrown landing strip behind it. Pike considered the airplane, then the surrounding land. The landing strip was obvious. The smugglers had smoothed a forty-foot-wide piece of desert for twenty-five hundred feet, pushing their rubble into a low berm along the runway's length. Now, all these years later, though the creosote bushes and bunchgrass returned, the landing strip created an unnaturally flat table of land with an unnaturally straight edge.

Pike took a deep breath, and waited for the desert's silence. The Jeep ticked and pinged, but the desert swallowed these sounds as deserts will do, muting them with its emptiness. Deserts held an emptiness that could not be filled, and as the metal cooled, the pops and knocks slowed like a clock running down until the desert was silent.

Pike took another breath, expanding his lungs ever farther, and slowed his heart. Forty-four beats per minute. Forty-two. Forty. Pike wanted to be as still and silent as the desert. The best hunters were one with the land.

Pike made his way through the cholla and creosote, and quickly located the remains of the fire Cole described and the tire print marked with an E. This would be Trehorn's track, with his friend's track next to it. Pike thought of these tracks as "friendlies," and would ignore them if he saw them elsewhere in the area.

Once the two friendly tracks were identified, Pike searched for the oversized quad tracks Cole described. These signs were not easy to find, the way you could see tracks on a sandy beach. The desert hardpack was made of shale plates scattered with sand, rocks, and sun-baked dirt. Though an occasional puddle of sandy soil held a clear track, the signs Pike found were mostly a few inches of thin line on a rock or a shadow pressed into the sand.

Pike worked carefully, and did not hurry. He eased into a push-up position, lowered his head, then changed position and lowered himself again. During his contract years, he was often hired to protect African villages and farm collectives from raiders and poachers. These missions involved tracking dangerous men through vast tracts of mopane scrub or arid savannah. Pike hired Masai warriors to track them. These were lean, mystical men who would study the tilt of a reed for an hour or touch a tree as if they could feel the heat left by a passing Bantu. They claimed the trees and grass spoke to them, and tried to teach Pike what they saw—*be one with these things, and you will see without looking*. Pike never heard voices or saw what they saw, but he learned what to look for, and that a man needed patience to find it. Joe Pike was patient.

He found three nine-millimeter casings almost at once, glittering like small copper mirrors. He found clear prints left by two pickup-sized vehicles, fragments of three different shoe prints, and then found the quad. Cole was right—two big tires mounted side by side, each maybe ten inches wide. A large truck had been here in a place where large trucks did not belong. Pike studied the dual tracks, and noted they lined up with the centerline of the landing strip. He followed them, noting more fragments of smaller treads, some crushed by the quad tracks, others cutting across them. The smaller tracks didn't follow a straight course, but swerved and curved into the brush. Some of these tracks showed a sideways skid as if the vehicles had been moving fast. Pike wondered why they had turned hard into the brush, but kept following the quad.

Twenty yards past the dead airplane, the quad tracks curved toward the road where his Jeep now waited. Pike thought this was probably how the truck left, so he reversed course, and followed the tracks in the opposite direction back past the airplane.

He was thirty yards beyond the crash when the clearing was suddenly crowded with shoe prints; mostly fragments—the crest of a heel, the edge of a shoe—but enough to see differences in their sizes and soles. The shoe prints overlapped as if many people had stood in a group. Pike lowered himself to study them more closely, and realized the shoe prints completely covered the quad prints. This meant the people were here after the truck.

Something about this bothered him, so Pike backtracked a few feet the way he had come, and discovered the tracks leading to the road were clear. A few feet farther away from the road, and overlapping shoe prints covered the tracks. The line between shoes and no shoes on the quad tracks was clear.

Pike realized he now knew the truck had come from the south, rolled up the centerline to this spot near the crashed airplane, and stopped. A group of people had gotten off or gotten on at the rear of the truck, after which the truck departed toward the road where his Jeep was now parked.

Pike said, "Mm."

Pike searched for a depression where the truck's weight would have pressed into the soil when it sat parked. He located the first depression, then two of the remaining three. He paced off the distance between the rear tires and the fronts, which gave him the wheel base. The truck was about twenty feet long with a fourteen-foot box. This was about the size used for local meat deliveries or rented to do-it-yourself movers.

Pike was considering the size of the truck when he noticed a long arcing skid where one of the smaller vehicles crushed a cluster of furry cholla cactus as it raced into the brush. Pike left the quad for a closer look, and saw a path of broken ocotillos and creosote. The creosotes were large, heavy plants, and would have damaged the vehicle, but the driver hadn't cared. Five more nine-millimeter casings were scattered along the hardpack.

The smaller track was easy to follow. Broken shrubs and deep ruts where the tires dug for traction led in a curving arc through the brush. Forty yards from the landing strip, Pike found four deep sideways skids where the vehicle made a hard, sliding stop. A few feet away, Pike spotted seven nine-millimeter casings and three yellow shotgun shells. Someone had driven hard to this place, stood on the brakes, then fired off rounds. Two guns, so Pike guessed two men. Chased something. Caught it. Killed it.

Pike circled the area, but did not have to go far. Twenty feet away, he found an irregular brown amoeba-shaped stain almost two feet across on the dusty shale. The brown had faded, and was almost the color of dust, but Pike had seen similar stains in similar deserts all over the world, and knew it had once been red.

Something bad had happened here.

Someone had died here.

And the shooters had taken the body.

Pike had been on the scene for one hour and twelve minutes. It was almost three o'clock. He marked the spot, then jogged back to his Jeep to call Elvis Cole.

ELVIS COLE:
four days before
he is taken

12.

The bathroom felt cold when Pike told me what he had found.

"Big group. Can't tell how many, but more than ten. Two or three smaller vehicles came hard for the quad. Looks like three, but I can't confirm."

"The quad was there first? The others came after?"

"The quad wasn't running. He was probably stopped when they hit."

"They followed him?"

"Or knew he would come and waited nearby. He parked, people got out, the bad guys hit."

"So everyone ran, but got rounded up and put back aboard?"

"Way it looks. At least one man went down. From the amount of blood, KIA."

"Jesus."

"Uh-huh."

"Anything else on the kids?"

"No, but I can stay longer."

I was thinking about it when a man in his thirties with neatly trimmed blond hair opened the door and told me Mr. Locano was ready. He had a faint Russian accent and wore a UCLA class ring. One of Locano's associates. I told Pike I would call back, and followed the man to Mr. Locano's office. As before, he was behind his desk when I arrived and came around to speak with me, but this time we did not sit.

He said, "There is a man."

"Isn't there always?"

"Rudy Sanchez. Rudolfo. Mr. Sanchez is well established, and is known to deal with groups."

"Thanks, Mr. Locano. This won't get back to you."

"Wait. You'll want his address."

He gave me a white index card on which he had written *Sanchez & Sons Towing*, along with a Coachella address. Both the address and the business surprised me.

"He lives in Coachella?"

"They tell me he's an American, and the business is real."

I put the card away. Maybe a man in the towing business would be confident driving a large truck over rough ground, but maybe the overlap of business and large trucks was only a coincidence. Maybe Krista's Sanchez and Rudy Sanchez weren't the same coyote, and maybe Mary Sue was wrong about Q COY SANCHEZ, and the Sanchez in the note wasn't a coyote, but a shy flirt who was after Krista's boyfriend. Rudy Sanchez might never have heard of Krista Morales, and she might never have heard of or contacted him.

I said, "I spoke with my associate while I was waiting. There appears to be evidence of some kind of abduction at the crash site."

"Evidence the girl was taken?"

"Nothing specific to Krista Morales, no, sir, but what he's found isn't good."

"Then let's hope for the best."

He pursed his lips as if wrestling with how much he wanted to say, then finally told me.

"Have you seen news accounts of the mass graves found south of the border?"

I nodded. Mass graves containing scores of murder victims were some-times found, and were so horrific they made national news in the U.S.

He said, "These were immigrants abducted for ransom, Mr. Cole. *Bajadores* leave no witnesses. Let us hold a good thought until we know more."

I thanked Mr. Locano for his help, and went out to my car. I wanted to talk with Pike about what he had found, but Starkey called as I got into my car.

"I got your DMV on that Mustang. Can you talk?"

"Sure."

"No one owns it."

"What do you mean, no one owns it?"

"The owner of record isn't a person. DMV shows it's owned by the Ar-rowhead Trust. That means whoever owns it didn't buy the car as an indi-vidual, but bought it through the trust or transferred title to the trust. Rich people do that for tax reasons."

"I know, Starkey. Thanks."

"I know you know. Just sayin'. You want the address?"

"Yeah."

She didn't give me the address Mary Sue found in Krista's computer. She gave me a Wilshire Boulevard address not far from UCLA, on a stretch of Wilshire lined with corporate high-rises.

"One-oh-eight-eight-six Wilshire Boulevard, tenth floor, Westwood, nine-oh-oh-two-four."

She repeated it without my having to ask. Though trusts can and did hold title to anything, Mustangs weren't typically the type of vehicle held in trust. Trusts were used to shelter high-ticket items like yachts, Ferraris, and multimillion-dollar homes from inheritance taxes.

I said, "Starkey, you at the office?"

"Yeah. I'm done for the day. You want to swing by and pick me up?"

"No. I want you to check a name for me. Rudolfo or Rudy Sanchez. Has a business in Coachella called Sanchez and Sons Tow."

I gave her the address, and explained his occupation. If Sanchez had ever been arrested in California, his history would show on the California Department of Justice system. I could hear Starkey curse as she typed, and I didn't blame her. Officers couldn't tap into the system any time they wanted for any reason at all. She would have to enter a case number and her badge number, which meant her supervisor would be notified of her request, and she would have to justify the search. Fabricating a reason for checking out Rudolfo Sanchez was no big deal, but the paperwork was annoying.

Then she stopped cursing, and lowered her voice.

"Who's this guy Sanchez to you?"

"If he's the right Sanchez, he may have had contact with a woman I'm trying to find. But he might not be my guy. I won't know that until I talk to him."

"Good luck with that."

"You found him?"

"I found him. No criminal record. Not even a ticket."

I was half a beat behind her.

"Then why is he in the system?"

"He was found murdered by gunshot last Saturday afternoon. They fished him out of the Salton Sea."

I felt the dropsick feeling you get when your stomach washes with acid.

"Is this the same Sanchez?"

"Yes, Cole, I'm sure. Rudolfo Sanchez of Coachella."

"Sanchez and Sons Tow Service?"

"Jesus, Cole, yes, I'm looking at it right here. Owner of Sanchez and Sons Tow Service, Coachella, California. That would be *your* Rudolfo Sanchez. They found him backstrokin' last Saturday afternoon."

Saturday. Krista Morales and Jack Berman disappeared Friday night.

Starkey kept going, reading from her computer.

"No suspects at this time, anyone with information contact Sergeant Mike Bowers of the Coachella Police Department, blah blah blah."

I thought about Pike and the desert, and what we have found there.

"What kind of gun?"

"Nine-millimeter. Plugged him five times with the nine, and put a load of buckshot in him. A nine-millimeter and a shotgun. You know anything about this?"

"Just what I told you."

"Who's the woman?"

"A college student."

"Anything I should know?"

"It's like I said, Starkey. I'm not even sure he's the right Sanchez. You know how many Sanchezes there are?"

"I know it's the eighth most common Spanish name in America. That's a lot of Sanchezes."

"Yeah. I better get back to work."

"And I know you better not leave me hanging on this. You understand?"

"I understand."

I hung up and stared at my phone. Then I looked at the address in Coachella. Sanchez & Sons. It was three minutes after four. I called Joe Pike.

"Still there?"

"Yes."

"I'm coming back."

13.

The I-10 pulsed through Covina to Pomona, but I was on the phone with the Information operator by Ontario. Information showed thirty-two Sanchezes in the desert communities. One was listed as Rudolfo Junior, one as Rudy. Rudy's address was the same as his place of business. Rudolfo Junior's address appeared to be a condo or apartment in Coachella.

I copied Junior's address and phone, then asked for the number for Sanchez & Sons Tow.

"Emergency or business?"

"Business."

She connected me, and a male voice answered on the third ring.

"Towing."

"Ah, hey, this is Billy Dale. I didn't know if you'd be open, considering."

"We're open."

"Ah, is this Rudy Junior?"

"Eddie. Hold on, I'll get him."

"That's okay. I thought you might be one of the sons, and wanted to pay my respects. I heard what happened, and, man, it just floored me."

Eddie hesitated for a moment, then sounded more relaxed.

"Thanks. I'm the middle brother, Eddie. It's hit us pretty hard."

Middle implied three. At least one other was on the premises.

"They get the guy who did it? I mean, they can't just let some bastard get away with this. Rudy was a great guy."

"No. No, they haven't made any arrests. Thanks for asking."

"Ah, listen, I had some business with your dad. Could I stop around for a few minutes?"

"We're open till six."

"That'd be swell. Thanks."

Swell.

Six gave me fifty-two minutes.

I phoned Pike as I raced through Fontana to Redlands, where the 10 dropped south to the Banning Pass. Pike, already in the desert, had gone direct to their address.

"I'm thirty out. You on it?"

"Block away outside a building supply, opposite side of the street. I'm not alone."

"What's that mean?"

"Taco stand on the opposite corner. Asian male in a tan Subaru. Windows up for his AC. Second time I passed, saw him with binos."

"Police surveillance?"

"Whatever. He's watching."

I wondered if the police had learned Rudy Sanchez was a coyote, or if they had always known it. The police would make dealing with the brothers more difficult, but not impossible.

"Okay. What's he seeing?"

"Five men on the yard, one just left with a wrecker. Multiple trucks. Small office in the rear. Looks like a real business."

"Locano said it's legit. I spoke with one of the brothers."

"You think they know?"

"We'll see. They close at six. I'm twenty-five out. I'll cruise the yard, then we can figure this out."

"There's a Ralphs market a few blocks west on the other side of the freeway. You'll see me."

Pike killed the call, and I picked up the pace.

Coachella was low, flat, and gray despite heavy irrigation. The buildings all seemed to be built of concrete block or stucco, and most were as charming as storage units. Thirsty trees struggled against the onslaught of dry heat, and patchy lawns were never quite green, as if their true color was hidden by a thin film of dust that the locals could sweep away, but never defeat. A gentle desert breeze dropped powdery sand from the sky like fairy dust. It left Coachella looking like an outlet mall.

Pike was gone when I arrived at Sanchez & Sons, but the man in the Subaru was parked a car-length away from a tiny white taqueria stand with an easy view of the tow yard on the opposite side of the street. He was slumped behind the wheel exactly as Pike described, wearing shades as if they made him invisible, and a stylish gray porkpie hat. Three scruffy, dusty men who looked like they worked hard were lined up for tacos. They ignored the hat man, and he ignored them. He watched the tow yard.

Sanchez & Sons Tow Service was a large truck yard on the wrong side of the freeway. A chain-link fence circled the perimeter with a small office building at the rear that used to be a gas station. Block-letter signs on the fence read: TURN JUNK INTO CA$H! WE BUY OLD CARS! 24/7 SERVICE! LOCAL AND LONG DIST TOWS! Six white tow trucks all bearing Sanchez & Sons logos were parked behind the signs. The trucks ranged from light-duty wheel-lift trucks to medium-duty wreckers with blue cranes on their beds to a couple of flatbed lifters large enough to piggyback an RV. A sliding gate for the trucks to come and go was open, with a drooping black bow to acknowledge Sanchez's death. A young guy wearing a greasy blue work shirt was hosing one of the trucks. An older man was working under the hood of a different truck. Neither appeared armed or particularly threatening, but I hadn't expected banditos. I was more concerned about the hat in the Subaru. The police would have come the day Sanchez's body was identified. Depending on what they knew, they would have informed the family, then questioned both his family and employees about his activities on the days leading up to his murder. If they maintained a surveillance, it meant they knew of or suspected Rudy's extracurricular activities, which might make it more difficult to get information about Krista Morales. Three minutes later, I pulled up beside Pike, and got out of my car. We stood between our cars to talk.

Pike said, "The hat?"

"Still there, in front of the taco stand like you said."

"Mm."

"I'm thinking I'll go in alone, while you keep an eye on the hat."

"What about the brothers?"

"I'll feel them out. They may not even know what their father was doing."

Pike turned away without another word, slipped into his Jeep, and left. Mr. Small Talk.

Sixty-five seconds later, I parked on the street across from the gate, and no one except the hat man paid attention as I walked to the little office. The young guy washing the wrecker kept washing while an older man I hadn't seen before climbed aboard a light wheel-lifter, and backed past me toward the street. Off to help a stranded motorist. I couldn't see Pike and didn't know where he was, but neither did they. Especially the hat in the Subaru.

Cold air hit like a meat cooler when I entered the office. Two men were seated at a desk, one behind it with his chair rocked back, and the other beside it with his legs stretched out. They turned when I entered. The younger was in his late twenties and the man behind the desk was in his early thirties. The younger wore a blue work shirt with *Eddie* stitched on his left chest. The older wore a bright green Islander decorated with yellow palm trees and pink flamingos. This was probably Rudy Junior. Both had bruised eyes, lumps on their cheeks, and Rudy's upper lip was swollen. I could see the resemblance even under the bruises.

I said, "Hey."

The older guy said, "Hey. Can I help you?"

"I spoke with Eddie here earlier. You Rudy Junior?"

Rudy arched his eyebrows at his brother, who recognized my voice.

"This is the guy who called. He knew the old man."

I looked from Eddie to his brother.

"My condolences."

"Eddie said you had business with our dad?"

"That's right. I'm looking for Krista Morales. Either of you know her?"

They glanced at each other, with Eddie shaking his head.

Rudy Junior said, "Sorry, friend. Should we?"

"I'm pretty sure your father knew her, or at least spoke with her. I was hoping one of you might know what they talked about. Here, she wrote this—"

I took out the note and held it so they could see. While they looked, I noticed a black-and-white picture on the wall showing Eddie and Rudy J with the young guy washing the wrecker outside, and a much older man. The older man would be their father. All of them were smiling.

Eddie read the note aloud.

"Q coy Sanchez. What's it mean?"

"It means ask the coyote Sanchez. She wanted to know about bringing people up from the south. Your dad say anything about it?"

I watched Rudy J when I said it, trying to gauge his reaction. Eddie stood first, but Rudy Junior followed, moving with measured purpose.

"Who are you?"

"The man who's looking for Krista Morales. She's my interest here. Nothing else."

Eddie said, "He's a federal fucking agent."

Rudy Junior shrugged.

"Doesn't matter what he is. He's got the wrong Sanchezes. There's a lot of us. We're like Smith and Jones, only brown."

I said, "Why don't we ask your other brother? Maybe he knows something."

Rudy Junior pointed at a round clock on the wall. It wasn't Pinocchio.

"It's six. We're closed. You need to leave, or I'll call the police."

Eddie said, "Asshole fed."

They were glaring at me when Eddie suddenly focused on something behind me, and his face sagged.

"Oh shit."

I turned as Rudy J reached behind his desk for a baseball bat, and then the door opened.

A tough-looking Asian man in a nice suit and sunglasses swaggered in first. He had been born with a thick neck and large bones, but time in a gym gave him sharp cuts and rude angles. He grinned when he saw the baseball bat, then stepped aside as two more Asian men pushed the third brother inside ahead of them. He couldn't have been more than nineteen. They were lean and hard with no-bullshit expressions, and something told me they weren't police officers.

The second man held the youngest brother by the upper arm, and spoke to Rudy J as if I wasn't present, even though I was only three feet away.

"We gave you much time. Now you pay."

He barked the words in a heavy accent, each word a separate explosion.

Rudy J dipped his head toward me. He was afraid, but he was more afraid of what they would do to his brother than what I might overhear.

"Let him the hell go. Don't you see we got people here? We're doing business."

The three men glanced at me as if I had been invisible until that moment, then the man holding the kid barked a broken-English command.

"Leave now. Come back tomorrow."

I looked from him to the brothers, and wondered what was between them. I didn't like the way they held the kid, or the way they assumed I would leave, or how they wore suits in the hundred-degree heat.

He barked again, louder.

"Leave now."

I said, "I'm from the government. I'm here to ruin your day."

Now he barked in a language I didn't understand, and the big man reached for my arm. He was heavier and probably stronger, but he didn't have time to use his weight or strength. I rolled his hand away, stepped into him with my left foot, and brought my right knee up into his liver. He went down as Joe Pike came through the door, kicked the legs from beneath the last man, and slammed him facedown into the floor. Then Pike's gun was out, and up, and on the talker, and so was mine. Start to finish, three-quarters of one second.

I smiled at the talker.

"Nice suit."

He let the boy go, and the boy scurried to his brothers. Then the man said something else I didn't understand.

Pike said, "Korean."

The Korean didn't look scared.

"You should go. Go now."

Pike took small pistols off each of them, and slipped them into his pockets.

I looked at the brothers behind their desk. They didn't look like banditos or criminal coyotes. They looked like three rabbits pinned by the headlights.

I tipped my gun toward the suits.

"Who are these people?"

Rudy J wet his lips, then shook his head. Too scared to speak.

I said, "Want to call the police?"

Rudy J shook his head again, but it wasn't good enough for the Korean.

"They owe us money. You should not be involved."

Rudy J said, "Man, we don't. I told you. The Syrian took'm. I don't know what else to say."

He was pleading.

The big guy was moving like he might try to get up. I cocked my pistol, pointed it at his head, but spoke to the talker.

"If he gets up too fast, I'll hurt him."

The talker stared at me as if deciding whether to continue, then kicked the big man hard in the back, shouting in more Korean. He kicked him twice more, and then we all heard a loud buzzing. The talker reached into his pocket, came out with a vibrating cell phone, and looked outside through the glass. Everyone else looked, too.

Three men climbed from a dark gray four-door sedan. Short-sleeved Arrow shirts and ties, carrying their jackets like men who didn't want to put them on. A lanky African-American and a bald, pale Anglo got out of the front. A trim, well-built man with crew-cut red hair climbed from the back. They moved slowly, scanning their surroundings like they were getting the lay of the land, or maybe they wanted to make sure no one was going to shoot them. It was obvious they were cops even before the black cop took a hol-stered snub-nose from the car and clipped it to his belt beside a badge.

Rudy J said, "That's the police. The black guy, that's Detective Spurlow."

The head Korean glanced at me, then pulled his two friends to their feet as Rudy J continued.

"That bald guy is Lance. They're the ones told us about the old man. I don't know that other guy."

Eddie said, "Lange. It was Lange, not Lance."

Outside, the officers slipped into their jackets, shaking themselves be-cause the cloth stuck to their skin.

The head Korean stepped close, and looked like he wanted to rip out my heart.

"You have guns. Give back now."

Pike said, "Not him. Me."

The talker glared at Pike for a moment, then smiled as if he was giving Pike a break, and swaggered out through the door. His minions followed. All three smiled as they passed the officers, climbed into a black BMW sedan, and drove out of the yard.

Pike said, "Watch."

As they passed the Subaru, the man in the hat nodded at the men in the Beemer. A moment later, the man in the hat sat taller and started his car.

Pike trotted past the brothers and left through the rear.

The officers had gotten themselves together, and were coming our way. None of them hurried, but they didn't have far to go.

Rudy was staring at me. His mouth worked as if he was terrified of what I might do.

I said, "Who were those guys?"

"I don't know, man. They were in with my dad."

He wet his lips, and glanced at the approaching officers, and I glanced at them, too.

"I'm coming back."

I left through the front door just like the Koreans, nodded at the officers the way strangers do, and mumbled something about the heat. Spurlow nodded back and Lange ignored me, but the red-haired guy locked eyes with me and didn't let go.

I kept walking, just a man going to his car at the end of the day, only I wasn't. Each step was careful and measured, and with each step I hoped they wouldn't stop me.

When I passed through the gate, Spurlow and Lange were inside, but the red-haired guy was in the door. He was watching me with eyes so narrow they looked like slits.

Joe Pike called as I reached my car.

"The Subaru climbed the first on-ramp. The Beemer is somewhere ahead."

"Which direction?"

"L.A."

"Find the Beemer. Follow it. I'll stay with the brothers."

I pulled around the corner, parked behind the taco stand, and waited for the police.

JACK AND KRISTA:
nine hours after
they were taken

14.

They were herded from blackness through a blood-red world, then into light so bright Krista closed her eyes. When she opened them, squinting against the glare, they were shuffling through a small house, Jack close behind her. Now in the harsh light, this was the first time she saw the others clearly. They were mostly Asian, but also a few Latins and people who might have been from the Middle East or India. One by one, they were searched as they walked. Belts and shoes were taken, and tossed into a growing pile. Six or eight men with shock prods and clubs pushed the crowd through the house. Krista did not look at them. She kept her eyes down, afraid to make contact.

The house was shabby, and empty of furniture. The harsh light came from hundred-watt bulbs in shade-less lamps. The shuffling line slowed, then was prodded into a small room.

Behind her, Jack's whisper.

"We're fucking trapped."

Heavy plywood panels were screwed over the windows, completely covering them. The floor was a stained wall-to-wall carpet, a narrow door revealed an empty closet, and the sickly blue walls bore crayon marks and holes where tape and nails had been removed. An empty plastic bucket, one roll of toilet paper, and a case of plastic water bottles waited in the corner.

Krista guessed they were in a boy's bedroom. The bedroom was small, filled quickly, and then the door closed.

No one moved. The people who now filled the crowded room stood as if waiting for something more to happen, as if they were too shocked or afraid to move.

Krista and Jack did not move, either. She turned to Jack, and he hugged her, and they stood without moving as people around them cried.

Krista cried, too, and felt Jack sob as he held her.

The man said, "I am Samuel Rojas. You may call me Sam."

Seeing she was Latin, he spoke to her in Spanish and she answered in the same, pretending to be a Mexican.

People were taken from the room in no particular order. The door would open, a man would come in, motion to someone, and take that person away. They always came back a few minutes later, and no one was hurt, so Krista wasn't afraid when the guard she would soon know as Mr. Rojas motioned her to him. Jack held her arm a moment too long, but she pried his hand gently away, and told him it would be fine.

The man brought her to the kitchen, and they sat facing each other on the dirty vinyl floor. Following Rojas to the kitchen, she saw other guards in paired conversation with prisoners in the living and dining rooms. Krista also noted the windows in these rooms were covered by the same heavy plywood, and the front door was sealed in the same way. She felt a hollow sickness in her stomach when she realized the entire house was a prison, and suddenly the kitchen felt hotter even though the AC was blasting.

Once they were seated, Rojas opened a spiral notebook. The cover showed a unicorn reared on its hind legs.

"What is your name?"

"Krista Morales."

"Where are you from, Krista?"

"Hermosillo. In Sonora."

"It is very pretty there. I have always wanted to see it. I am from Torreón, in Coahuila. It is not so pretty there."

Rojas made notes in the spiral notebook as they talked. He had a reassuring smile and a gentle voice.

Krista heard the Asian language in the next room, and a frustrated conference in Spanish between two of the guards. None of them spoke the language, so they had no way to communicate with the prisoner.

"Do you have family there in Hermosillo?"

"No, I am the last. The aunt I lived with, she died."

"That is such terrible news. Is this why you are traveling north?"

"Yes. There is nothing for me at home."

"Do you have family in the north, or a job?"

"My mother."

Rojas smiled, and Krista knew she had said the right thing. She had desperately been trying to recall everything she knew about how *bajadores* operated, and what the people from Guatemala had told her.

"Ah, that is very good for you. A mother in your new home. Where is she?"

"Los Angeles. A place called Eagle Rock."

"Ah, good. She is waiting for you?"

"Yes. She sent her friend's son to pick me up."

Now Rojas cocked his head.

"What friend is this?"

"Her friend's son, Jack Berman. The Anglo boy who is with me. He was waiting at the airplane when you took us."

Rojas wet his lips, and glanced toward the living room before going on.

"This boy, he is here?"

"Yes. In the room."

Rojas went to the entry, and gestured to someone in the living room. A moment later, a dark man with long hair and tiny, jet black eyes joined him. The man stared at Krista as Rojas whispered in his ear. They had a quiet conversation, then the man walked away, and Rojas returned to resume their conversation.

"Does she have a good job, your mother?"

"She is a housekeeper."

"That is good, steady work. Do you have other family? Aunts, uncles, cousins?"

"No. There is only my mother."

Rojas scribbled quickly.

"What is her name and phone number?"

"Why do you wish to know this?"

"She will have to pay our expenses before we deliver you. Unfortunate, but once she has paid, we will let you go home."

"She is a housekeeper."

"This is good, steady work, so she probably has savings, and maybe a generous employer. We will let you call her. Not now, but later."

Krista gave him her mother's name and cell phone number. As Rojas was recording these things in his ledger, two men entered from the utility room, which was the same door through which Krista and the others were brought into the house. The first man was tall and dark, with hollow cheeks and the face of a hawk. Krista thought he was a deeply tanned Anglo, then realized he was Arab. The other was a shorter, burly Latin, with broad shoulders and a large stomach. The tall man glanced down at her, but paid no attention. He wore tight designer jeans and a knit shirt that showed overdeveloped arms and shoulders. His long, black hair was pulled back into a ponytail. One glance at her, and the tall man strode across the kitchen to the entry, and called for someone named Vasco. The man with tiny eyes reappeared almost at once, smiling broadly as he greeted the new man. Krista saw that his teeth were jagged and broken, as if he had been in many fights, and never had them fixed. The two men disappeared as they moved into the house.

The burly man nudged Rojas with his toe, and spoke.

"Got the food out here. C'mon, the Syrian doesn't want to spend the night."

Rojas answered in English.

"Fuck you, Orlato. I'm not your bitch."

"You can tell it to The Man when I tell him why he has to wait. Then we'll see whose bitch you are."

Orlato toed him again.

"C'mon, make this *puta* here help. It's only a few pies. How many you get?"

"Thirty-two."

"Cool."

Rojas switched to Spanish when he told Krista to follow him. He led her out of the kitchen into the utility room and then into the garage. The utility room held a washer and dryer. A door that probably opened on the side of the house was covered by plywood just like the windows. There would be no way to open the door without removing the plywood, but a dozen wood screws held it in place.

Earlier, when they arrived at the house, the big truck had backed up to the garage, and black plastic hung to hide its cargo as they unloaded. Now, the truck and the dim red lights that illuminated the garage were gone, and the garage held a charcoal gray Lexus SUV and a long blue BMW sedan.

Rojas said, "Smells like pepperoni. Yum!"

The BMW's back seat was filled with three stacks of giant pizza boxes, five boxes per stack. Rojas handed five boxes to Krista, took ten for himself, and also two plastic grocery bags. When she followed him back between the cars to the utility room, she saw a switch mounted on the wall by the door inside the garage. Wires ran up the wall from the switch, across the garage ceiling, then down to the overhead door's motor. Krista instantly knew this was a switch to open and close the garage door.

Krista's heart beat faster as she considered the switch. The door would be noisy, and would take precious seconds to rise, but one push, and she could be free.

Then they were through the door and inside the utility room. Like the rest of the house, it was small and cramped, and Rojas clumsily bumped into the washing machine with his stack of pizzas. The top two boxes fell, Rojas tried to catch them, and three more boxes hit the floor with a crash. Rojas cursed, and told her to help him pick up the food. When she set her own boxes on the washing machine to help, Krista noticed a square access door in the ceiling. It had not been blocked or screwed shut, and would open into the attic so people could service air-conditioning ducts or pipes or whatever was in the crawl space.

It was in the ceiling, but she could reach it by climbing onto the washer.

Krista Morales, who was smart and resourceful, began to work out a plan.

15.

Five seconds after they took her, Jack pushed to the door and tried the knob, but it was locked. He twisted as hard as he could, pushed, jerked back and forth, but it was no good. These weren't ordinary interior doorknobs and locks. The knobs had been changed so the doors could be locked from the outside, and the locks were deadbolts. Jack punched the door in frustration and edged through the crowd, trying to burn off his fear, but had no place to move. He finally made his way to a spot against the plywood, and leaned with his back to the wall, studying the other prisoners.

The little room felt like a steam bath. A laser of cold air blew from an AC vent in the ceiling, but was immediately swallowed by the heat of so many bodies crowded into the tiny space. Their smell was making him sick, and he wondered how many days they had been traveling.

Thirteen people were wedged into the room. Jack and Krista made fifteen. Nine were Asians who appeared to be in their twenties or thirties, though three were much older. There were two singleton Latins and the Guatemalan couple. All of them looked hungry, tired, and poor. Their shabby, sweat-stained clothes were either too thin or too coarse, and their eyes were frightened. A few hugged meager cloth bags, but these had been looted when they were taken.

The Asians had clumped in the opposite corner, most skinny young women and men who sat on their heels with vacant expressions, but one sat to the side by himself. He was young, too, but didn't look like the others. He was muscular and fit, with nice clothes and glistening hair that was short on the sides and straight up on top. His eyes were hard and angry, and his face rippled as he clenched and unclenched his jaw. He must have felt Jack's stare because he suddenly looked dead into Jack's eyes, and Jack glanced away.

Jack said, "Does anyone here speak English? Any English speakers?"

The Guatemalan man answered.

"I say a leetle some."

A slim Asian girl raised a delicate hand.

"I understand some. My speaking not so well."

"Where are you from?"

"Korea. Are we close to Olympic Boulevard? We go to Olympic Boulevard."

Her accent was so bad Jack did not understand her at first, then realized she was saying "Olympic Boulevard." So many Koreans had settled between Olympic and Wilshire in the midtown area, the neighborhood was now known as Koreatown. Jack and Krista had been twice, once for *galbi* and once to a karaoke bar. Neither of them had sung, but it had been fun to watch.

They were interrupted when the door opened, and two guards entered. The first guard was a short, muscular African-American. He cast his eyes around the room, then pointed at the tough-looking Korean kid.

"You. Yeah, you, c'mon, get up."

He spoke perfect English, but Jack couldn't tell if the Korean kid understood English or not. The guard motioned him to get up, so he slowly stood. The guard motioned him closer, so he went closer. He didn't shuffle forward with downcast eyes like the others. He held himself erect and met the guard's eyes. The guard took his arm, and they left.

Two minutes later, the door opened again, and Jack felt a rush of relief when he saw Krista. Her eyes told him to play it cool, so he showed no emotion as she came toward him.

The guard who had taken her stepped in, looked at Jack, and motioned him over.

"Jack Berman?"

"Yeah, that's right."

As Jack passed through the crowd, Krista blocked his path for one second with her back to the guard, just long enough to whisper.

"Remember what I told you."

Then she moved aside and sat with the Guatemalans as Jack followed the guard, trying hard to remember what Krista had told him.

The man led him to the big room off the entry of the house near the kitchen. Once upon a time this had been a living room, but now it was a box with the doors and windows covered by heavy sheets of plywood. Jack caught a strong smell of pizza that left him feeling hungry.

The man pointed at a spot on the floor near the entry, and told Jack to sit. The tough Korean kid was with two guards in the far corner, and another guard was speaking with a Latin woman in the opposite corner. The Korean glanced at Jack, then glared at his guard.

"My name is Samuel Rojas. You can call me Sam."

Jack nodded, but said nothing. Rojas had a spiral notebook and a pen.

"There was a silver Mustang. Was this your car?"

"Yeah. Where is it?"

"You're a U.S. citizen?"

"Yeah. What did you do with my car?"

"How do you know Krista?"

"I don't. I know her mom. She and my mom are friends. What the fuck is going on here? Who are you?"

"What's your mother's name and phone number? We'd like to call her."

"Good luck. She's in China."

Rojas looked doubtful.

"She lives in China?"

"A tour. She went with our church group. Why are you asking this stuff?"

"Your father?"

"He died last year. Why are we in this boarded-up house?"

While they spoke, a tall man with a ponytail and a shorter man with bad teeth emerged from the hall and stopped in the entry. They spoke softly in Spanish, but the tall man didn't look Latin.

"You have brothers or sisters?"

"I'm it."

"When will your mother be back?"

"A couple of weeks. Two."

Rojas studied Jack, and Jack wondered what he was thinking. Then Rojas glanced in his notebook, turned a page, and looked up.

"The Mustang is a nice vehicle. How did you pay for it?"

"My mom bought it for me. Why does this matter? Why are we talking about this?"

"You had no driver's license. Don't you have a driver's license?"

"I left it in the car."

Rojas shook his head.

"There was nothing in the car."

"Dude, I left it in the car with my wallet. My wallet, my credit card, my money. What happened to that stuff?"

Rojas told Jack to stay where he was, and joined the tall man and the man with bad teeth. Jack did not understand what they were saying, but the tall man frowned at Jack, and seemed to do most of the talking. Rojas did most of the nodding, as if he was receiving instructions.

Jack was watching them when the tough Korean shouted, his words exploding like rapid-fire gunshots. The Korean was on his feet when Jack turned. Two guards hit him with their shoulders down, driving him into the corner. A third guard joined in, jabbing a shock prod into the Korean's ribs that crackled so loud when the current discharged, Jack heard it across the room. A second shock prod appeared, and the third guard swung a club. The Korean went down, but the club kept falling and the shock prods popped and snapped as the Korean pulled himself into a ball. The kicks and punches and electric snapping went on forever, until Jack lurched to his feet.

"Stop it! He's down!"

Jack took a step, but something hit him hard from behind, and staggered him forward. An arm wrapped his throat and lifted him off his feet.

"You want some?"

He crashed belly down on the floor. The man with the bad teeth was on top of him, raspy voice in Jack's ear.

"You want it like him? I got some, you want it."

In that moment, Jack saw the Korean. They were both belly down on the carpet. The Korean was looking at him. The three men on his back were tying his hands behind his back.

The man with bad teeth punched Jack in the side, the back, and the back of his head, and Jack clenched his eyes. He was jerked to his feet, spun around, and the man slapped him. Jack tried to cover his face, but the man slapped him again, then pushed down his hands.

"You want me to tie your hands? I tie your hands, you'll shit in your pants. You want that?"

"No."

"What did you say?"

"No, sir."

"You gonna give me trouble?"

"No, no trouble."

The man held Jack by the back of his neck with a grip like pliers. He pushed Jack out of the living room, down the hall, and into the bedroom. He stopped in the open doorway, holding Jack as he stared at Krista. He was very close. His teeth were so jagged and crooked they looked like the teeth carved in a pumpkin. He looked from Krista to Jack, then leaned so close the warmth of his breath tickled Jack's ear.

"I got my eye on her. You give me bullshit again, we see what happens, huh?"

The man shoved Jack hard into the room, then slammed the door. The lock bolt thudding home sounded like a headsman's ax hitting the block.

Jack tried to make it to the bucket before he threw up, but didn't.

ELVIS COLE:
four days before
he is taken

16.

The police stayed with the Sanchez brothers as the day settled into darkness, and the cooling air grew silky. I bought a Diet Coke and two chicken tacos while I waited. The tacos were Mexico City style. Two small corn tortillas wrapped around chicken, onions, and cilantro, with a generous helping of fresh jalapeño and salty green tomatillo sauce. No beans or cheese. Beans and cheese were for sissies. The tacos were hot and juicy, and the heat increased as I ate. So good I ordered two more. Delicious.

I saw movement in the office from time to time, but my angle was bad to see more. Eighteen minutes after I ate the last taco, the red-haired cop came out to their car. He took a briefcase from the back seat, took out a folder, then put the briefcase back. He started back to the office, but abruptly stopped and studied the street as if he sensed someone watching. I stepped farther behind the taco stand, watching him through the sliver of space between the stand and a telephone pole.

My phone buzzed in my pocket, but I did not move.

He did a slow three-sixty until his eyes settled on the taco stand. A middle-aged Latina was ordering food. The red-haired cop was forty yards away, but I still saw the lines that trapped his eyes like spiderwebs.

The phone buzzed like an insistent alarm clock. I worried the woman would hear it, and turn from the window to look. I covered the phone with my hand, and waited.

He stared at the stand for eight or ten years, then abruptly returned to the office.

I checked the call, and found a message from Carol Starkey.

"Dude. What the fuck? Call me."

Starkey talks that way.

I called her back.

"It's me."

"Are you *trying* to fuck me, you moron?"

She didn't sound happy.

"What's up?"

"I had the Feds in here, man. ICE. The Immigration police? They pinged my search on your boy, Sanchez. They wanted to know my fucking interest."

"What did you tell them?"

"Oh, are we worried now? Are we *scared* I ratted you out?"

"I know you wouldn't rat me out, Starkey. What's the fallout on you? What did you tell them?"

"The name came up in a Green Light hit I'm working in Hollywood. Told'm I ran the name for due diligence, but my Rudy Sanchez lives in Venice, not Coachella. He wasn't my guy."

Green Light hit meant Mexican Mafia. *La Eme.* Dropping their name lent credibility to her search for a Spanish surname.

"Good dodge."

"Did you know he was a coyote?"

"Yeah."

"You asshole."

"I wanted to find him, Starkey. What difference is it the kind of criminal he is?"

"Yeah, well, ICE was all over this fuckin' criminal. He was involved with the Sinaloa cartel. Is there anything else you should tell me?"

"Who killed him?"

"If they know, they didn't tell me. You got an idea?"

"Did they mention Korea or gangsters from Korea?"

"What are we talkin' about here, the U fuckin' N? Do you know something about this?"

"Not yet. I gotta go, Starkey. Thanks."

"Don't leave me hanging."

"Gotta go."

The three officers came out to their car as I put away the phone. I thought they would bring one or more of the brothers in handcuffs, but the brothers stayed in the office. Twelve minutes later, the youngest brother, James, came out, mounted a motorcycle parked beside the office, and buzzed through the gate. Eight minutes later, Eddie and Rudy Junior came out together, but went to separate cars. Eddie drove away first. Rudy J eased through the gate, but stopped in the street, pulled the gate closed, and locked it with a padlock. By the time he locked the gate and got back into his car, I pulled around the side of the taco stand, and turned out behind him.

Three-quarters of a mile later, Rudy Sanchez Junior pulled into the Ralphs where Pike had waited for me. Coincidence.

He was out of his car and heading inside when I pulled up alongside him.

"Get in."

He started around me, so I tapped the gas, cutting him off.

"I'll be here when you come out, Rudy. Get in."

"I'm not getting in there with you."

"All we're going to do is talk."

He started the other way, but I squeaked the rear end, cutting him off again.

"Talk, Rudy. I'm not going to lump up your face or arrest you. I might be able to help."

He studied me.

"You're not a federal agent?"

"I'm looking for Krista Morales."

"I don't know who she is."

"That's okay. It's enough that I know. C'mon. Get in the car."

Rudy stared at me for five heartbeats, then walked around the front of my car and got in. I drove to the far side of the Ralphs, and parked in a pool of shadow. He sat quietly, staring straight ahead as if an enormous weight was crushing him and he didn't know how to stop it.

"Are you and your brothers part of this?"

He shook his head.

"No. The old man kept us out. It was his thing, not ours. He didn't want us involved."

"Bringing people north."

"Yeah. North. He started when he was a kid, bringing up his cousins. He was born here. They weren't. I guess he liked doing it."

"Who were the Korean guys?"

"People with guns."

"Gangsters?"

"Jesus, look at my face. I don't know who they are. I never saw those guys before a few days ago."

"Did they kill your father?"

"Not them. They paid to have people brought up, and their people didn't get here. Two hundred thousand dollars. Two *hundred*. Now they want their money or their people, and they sure as hell aren't paying a ransom to get them."

I flashed on Nita Morales, getting the ransom demand.

"The people your father brought up that night were kidnapped?"

"That's what *bajadores* do. They steal people, then milk their families. The old man was hijacked."

"How do you know a *bajadore* took them?"

"Some cartel assholes came to see us. They told us a *bajadore* ripped off the *pollos*."

The feds had told Starkey Rudy J's father was involved with the Sinaloa cartel.

"He worked for Sinaloa?"

"How'd you know that?"

"I know stuff. I'm a swami."

"Not by choice, man. Those Sinaloa pricks stole his business."

This fit with what Thomas Locano had told me.

"So he wasn't a freelance coyote? The Koreans gave their money to the Sinaloas?"

"Hell, yeah. Shit, we didn't even know the old man went out that night. Then some kids found him in the lake. That's when Spurlow and Lange came to see us. That's how we found out. Then the Sinaloas came around and told us the *bajadore* got him—some guy called the Syrian."

Starkey was right. It was beginning to sound like the United Nations.

"A Syrian from Syria?"

Rudy J rubbed his face with both hands.

"Who the fuck knows? They made it sound like this guy rips them off all the time. Mostly, they told us they'd kill us if we talked to the police."

"And let you hang with the Koreans?"

Rudy J slumped, and shook his head.

"They said they'd take care of it, but you saw. I think Sinaloa is scared of those guys, but they ain't giving out refunds."

"So the Koreans are looking to you."

Rudy blinked hard, and I knew he was blinking back tears. He suddenly shouted.

"FUCK!"

I watched him there in the shadows, and believed him. Rudy J and his brothers had not known what their father was doing that night, were not part of his father's business, but were now held hostage by the events of that night like Nita and Krista Morales.

I said, "You know the old crash site where a drug runner's plane went down, south of here in the desert?"

Rudy J slowly looked at me.

"I used to go out there when I was a kid. All of us did."

"Did your father use it as a transfer point?"

Rudy J frowned, but I could see he was thinking.

"Sometimes. Coyotes and smugglers used that old wreck all the time, then no one used it for years. I remember him saying, man, why waste a good spot?"

"What about the night he was killed?"

"I don't know. It's not like he told us his routes or anything, but he liked that spot. He said it was easy to find."

Maybe too easy.

I could see Rudy Senior's big truck lumbering out of the desert, and a man called the Syrian moving in fast to hijack his human cargo. It was easy to see Krista and Jack being caught in the Syrian's net.

"Maybe we can help each other, Rudy. The Sinaloas who came to see you, can you reach them if you have to?"

"You're not a fed?"

"Would it matter if I were?"

He studied me a moment longer, then turned away as if he was embarrassed to admit the truth.

"Not at this point. No. I just want to get out of this nightmare."

"If I need to talk to them, will you set it up?"

"Yeah. Yeah, I'll set it up. They gave me a number."

I brought him back to his car, dropped him off, then drove home to the city. Everyone had a story, and the stories were fitting together, but I needed more, and I wanted it fast.

Krista and Jack had been taken. They had been taken by a *bajadore* the Sinaloa cartel called the Syrian. I had done good work that day.

I gazed into the black landscape beyond the freeway lights, and knew Krista and Jack were out in the darkness. If I found the Syrian, I would find them.

I drove with the windows down, and the clean roaring wind, until I was free of the desert, and called Joe Pike.

17.

The silky night air was cool as I drove west toward Los Angeles. The wind's heavy scream carved a peaceful place in the world when Joe answered my call.

"You on the hat?"

"The hat joined up with the Beemer, and followed it to a *soju* bar on Vermont north of Olympic. The hat and the suits went in, so I'm watching the bar."

Soju was a Korean liquor.

"Is that in Koreatown?"

"Yes. The Blue Raccoon."

I jotted the name.

"What are they doing?"

"Unknown. They're inside, I'm a block off. The bar's in a two-story strip mall. A barbeque place. *Noraebang* studios. A couple of businesses. Valet. Upscale place."

I sketched out what I had learned from Rudy J about the Koreans and Sinaloas, and how the brothers were caught in the cross fire.

Pike said, "Is he telling the truth?"

"I think so, yes. The police are on them, the Koreans are jamming them for the two hundred thousand, and the Sinaloas are letting them hang. That can be good for us. If the Sinaloas told the truth about this guy they call the Syrian, it's possible the Syrian scooped up Krista and Berman along with the hijack. Rudy confirmed his father sometimes used the crash site as a transfer point."

Pike grunted.

"Would the Syrian take them south?"

If they were south of the border, it would be more difficult to find them and reach them.

"I don't know. I don't know anything about the Syrian, and neither do the brothers. All they know is what the Sinaloas told them."

"Can you find out?"

"I'm on it. I'm calling Locano as soon as we hang up. If he can't help, we'll find another way. If we have to, we'll go straight to the Sinaloas."

Pike grunted again, and this time I knew he liked it. Pike was a straight-ahead person.

I said, "We need intel on the Koreans, too. Can you get the tags off the Subaru and the Beemer?"

"Stand by."

Pike recited the two tags as I copied them.

"How long can you stay with these guys?"

"Whatever it takes."

"Stay with the Beemer. He goes home, get the address."

Pike hung up without another word, and I called Thomas Locano. It was after office hours, but I called his office first, and left a long, meandering message. I wanted to give him time to pick up in case he was working late, but he didn't. I looked up his unlisted home number, and that's where I reached him.

Mr. Locano sounded disturbed.

"We're unlisted. How did you get this number?"

"I'm a detective, Mr. Locano. I had it in two calls."

He still didn't like it, and now sounded impatient.

"Well, what? We have guests. We were about to sit down."

"Rudolfo Sanchez is dead. He was murdered on the same night Krista Morales and her boyfriend disappeared."

"Oh my God. Hold on. I have to move to another room."

I heard movement, then he came back on the line, talking as he walked, though his voice was low and guarded.

"All right, I can talk. Are these two things connected?"

"I believe so. Sanchez wasn't a freelance operator like you were told. He used to be, but a cartel took over."

"Which cartel? The Bajas, Tijuana, the Beltrán-Leyva, who? There are many."

"He was bringing people north for the Sinaloas. They believe he was hijacked by a *bajadore* they call the Syrian."

"How do you know these things?"

I told him about Rudy J and his brothers, and how Rudy Senior had sometimes used the crash site as a transfer point to deliver the people he brought north.

"We know Krista and Berman stayed at the crash site after their friends returned to town. If they were at the scene when Sanchez arrived, it's possible they were swept up in the hijacking."

"You believe the *bajadore* has them?"

"Yes."

I described the cartridge casings and tracking patterns Pike and I found in the desert, and how they indicated three smaller vehicles had assaulted a larger vehicle. I told him about the brown stain Pike found, and the footprints indicating a large number of people had clustered at the back of the larger truck.

"It would explain the ransom calls Nita received from her daughter. That's how *bajadores* work their kidnappings, isn't it? They force the victims to call their families."

"Yes. This is how it is done."

"Have you heard of this guy before, the Syrian?"

"Never. Is he from Syria?"

"No idea. They didn't use his given name or say why he was called the Syrian, and Rudy didn't ask. He just wanted them to leave."

Locano was quiet before speaking again.

"Were the sons involved?"

"Rudy says they weren't, and I believe him. They're scared. They're caught between the cartel, the police, and Korean gangsters who had people on the truck. I need a lead on this guy, Mr. Locano. If he has Krista Morales, then I need to find him."

Mr. Locano was quiet for several long moments, but I knew he was thinking, and I knew he would help.

"I have helped people who were with the Sinaloas. Let me speak with them."

"That would be great."

"May I have your home phone? I might call tonight, or early tomorrow."

I gave him my cell and my home, then asked for a second favor.

"I'm going to phone Nita, but I would like you to call her, too. She could use some reassurance."

"Because she has no documents?"

"Yes, sir. She has enough on her mind without having to worry about losing her home and her business."

"She'll lose neither. The Immigration courts are overloaded with violent criminals they can't deport fast enough. A woman like Nita with an established business and employees can easily get a stay of removal. These things are at the judge's discretion. We see this all the time."

"Will you explain this to her?"

"Should it come to that, I will represent her."

"Thanks, Mr. Locano. For that, and for everything. Anything you find out about the Syrian will help."

"I'll get back to you as soon as I can."

I put down the phone, and took a deep breath. I wanted to call Nita Morales, but wasn't yet sure what I was going to tell her and how I was going to say it. I rolled down the window and filled the car with the thunder of rushing air. The tail lights ahead were frozen red eyes; the oncoming headlights were screaming white tracers. I had been racing hard all day, maybe too hard, maybe so hard I needed to slow down before I made a mistake that cost Krista Morales her life.

Pike had given me the tags off the Subaru and Beemer. I rolled up the window, found the scrap with the numbers, and called an L.A. County Deputy Sheriff I knew who worked the West Hollywood night watch. She was fast, efficient, and happy to cooperate for two guaranteed Dugout Club seats to a Dodgers-Giants game.

The DMV showed the Subaru was registered to a Paul Andrew Willets in Northridge, California. I wasn't an expert on Subarus, but the DMV showed Mr. Willets as owning a blue Subaru, and the hat man's car was tan. This told me the hat man was driving a stolen car, and had swapped plates with Mr. Willets's vehicle.

The BMW told a different story. It was registered to something called Yook Yune Entertainment with a Wilshire Boulevard address showing a suite number. The suite might be an actual office, but I suspected it was a mail drop. I used my iPhone to google Yook Yune Entertainment, but found no website, business listing, or mentions of any kind.

Joe Pike was still parked one block from the strip mall when I called to fill him in. Neither the Beemer nor the Subaru had moved. It was seven minutes after ten that night.

Pike said, "Yook is a family name. Don't know about Yune."

"Forget the hat. Follow the Beemer when it leaves. A residential address might help us get an ID."

"Remember Jon Stone?"

"Sure."

"Jon speaks Korean. He spends time here. He might be able to help."

"Great idea. Call him."

Pike hung up without waiting for a response, and left me with no one but my phone and Nita Morales. I went through what I was going to say, then dialed her number. There was much to tell, and most of it was bad. Even tough-guy detectives like me hate to spread the bad word.

But when she answered my call, her voice was as brittle as dried parchment, and my rehearsal was useless. She had already heard something far worse than what I was going to say.

"This is real, isn't it? Krista's been kidnapped."

"What happened?"

"She called this evening, in that funny voice with the accent. When the man took the phone, he demanded more money. I told him they had gotten their last cent from me—"

Her voice broke when she said it, but she pushed through the sob.

"They made her scream."

I said, "Did you wire the money?"

"Not yet."

"Pay them. Pay, and keep paying, and they will keep her alive."

"Did you know this was real?"

"Yes. Yes, I found out what happened, and how, and I know who took her."

"Who did this?"

"A *bajadore* called the Syrian. You know what that is, a *bajadore*?"

"Yes, yes, of course. Where is she?"

"With the Syrian. I'm looking for him. When I find him, I'll find Krista."

"What are you going to do?"

"Bring her home."

"How? How will you do that?"

"I'll take her. Trust me, Ms. Morales. I'll find her, I'll take her, and I will bring her home."

"Please. Please, Mr. Cole—"

Her voice broke, and was swallowed by tears.

"Cry, Nita. Cry all you want. Talk. I'm with you. I won't let you go."

I pushed on through the darkness, whispering to Nita Morales until her signal was lost in the roaring black night, wondering what they had done to make Krista Morales scream.

JACK AND KRISTA:
four days after
they were taken

18.

Jack spoke louder than necessary when he asked for the soap.

"Can I have some soap? I got a mess back there."

Her answer was just as formal.

"Sure, but I need it back. I have all these pots."

"I'll bring it right back. Promise."

They were in the kitchen in open view of two guards, one who sat in a lawn chair in the entry, and another who leaned against the dining room wall at the opposite end of the kitchen.

Jack checked to make sure the guards weren't watching, and lowered his voice.

"Did you see? Piece of cake. They let me come."

"Shh."

Krista gave Jack the bottle of Dawn dishwashing liquid. He started away, then turned back.

"Could I have some of those paper towels, too? I'm going to need more than toilet paper to get up this mess."

"Okay. Sure. Take the roll."

She gave Jack the roll of paper towels and watched him walk back to the bathroom at the far end of the house. Krista worked in the kitchen. Jack's job was emptying the bucket of urine from their room. It was a disgusting job, and the contents of the bucket weren't always liquid. Jack was allowed to carry the bucket to the bathroom three or four times a day, where he flushed the contents and cleaned the bucket in the bathtub. A few minutes earlier, he had spilled some of the contents onto the toilet seat and floor so he could come to Krista for the soap and towels. He had done this on purpose to see if the bathroom guard would follow him to the kitchen or let him go alone. The guard had let him go by himself.

Having the soap and the towels would also allow Jack to return, which was part of their plan. Krista wanted Jack to have a few minutes alone in the utility room. She had been unable to pry open the service hatch in the ceiling, so now Jack would try, but he needed a reason to be in the utility room.

Krista returned to the sink and continued washing the pots.

The guards had assigned jobs to the Spanish and English speakers. Only two of the Koreans spoke English, and none spoke Spanish, so the Koreans were kept in their rooms. Now, on the fourth day, Krista still did not know how many people were in the house even though she and two other women cooked for them. She rarely saw the second group of prisoners, and the number of guards kept changing, sometimes six and sometimes eight. Krista guessed the total number living in the house was over forty.

The prisoners were given one meal a day, in the late afternoon. Krista and two other Spanish-speaking women prepared the meal, served it, and cleaned up afterward. This was good because Krista had more freedom than Jack and most of the others. They cooked large pots of beans or soup with huge quantities of rice or noodles. There was little meat, though sometimes a guard brought extra beef or chicken for himself and the other guards, and often brought takeout pizza or tamales. They never shared.

The cooks were given three large dented pots, one enormous skillet, two peelers, and a bucket of battered spatulas, ladles, and spoons. They were not given a knife. If onions or cabbage needed to be chopped, a guard chopped it, or let one of the women use his knife while he stood by. This was the guard in the lawn chair, whose name was Miguel. For cleaning, they were given a box of S.O.S soap pads and the large bottle of Dawn soap. Blue.

Krista's duties took three to four hours, start to finish, which she spent in the kitchen and utility room with its ceiling hatch and door to the garage. Miguel had wheeled a large plastic garbage can into the utility room at Krista's request, which made it easier to dump the heavy amounts of peelings, garbage, and leftovers. It also made it easier for her to chart the guards' comings and goings, learn how they moved through the house, and sneak glimpses into the garage when they opened the door.

Currently, Miguel occupied the lawn chair, a reed-thin guard she called the Praying Mantis loafed in the dining room, and a third guard slept on a futon on the living room floor. Miguel dozed off after lunch every afternoon. She had watched him. His eyes would close, his chin would lower, and he would fall asleep.

Watching Miguel nod out made Krista smile.

The remaining guards were in the back of the house by the prisoners. One usually floated in the hall to watch the bedroom doors and take people to the bathroom. If a prisoner needed the bathroom to make number two, they weren't allowed to close the door. You had to do your business while the guard watched from the hall. Sometimes two or three guards gathered at the door, and leered at the women. It was humiliating and frightening, and some of the women now did their business in the bedroom buckets while other women held up shirts given by the men in a kind of sorrowful privacy curtain.

During the day, the only time the bathroom door closed was when someone was brought inside to make a call for money. Samuel Rojas had taken Krista into the bathroom twice. The first time, she had been scared when Rojas closed the door, but he explained he did this so they wouldn't be interrupted or disturbed. Both calls had been low-key and calm. People were brought in to call throughout the day, so the door was closed a lot.

Krista put the last pot aside to dry, then brought leftover beans to the refrigerator. From the fridge, she could see beyond Miguel through the hall to the bathroom. She couldn't see Jack, but she knew he was inside toweling up the mess. As she watched, Rojas and the guard with the bad teeth approached the bathroom. The guard with the teeth made her skin prickle. His name was Vasco Medina, and he was in charge. He drifted through the house telling the guards what to do, or kicking them when they fell asleep. She found him all the more creepy because she never knew when he would appear. She would turn around or look up, and find him staring at her as if his thoughts were a thousand miles away or leering as if his fantasies were licking her skin. He made her shudder.

Medina said something to Jack, then he and Rojas stepped away as Jack emerged with the bucket. Medina glanced into the bucket, then let Jack pass.

So far, so good.

Krista busied herself with the pots until Jack reached the kitchen, where he made a show of holding the bucket away from her.

"Don't touch this. It's really gross."

She made a show of backing away, and pointed at the utility room.

"Ugh. That's disgusting. Throw it in there. There's a garbage can."

Miguel roused enough to squint at them.

"What you got there?"

Jack held the bucket toward him.

"Paper towels soaked with piss and crap. I gotta toss it. It'll stop the toilet."

Miguel made no move to rise.

"Put that shit in a plastic bag, man. We gonna smell it all night. Tie it tight. I'll put it out later."

Krista said, "There's a roll of garbage bags on the washer. Right on top."

Jack carried the reeking bucket into the utility room, and Krista turned back to the sink. Miguel never moved from the chair, but the Praying Mantis had disappeared.

Jack's time in the utility room would be short, so she returned to the fridge to keep watch. Miguel nodded out again, but Rojas had unlocked the door to the other group's bedroom, and called a young Latina into the hall. She was one of the women from Guatemala. Medina joined them, and he and Rojas spoke for a moment. Rojas handed Medina the phone, then Medina took the woman by the arm and brought her into the bathroom. The door closed, and Rojas walked away.

Krista had never seen Medina take someone into the bathroom.

Miguel suddenly snored, a single snurfling snort, and jerked awake.

"Where's that kid?"

"He's coming. He couldn't find the bags. I had to show him."

Loud enough for Jack to hear and get his butt out here.

Krista returned to the sink just as Jack came out of the utility room, looking grim. He locked eyes with her, shook his head once, and whispered.

"I couldn't get it. It started to give, but I needed more time."

"Shh. In the room."

"One minute, I would've had it—"

"Shh."

Jack put the bottle of soap on the counter, washed his hands, then took the bucket back to their room. Krista watched as the hall guard let him in, then locked the door behind him.

Prison.

She put the last pot away, then turned to Miguel.

"I'm done."

"Put them beans away?"

"In the fridge. There isn't much left."

"I might eat'm later. They were pretty good."

"Can I go?"

"Sure. You did good with them beans."

Miguel stood to stretch his legs as Krista went back to her room. She was two steps past the entry when she heard the woman's muffled plea from the bathroom.

"*Por favor!*"

Please.

Krista stopped, rooted in place as if she had seen a snake.

"*Oh Dios, por favor pare!*"

The begging snapped into a sharp muffled shriek, just one, just the one terrible muted cry.

Krista couldn't move. She stared at the door as if it were a nightmare painting from Hieronymus Bosch's personal, tortured hell.

Then the door opened, and Medina pulled the woman out. She was bent over, and whimpering.

Rojas appeared as Medina saw Krista. He looked at her, looked into her eyes, and showed his sharp jagged teeth. He pushed the woman at Rojas, gave him the phone, and handed Rojas a pair of pliers with red plastic grips.

He held the pliers out and up as he gave them to Rojas, showing them to Krista as he smiled the horrible jack-o'-lantern smile.

Rojas pulled the woman away, and took her to her room.

Krista still didn't move. She wanted to, but she couldn't. She tried to move, but her body did not respond.

Medina smiled wider. He ran his tongue over his broken, rotten teeth, then kissed his finger and pointed at Krista Morales.

Then he wiggled his finger at her—bye-bye—and disappeared into the guards' bedroom.

Krista took one step. She stepped again. She put one foot in front of the other until she reached her door. Rojas had returned by then, but Krista stared straight ahead at the door.

"I would like to go in now, please."

Samuel Rojas let her into the crowded, dank room, and locked the door behind her.

19.

Jack returned to the room furious with himself. He had been *this close* to opening the hatch, but the warped wood had been painted over so many times the hatch was wedged tight in its frame. He could have pushed harder, but had been scared of the noise, and finally chickened out, so here they still were. Stuck.

Jack put the bucket back in its corner, then went to the far wall and slumped beneath the boarded-over window. A young Korean man hurried to the bucket, and urinated as if he had been holding it for hours. His eyes were downcast in shame, and he tried to shield himself from view, but there he was, pissing in a bucket in plain view of a room filled with people. No one looked. Everyone had the good grace to ignore him. Next time, it would be them.

Jack tried not to hear it and closed his eyes. He tried not to smell the stink of all these unwashed people. He concentrated on the hatch. If he had been stronger or braver, he might be dropping down the side of the house right now. He might be waving down a car, or using a neighbor's phone to call the police. They might be free.

When Jack opened his eyes, the tough Korean kid was watching him, Jack in his usual place below the boarded-over window, the Korean in his spot against the adjoining wall. After four days, everyone had their own personal space on the floor. Use the bathroom, get food, go with Rojas to make a call—everyone returned to their spot, the same spot, and no one ever took anyone else's place. Your spot was your home.

One of the Korean girls who spoke some English told Jack the tough kid's name was Kwan. She didn't know more than that, though they had been traveling together since their group boarded a plane in Seoul for Bogotá, Colombia. Kwan kept to himself, said little, and had nothing to do with the others.

Jack met Kwan's eyes, glanced away, then looked back. Jack nodded once, kind of like saying hi, but Kwan did not respond. His lean face was all planes and angles, and as warm as a granite mask. He also had a split lip and a heavy purple bruise on his cheek from the guards.

Jack looked away, which is when the door opened and Krista came in. He knew something was wrong when he saw her. She carried herself stiffly, as if balancing a plate on her head, and her skin was the color of dough. He sat up, staring, as she came to him, and stood when she reached him because he thought she would fall. She shook like a leaf in high wind, closed her eyes tight, and pressed her forehead into his chest.

Jack felt a flush of true panic.

"What happened? Kris, are you all right?"

She sank to the floor, and he sank with her, the two of them clinging to each other in their spot.

"Krissy?"

She pulled back just far enough to see him, keeping her voice low and her back to the others.

"We have to go. We have to get out of here."

Jack's panic spiraled into a head-splitting tornado.

"Did they hurt you?"

"The other girl. You didn't hear her?"

"What happened?"

"He took her into the bathroom. You didn't hear?"

"Nothing. I didn't hear anything."

"He used pliers on her. He hurt her with pliers. She was crying when she came out, all hunched to the side."

"Rojas?"

"The one with the teeth. Medina."

The throbbing in Jack's head eased.

"We're gonna go. We'll get out of here soon. I'll try the hatch again."

"The garage is better. Let's just use the garage."

"Don't panic, Krissy. C'mon. We've been over it a hundred times."

Maybe two hundred, since the first day when Krista told him about the door to the garage in the utility room, and the service hatch in the ceiling, they had planned and re-planned how they would escape, and had worked out two possible plans, one where they got into the garage and raised the garage door, and the other where Jack climbed into the attic and escaped through a vent. The garage door was slower and riskier, so Jack didn't like it. The door from the utility room to the garage was locked except when the guards used it to take out garbage or bring in food, or come and go on their business. This meant Jack and Krista would have to be in the kitchen when the guards were using the door. They knew from experience there were brief windows of time when an incoming guard left the door unlocked while he stepped into another room. Plenty of time for Jack or Krista or both to step into the garage, but then they would have to open the garage door. The garage door was noisy. Krista heard it opening and closing when she was in the kitchen. You pressed the button, and the door lurched with a rattle. The little electric motor whined as it pulled the rattling door slowly up its squeaky tracks. They only had to wait for the door to rise a foot or so before they slipped under, but waiting those few seconds could take forever if the guards heard the door. And even if they made it under the door, Jack wasn't sure they could run far enough fast enough before the guards chased them down. Especially Krista.

Jack thought the service hatch was safer. The heat in these desert attics was hellacious, so the heat had to be vented. The bays between the rafters would be packed with thick insulation, and air-conditioning ducts would twist through the attic, but Jack knew these older desert homes had large vents cut into the gables. If he could get into the attic, he could push out a vent cover, drop to the ground, and run to a neighboring house where he would call the police.

The attic was safer, faster, and better than using the garage, only he hadn't been able to open the hatch.

Krissy said, "Tomorrow morning."

"What?"

Jack had been thinking about the attic.

"When you empty the bucket tomorrow morning. Miguel told me they're bringing more toilet paper and cooking oil and things in the morning. He's going to come get me to put it away. You can empty the bucket, and come for more soap. If they leave us alone when the door is unlocked, I want us to go."

"I want to try the hatch again."

"We have to go."

"We'll go. I just want to try the hatch again."

Krissy started crying.

"We have to go as soon as we can. We cannot stay here."

"We'll go. We'll go as soon as we can however we can, I just want to try the hatch again. If I can't get it open, we're stuck with the garage anyway. Okay?"

"I don't want to wait, Jack. He hurt that girl with these pliers. He showed them to me. He pointed at me."

Her eyes were red, and wet, and the wet ran free down her beautiful face.

He held her arms, and nodded as he tried to calm her.

"The first chance we get. If we can get in the garage, we'll run right out that door. Okay? We'll do it, Kris. The first chance we get."

"I want to go."

"If you can get into the garage without me, get in and go. Don't wait for me, okay? If you're in the kitchen and they leave the door unlocked, you get in and go. Take off. I mean it."

She cried harder, and nodded, and Jack sensed she was coming apart.

He held her close and stroked her hair. She had the softest hair in the world. Softer than any hair ever in the entire history of the world.

Kwan said, "You need purpose?"

Jack looked over, and Kwan was watching. His granite face was unreadable.

Jack didn't understand, and shook his head.

Kwan said, "For guards. You want go kitchen?"

He glanced toward the kitchen, then came back to Jack. Jack wondered how much Kwan had heard, and how much he understood.

"Yes. I need to go back to the kitchen."

Kwan stared as if Jack's words were settling through deep water to reach him.

He said, "O. Kay."

His face closed like a fierce steel trap, and he pushed to his feet. A middle-aged Korean man was now using the bucket, but Kwan stalked across the room, jerked him away, and scooped up the bucket. He brought it to the door, and pounded hard with his fist, shouting aggressively. When the guard pulled open the door, Kwan threw the piss on him, tossed the bucket aside, and shouted at the guards in Korean. They swarmed him as they had before, driving him backward into the room and onto the people who were huddled in the center of the room.

The guards came in hard, and beat down Kwan. It took four of them to subdue him, and when it was done, Medina looked at the piss all over the floor.

Jack said, "I'll get the paper towels and a plastic bag. I'll get some soap."

Medina waved him past, then spun toward Kwan and kicked him hard in the side while the other guards held him. Medina kicked him three times, then dropped to his knees and punched. He punched so hard he grunted each time he threw a shot, but Kwan only stared into the floor and took it. It was crazy the way that kid took it.

Jack locked eyes with Krista, then hurried down the hall to the kitchen.

He scooped up the Dawn and a roll of paper towels, then ducked into the utility room.

Jack's heart pounded. He didn't want to leave Krista, but if he could get into the garage, he was going to slap the button to open the big door and run like hell—dive under the opening door, slide through, and run into the street screaming and shouting and waving his arms, stop a car if he could or run to the closest house.

The door to the garage was locked. He shook the knob and twisted, but the guards had thrown the deadbolt.

Jack glanced up at the hatch, then climbed onto the washer. He paused, listening to hear if anyone was coming, hunched under the hatch and put his shoulder under it. He pushed with his legs as hard as he could. He pushed so hard the washer rocked, and slid an inch with a squeal.

Jack's heart clutched at the noise, and once more he listened.

Nothing.

Jack set his shoulder to the hatch, and tried again. They would come looking for him soon, but he had to try. He couldn't just quit.

He pushed as hard as he could. He pushed harder, and kept pushing. He pushed so hard his vision blurred and his head throbbed, and the washing machine suddenly squealed sideways. Jack lost his balance, teetered, and dropped to the floor.

The washer had twisted a foot out of whack.

Miguel's voice came from the entry.

"Get this shit cleaned up. Where them towels?"

Jack shouted back.

"I'm getting the plastic bags."

He put his weight to the washer, frantic to push it back into position, and that's when he saw a slender black shape matted with the years of dust.

Jack slid it from beneath the washer, and discovered he had found an old fisherman's knife with a black plastic handle. It had a cutting edge on the bottom of the blade and a file edge on top for scaling fish.

Miguel's voice was close.

"Them bags are right on the washer."

Jack pushed the washer into place, and snatched up the box of garbage bags as Miguel appeared in the door.

Jack held up the box.

"Found'm. I thought they were in the kitchen."

"C'mon, clean up this mess. The whole fuckin' house smells like piss. Don't forget that soap."

Miguel had already turned away.

Jack slipped the knife into his pants, and followed Miguel back into hell.

JON STONE:
three days before
Cole is taken

20.

This time of morning, still more than an hour before sunrise, Jon Stone watched Los Angeles turn gold from his home in the hills above the Sunset Strip. The ocean to his right was a black smudge dissolving into a murky night sky as the first glow of the new day seeped over the horizon. Soon, the eastern faces of downtown skyscrapers would catch the light, and as Jon watched, their golden fire would jump to Wilshire Corridor high-rises to the buildings along Hollywood Boulevard and on to the twin towers of Century City.

Jon stood naked on the tile deck at the edge of his pool, raised his hands to the city, and shouted as loud as he could.

"KISS. MY. ASS."

Then Jon Stone shouted even more loudly.

"KISS! MYY! ASSSS!"

Jon loved Los Angeles, he loved his house, and he loved being home. It was great to be back.

Then he lowered his arms, and spoke quietly in a soft voice.

"Made it again, you bitches."

Jon did a forward flip into his pool, tucked in tight for a fast rotation, hit the cold water, touched bottom, then pushed up and out in a single motion, back on the deck no problemo, dripping. It was a small pool, but still—Jon was built like a diver, but had never dived or swum competitively. He had played football and baseball in college, pole-vaulted all four years, and was captain of the judo and fencing teams. Junior and senior years, he part-timed as a bouncer. Jon Stone was good with his body, and enjoyed being physical.

Jon padded inside to his living room bar, and dug around in the fridge for a carton of apple juice. His house was dark except for the royal blue LED strip under the bar and bar cabinets. Mood lighting, to bounce off the steel tile and black marble counter. Earlier, Jon had pushed the four heavy glass doors into their wall pocket, joining the terrazzo interior with the tile deck to open his home to the pool and the city beyond.

Jon had purchased his house at the beginning of a down market: a twelve-hundred-square-foot, two-bedroom fixer on a tiny lot on a small street off Sunset Plaza Drive with an epic view and stellar privacy. Jon made a good living, but the house had been beyond his means, both then and now, so he funneled almost all his earnings into its re-creation. Floor-to-ceiling glass sliding doors, terrazzo floors, Italian tile deck, and French gray pool. The two tiny bedrooms had been transformed into an amazing master suite with a view of the city, a whirlpool tub, an oversized steam shower, and a walk-in, walnut, twenty-foot closet in which hung almost no clothes. Check out *Casa Stone*: black marble counters, German fixtures, Japanese toilets, and a full-on commercial kitchen. State-of-the-art, computer-controlled audio, video, climate, and alarms. Jon put his money into the house. It was his passion. A work of art in progress. An obsession with a home in which he did not live.

He kept his guns elsewhere.

Most of them.

Jon grabbed a carton of juice, then returned to the deck where he dropped onto a chaise lounge, still wet from the pool. The pool had been cold, and the pre-dawn air even colder, but Jon didn't mind. He had spent twenty of the past twenty-one days above 12,000 feet in the Hindu Kush of Afghanistan, not far from the Khyber Pass and close to the Pakistan border. It had been a lot colder than his beautiful house high above the Sunset

Strip. He could see the Whisky from here. He could see the big red, blue, and green buildings of the Pacific Design Center on Melrose where he had bought most of his furniture for cash.

Jon Stone was a professional military contractor—a PMC, also known as a mercenary. These days, he made most of his money by placing other professionals in contract jobs for a fifteen percent fee, though occasionally he still worked as a special teams operator for certain corporations and governments, namely the good ol' U.S. of A.

Stone had the credentials to do this, and, like many elite soldiers, his credentials were surprising. He had attended Princeton University on a National Merit Scholarship, where he studied history and philosophy, though most of his time was spent drinking beer and playing sports. His course work was an afterthought, but completed with honors, after which he enlisted in the United States Army. No-brainer. His passion in history had been the great wars and generals, and the monumental land and naval campaigns that carved world history and elevated some few men to greatness.

God DAMN, but Jon loved that stuff!

OCS. Airborne, Ranger, Special Forces, Delta. Delta was a bitch, but everything else had been pretty easy. High-speed assault. Explosive entry. Hostage rescue. Jon ate it up. Loved being a soldier, loved the company of like-minded men, loved the noise and the skills and the crazy wild-ass adventure lesser men feared.

Lesser.

Men.

Made Jon smile, even now, gazing out over his city.

Thirteen years in service, the last four with Delta, and Jon had gone private. Time to see and do something else. Get a little diversity in his life. Jon had been married six times. Long-term commitments weren't high on his list. He loved having a mission, and completing that mission, and if he got to kick a little ass along the way and make a few bucks, so be it. If things got hairy and his pulse spooled up, it was better than getting clogged arteries.

Now, eighteen hours off the plane from Afghanistan, and Jon was already thinking about what would come next, there on his deck as the city twinkled and his slug-butt neighbors slept.

His phone vibrated. A faraway buzz on the tile beneath the chaise lounge.

Stone checked the Caller ID, recognized Pike's number, and immediately answered. Jon had booked Joe Pike in the past, and had worked with him, too. Jon could book Pike at two thousand a day, twenty G minimum, up front and guaranteed. Special assignments, the sky had no limit. And Pike was very, very special.

"Let's go make some money, bro. I'm smellin' green."

Pike's low voice came back.

"You speak Korean, right?"

"Juh nun han gook mal ul mae woo jal hap ni da, moo aht ul al go ship eu sae yo?"

Jon saying he spoke Korean perfectly, and asking what Pike wanted to know.

"How about Korean organized crime?"

Jon had spent time in both South and North Korea, and could read Hangul, the modern Korean script. But coming out of the blue like this, the question made Jon wary.

"Depends. Here or in Korea?"

"I'm watching a place on Olympic. The people I'm on could be OC."

Stone tried to sound noncommittal. He knew Koreatown well. Liked the women. Liked karaoke. The Koreans were big on *noraebang*.

"I might know something. I'd have to see."

"You know something or not?"

"Maybe."

"You good with Arabic?"

Bam! Out of left field, and now Stone was smiling. There were many Arabic dialects, from Moroccan Arabic with Berber words which often did not even sound Arabic, to the aristocratic Arabic spoken by the Saudi royal family, which was different from the Arabic spoken in the streets.

"enta bethahraf aina be naifham kuiais. eish auzanee le olak bel logha arabeia."

Jon answered in street Arabic, saying Pike already knew he was fluent, and asking what he wanted translated.

Jon Stone was fluent in English, Arabic, Korean, Chinese, Spanish, Russian, and French. He could get by in Farsi, Japanese, German, and three different African dialects. He had studied only English and French in school.

Pike said, "Copy the address. Come down and see."

"I didn't hear a ka-ching."

"Come down."

"I've been away, man, c'mon."

Pike didn't respond, and Stone knew Pike was waiting him out.

"Twenty of the last twenty-one. I still smell like camels."

"You miss it already."

Stone stared at the faint eastern light and admitted Pike had him. Eighteen hours at home, and he already wanted to go.

"What about the money?"

"No money. It's Cole."

"That lame-ass turd works for shit. Why you waste your time with that guy?"

"If you can't help, you're gone. I'll owe you a favor."

Now Stone perked up. Pike's favors meant money. He made a big deal of sighing, as if doing it was some monstrous pain in the ass, but he was already committed.

"Okay. All right. Where are you?"

Pike gave him an address.

Stone didn't bother writing it because he would not forget it. Jon Stone never forgot anything, and never had. He could still recite junior high textbooks, operating and maintenance manuals for the M249 SAW light machine gun and twenty-seven other personal weapons systems, and both volumes of *Mastering the Art of French Cooking*, by Julia Child. Every word.

Every word of every document, book, newspaper, and article he had ever read. School had been easy. Delta had been hard. Jon liked it hard.

"Be there in thirty."

Stone placed his phone back on his belly. Far to the south, a line of bright lights descended toward LAX. Eighteen hours ago, he was strapped inside one of the lights.

Jon cupped his hands around his mouth, and shouted as loudly as he could.

"KISS MY ASSSSSS!"

Far in the canyon below, another voice answered.

"Shut the fuck up, asshole!"

Jon Stone laughed, naked there in his backyard overlooking a golden city, then went inside to dress for the day.

PART 2

ELVIS COLE:
three days before
he is taken

21.

Thomas Locano phoned me at six the next morning, so early the canyon behind my house still held the fading threads of yesterday's fog. I had slept on the couch.

"I didn't expect to hear from you so quickly. Is everything all right?"

"My apologies for the hour, but I told you I might phone early."

"Yes, sir, you did. This isn't a problem."

"Can you meet me in Echo Park by seven?"

I rolled off the couch, and went to the kitchen. This black cat who lives with me was waiting by his dish, but he wasn't waiting for me to feed him. He had brought his own. A fourteen-inch piece of king snake was on the floor by the bowl. It was still twitching. Maybe he wanted to share.

I said, "You found something about the Syrian?"

"I found someone who knows of this man. We will see him together if you will meet me, but it has to be now. He has other obligations."

I took the snake outside and dropped it over the rail. The cat let out a long, low war growl, then slipped off the deck after his kill. He would hold it against me.

I checked the time.

"I'll be out the door in fifteen. Where do we meet?"

"On the east side of the lake, where they rent the paddle boats? You will see me."

I shaved, changed shirts, and was making a fast cup of instant when Joe Pike called.

He said, "Jon's in. He knows these people. Come down, he'll fill us in."

"Locano called first. I'm heading out now. He may have a line on the Syrian."

"We'll stay with the Beemer. Come when you can."

I tossed the phone on the couch, locked the door, and followed the Hollywood Freeway south toward downtown Los Angeles. It was exactly the same route I drove when I first met Nita Morales, but this time I dropped off the freeway at Echo Park, an old and long-established community built around a decorative lake. The lake is encircled by a narrow green area split by a bike path. In the early days of Los Angeles, the silent film industry was centered in Echo Park before it moved to Hollywood, and the nearby Elysian Hills and Angelino Heights neighborhoods were home to the rich and famous. The makeup of the area has slowly changed since the film people left, and is now mostly home to working-class immigrants from Asia and Central America.

I made my way to the east side of Echo Lake, parked on a nearby street, and hurried to the boathouse. Even at this early hour, joggers and walkers circled the lake, and short brown women pushed baby carriages in schools like fish or stood talking to friends with their carriages parked like cars at a demolition derby.

Thomas Locano stood between two palm trees at the edge of the water, and wasn't alone. A skinny Latin kid wearing white pants and a white T-shirt was with him. The kid was bald, maybe five four, and couldn't have weighed more than a hundred ten pounds. He was also sleeved out and necklaced with gang ink, and couldn't have been more than fifteen years old. They watched me approach, and Mr. Locano spoke first.

"Mr. Cole, this is my friend Alfredo Munoz. Fredo, this is my good friend Mr. Cole. He is also close to another good friend, Nita Morales."

"Hey, Fredo. Good to meet you."

"Uhn, yeah, you too."

Fredo met my eyes, then glanced away as he offered his hand. His grip was limp, as if he was vaguely embarrassed. Up close, I saw a fine dusting of white powder on his face and neck and upper arms. Flour. His hands and forearms were clean, but he hadn't washed above his elbows. Locano went on with his introduction.

"Fredo works as a baker's apprentice here on the next block. Every morning from five to seven, then school by eight."

I nodded, trying to look encouraging.

"Man, that's early. That's some schedule you have, Fredo."

Fredo glanced away.

"Uhn. It's okay. It's good. Mr. Locano set it up."

I stared at Locano, my expression asking why we were here with this boy, but then the boy spoke again, and when I looked back he was staring at me.

"That Syrian guy killed Raoul. I know about that guy. I tell you what I know."

I blinked at him, then looked at Locano again.

"Raoul was Fredo's brother. Raoul and Fredo were born here, but their parents weren't. I represented them in a deportation hearing."

"One outta two, that ain't so bad."

Locano looked embarrassed.

"Their father was relocated, but we made arrangements for their mother to stay."

"He got her a work visa. That ain't so bad."

Mr. Locano cleared his throat.

"Raoul worked with Sinaloa here in Los Angeles and in San Diego. So did Fredo."

Fredo said, "Uhn. Eastside Kings."

The Eastside Kings were a Latin gang with ties to the Mexican Mafia.

I studied Fredo.

"How old are you?"

"Uhn. Don't let that fool you, but I'm done with all that. I'm looking to the future."

Locano filled in the blanks again.

"The different cartels have members all through the United States. They form partnerships with local gangs for the manpower and connections. One such partnership was with the Eastside Kings here, and a Kings affiliate in San Diego. Raoul and the other Kings were drivers. They brought marijuana and cocaine north up through San Diego."

"I made that trip lots of times. I coulda been with him that day. Uhn."

I stared at Fredo, and decided he was a million years old.

"Have you met the Syrian?"

"No, uh-uh. Uhn. I wanted to, though, I tell you that, but now I wanna get right."

"Then how do you know about him?"

"The shot callers told us what happened, and these Sinaloa Mexicans came up. Two of our guys got away, and the Sinaloas wanted to hear it first-hand. They said it was him, this Syrian dude and his crew. They popped Raoul and this dude Hector, double-tap right here—"

Fredo touched his head, not even slowing.

"—and took the truck, and that was two hundred pounds of cocaine, that's what they say, I never saw it. Jesús and Ocho, they got away. Those Sinaloa pricks, they thought Jesús and Ocho was in on it or some crazy shit, tol' the Syrian where to find the truck or some shit, and those Sinaloas fucked'm up real good. They cut off Ocho's fingers, uhn. Those Sinaloas, they said how did he know which truck? He had to get the information from somebody, and they put it on Ocho. I watched that shit happen. That's when I'm gone, dude, uhn. I don't need some dog shootin' my back. My mama, she called Mr. L here, and he's helpin' me get right. He tryin' to get my father back in, too. That ain't so bad."

Locano nodded when Fredo finished, and thoughtfully crossed his arms.

"When you mentioned the connection to Sinaloa, I remembered Fredo and Raoul."

I stared at Fredo, then Locano, then went back to Fredo who looked like a child.

"Jesús and Ocho personally knew the Syrian? They recognized him?"

"The Mexicans had this picture—"

He held up his hand as if he was showing me a picture, and pointed at air as if he could see it.

"—this him? This dude took you down? Jesús and Ocho, they both say yeah, that was him, who in hell is this guy? Those Sinaloa Mexicans, they called his name, said he used to work with them."

"He worked for the Sinaloas?"

"With, not for. He was a coyote, uhn, whatever they call it in Syrian, over there on the other side of the world. He brought people from over there to Mexico, and got'm where they wanted to go, but I know what happen—they took his bitch-ass business, and he said fuck you, I ain't workin' for you, so he started stealin' their shit. Not just them. The Bajas. The Pacific Cartel. Whoever runnin' stuff up. That Sinaloa, he said what we got is a rogue coyote, and we gonna put his ass down."

I thought it through, and wondered if the Sinaloas had been right about Ocho and Jesús.

"So how did he know where to find your brother's truck?"

Fredo glanced at Locano, then back, and smiled.

"Only one way that flies. He buys the intel. The Sinaloas got that part right, they just ain't right about Ocho and Jesús."

"The Syrian pays for tips?"

"That's what they do, the *bajadores*. You can't steal something 'less you know where it is, uhn. They pay. I met this dude, Wander, he say the Syrian pays better than anyone else."

Locano fixed his eyes on me, and nodded.

"This was not long ago, after Fredo left the Kings. This is recent information."

Fredo nodded, hanging on Locano's every word.

"This dude, Wander, he works over here. He used to be Latin Blades, but he jumped out, too. When he heard I was a King, he knew we were with Sinaloa. He said I could pick up some cash, you know? I didn't say I was on the outs, uhn. I just let him talk, tucking it away, thinking about Raoul. I said, dude, you crazy, you know Sinaloa wants to kill that Syrian bitch? But Wander, he says he feeds tips to all these cartel *bajadores*, and they killin' each other left and right. He said the Syrian, he pays a lot more. He told me if I get something to sell, he can make it happen, put good money in both our pockets."

I studied Fredo.

"You think it's true, that Wander sells to the Syrian?"

Fredo shrugged.

"He drives a nice car. He's got a silver buckle big as a plate, and a fat rock here on his thumb. I been asking. He's been paying people for tips, that much is true. He's gettin' cash somewhere, so I'm thinkin' the rest is true, too."

Locano said, "When the Sinaloas came up, you said they called the Syrian's name."

"Uhn. Ghazi al-Diri. It was hard to say in my mouth, but I practiced to make it right. Ghazi al-Diri killed my brother, Raoul, shot him two times right here."

He touched his head again.

I said, "If I wanted to see Wander, could you find him?"

Fredo studied me, and did not look away.

"What would you say?"

"I might have something for the Syrian. I might want to meet him."

Fredo nodded slowly, his eyes never leaving mine.

"Why he wanna meet you?"

I didn't have much to say, so Fredo shrugged.

"Lots of people trying to find him, and can't, uhn. Just 'cause you say you want to see him don't mean shit. Why he want to see you? You gotta give him a reason."

"I'll find a reason."

"It's gotta be good. He ain't in business to mess around."

"I'll find a good reason. What I'm asking is, can you put me with Wander?"

Fredo kicked at the ground, then looked at the lake.

"I've been thinkin' 'bout this thing Wander told me, him being up with this Ghazi al-Diri, trying to figure out what to do. I could give him up to the Kings, give him to the Sinaloas—they all want his ass dead. But here I am trying to get right. I have to put this stuff behind me."

I nodded. I knew where he was going.

He looked at Locano.

"Mr. L, he says you're trying to find some girl this dude took?"

"Yes. I am."

"Okay, I'll help you do that. Raoul and I, we can help. If I help get her back, maybe it helps me get right with myself. You see?"

"I see, Fredo. I get it, for real."

He seemed to notice the flour on his upper arms for the first time. He brushed at his arms and neck and face.

"I look like a clown."

Locano said, "No, Fredo. From this flour you make bread, and bread gives us life. This is not the makeup of a clown."

Fredo fluffed his hair, and squinted at me through the dust.

"I gotta get to school. You find a good reason. Find a reason so good the Syrian can't pass it up, I'll put you with Wander, uhn."

"I'll let you know."

Fredo offered his hand again, shook with Mr. Locano, and then trotted up along the lake. I watched him until he was gone, then looked at Locano.

Mr. Locano had watched him leave, too, and now sighed.

"That boy is fourteen years old. He is only fourteen."

I told him I would let him know soon, then drove across town to meet with Joe Pike and Jon Stone, hoping we would find something so good the Syrian could not pass it up.

22.

Jon Stone leaned forward between us, and pointed a chopstick at the two men climbing into the Beemer. He was eating *bulgogi* heaped with *kimchee*. *Bulgogi* was thinly sliced barbequed beef in a bowl, which Stone had covered with a sweet, fire-hot mound of pickled cabbage. Stone knew the best barbeque places in K-town. He also knew the best bars, karaoke clubs, restaurants, and markets. He had bought me a *galbi* bowl filled with barbequed short ribs, and Pike a bowl of grilled vegetables and rice. Jon Stone was a K-town regular, and had spent the morning before I joined them speaking with friends.

Stone touched the air with the tip of his chopstick as if he was dotting an *i* with a quill pen.

"Your talker there, he's Sang Ki Park. He doesn't run the gang. That would be his uncle, Young Min Park. Sang is the second in command. They're Ssang Yong Pa—the Double Dragon gang—straight out of the R-O-K. Hard-core and nasty."

ROK was the Republic of Korea.

I watched the men as I listened. The big guy I put on the floor in the desert opened the Beemer's door for the hard young guy who had done all the talking, then climbed in behind the wheel.

"Hard-core and nasty as in violent?"

"That's affirm. All your Asian gangs are bad, but the Koreans are worse. It's China. You grow up staring down China, it fucks with your brain."

Pike said, "Please."

"Please what? Remember those ex-ROK troopers in Africa? Why'd you send'm home?"

Stone turned to me before Pike could answer.

"The company sends us these three ex-ROK Special Forces turds who did nothing but fight. I'm not talking about fighting the people we were paid to fight, I'm talking about our own guys, the friendlies, even each other. Fuckers loved to fight. Pike here damn near killed two of them before he sent them home."

Stone looked at Pike.

"If I'm lying, I'm dying. Am I right?"

Pike simply stared ahead as we followed the Beemer, so Stone turned back to me.

"You see? He knows it's true. These fuckers are pit bull aggressive. You want more of this *kimchee*? It's the best."

I held up my bowl, and thought about it as Jon shoveled on *kimchee*. He was right about the *kimchee*. It was world-class spectacular.

"Sanchez told me they paid Sinaloa two hundred grand to bring up their people. You think they'll pay the Syrian's ransom?"

"Not in their nature. Your Syrian's gonna be stuck with twenty or thirty people no one will pay for. And the Sinaloas are shit out of luck, too, 'cause if these boys here don't get their money or people, they'll go all World War Three."

Rudy Sanchez had already told me the Sinaloas were worried, and worry wasn't something normally associated with the Sinaloa drug cartel.

Pike glanced at Stone in the mirror.

"Why bring in so many people?"

"They need'm."

I said, "For what?"

"Staff. The Dragons have been buying bars and restaurants as fronts for dealing dope and whores. They cater to Korean businessmen, so they want people who can speak the language, and they also want people they can trust. It's the same way with the Tong in Chinatown. They bring people from back home who are scared shitless of the police, and they're completely dependent on the gang for food, shelter, and protection. To a guy like Park here, people from back home are more trustworthy than Americans, and you know goin' in none of them are federal agents."

Pike glanced at Stone in the rearview.

"Where'd you get this?"

Stone had more of the *kimchee*.

"A couple of ex-ROK paratroops at a *soju* bar over here a few weeks ago. Double Dragons have these twin dragons inked on their arms, and these two assholes wanted to impress me with their ink. Hence, they gave up the farm."

Stone grinned.

"Too much *soju*. Just like those shitbirds in Africa."

We followed the Beemer only six blocks until it made a left, went two more blocks, and pulled to the curb outside a *soju* bar.

Stone broke into an even nastier smile.

"Is this too perfect or what? That's the place right there—where I talked up the ROKs."

The big guy stayed in the car, and Park went inside. He stayed for almost twenty minutes before he and another man came out. The other man was much older, with a leathery face, steel gray hair, and his eyes almost hidden by wrinkles. He didn't look happy, and neither did Sang Ki Park.

Stone tapped the air with his chopstick.

"That would be the uncle, Young Min Park."

"The boss?"

"That's the man. This was the first bar the Dragons took over. He owns it."

I twisted around, and looked at him. Stone shrugged.

"Those ROK guys wouldn't shut up, bro. They just could *not* stop talking. You hear shit, you tuck it away, you never know."

I turned back to the Beemer.

Jon Stone looked like a demented surfer with his spiky, bleached hair and pierced ear, but I knew his background with Delta. Sometimes you forget what that means. Most people think Delta, they're thinking of Rambo, with the big gun and even bigger muscles. D-boys are deadly warriors, for sure, but you won't find many who look like Rambo. This is because you can't rescue hostages or snatch high-value targets from hostile villages unless you find them, so D-boys are also selected to gather intelligence. They are off-the-charts smart, look ordinary, and are trained to blend in anywhere with anyone. This is why D-boys are called operators. Jon Stone had worked the two drunk ex-ROK gangsters for no other reason than gathering intelligence was in his nature.

As we watched, the older man shook his finger angrily under Sang Ki Park's nose. Park didn't like it, but took it. The old man steadily grew more angry until the finger wasn't enough. He slapped Park's face hard, then stormed back into his bar.

Stone said, "The old man isn't liking his nephew so much these days."

Pike said, "What were they saying?"

"Couldn't hear, but it's an easy guess. The nephew here just lost two hundred thousand and a boatload of workers. They probably weren't talking about a promotion."

Their next stop was a large two-level strip mall on Vermont. The strip mall was in the final stages of being remodeled, with a club and a restaurant taking up most of the upper level and what looked like another bar and a karaoke lounge on the lower level. A large sign in Korean script and English hung across the front of the karaoke lounge: OPENING SOON.

Stone said, "Y'see? This is what I was talking about. You can't open for business without the right staff."

I liked it. Under construction was good. Opening soon was good. The more pressure Park felt to recover his people, the more desperately he would look for ways to do so.

We stopped at two more strip malls and a large commercial building on Western Avenue. Park met people at each site, and toured the properties as if checking their progress, but no one looked happy, especially Park.

One hour and thirty-six minutes later, we followed his Beemer eleven blocks north to a small Craftsman home between Beverly and Melrose, not far from Paramount Studios. The house and front yard were small, but neat and clean with an attractive flower bed surrounding a crepe myrtle tree. A black Porsche Cabriolet was parked in the drive. The Beemer pulled in behind it, and parked. The drive was so short, the Beemer's tail hung over the sidewalk.

Park got out, went to the front door, and let himself in without a key. The big man rolled down both front windows, and stayed in the car. He would be there for a while.

I said, "Here we go."

Pike stopped in front of the neighboring house, and the three of us got out quickly and quietly. We crossed the neighbor's drive and walked directly to the Beemer, Stone to the passenger side, and Pike and I to the driver's side.

The big man glimpsed movement, and turned, but by then I had my pistol out.

"Remember me?"

He jerked sideways, but grew still when he saw the gun.

From the other side of the car, Jon Stone spoke Korean. The big man gripped the wheel, both hands, ten and two. Stone slipped into the passenger side, holding a .45 caliber service automatic. They had a brief conversation, then Jon explained.

"He's seeing a girlfriend. I'm good here. Go."

"Does she have kids?"

Stone spoke again.

"No kids. Go."

Pike and I went to the front door and quietly let ourselves into a classic Craftsman living room. The wood floors and doors and trim around the windows were so dark the wood was almost black, so we followed their voices. I thought we would find them in her bedroom, but they were in a sunroom at the end of the hall.

Sang Ki Park and a young woman were sitting at a small round table framed in a glass bay window looking out at an avocado tree. The woman was slender, Asian, and probably in her twenties. Park had taken off his suit coat, and rolled his sleeves. She was laughing at something he said, and Park was smiling. Then I stepped inside, and their laughing stopped. The girl made a surprised gasp, and Park pushed to his feet. He was smart enough not to reach for a weapon, but he grew angry, squared himself, and shouted a belligerent stream of Korean. I held my gun to the side, pointing away.

"Take it easy. We're here to talk."

Pike entered and moved to the right. I drifted left, and pointed my gun at the ceiling. Then I let it fall free on my index finger to hang upside down, telling him he had nothing to fear.

"We owe you three guns. We brought them back."

Pike placed the three guns on a small wicker love seat.

Sang Ki Park watched him, then glanced at my pistol. I put it under my shirt and showed my empty hands.

"Okay?"

His rage had turned to suspicion, leaving him watchful, but curious.

"Why you here?"

"You lost two hundred thousand dollars to the Sinaloa cartel."

He stared, but said nothing.

"The Sanchez brothers don't have it, so you can't get it from them. The Sinaloas have it, but you'll have to fight them for it."

"Yes."

"They will probably negotiate a settlement with you, go in halves, but you still won't have your money or your people. I think you want your people."

Park nodded once, such a small nod his head barely moved, so I went on.

"A man named Ghazi al-Diri has them. He is demanding a ransom."

"We will not pay."

"They will die."

"We do not pay."

He was hard and immutable, which was good.

"Just as well. He will milk you until the money stops, then kill them. That is what he does. He will not free them."

His left eye flickered, which was the first sign of strain to escape from his fortress. He wanted his people. He needed them more than he needed the money, and I wondered if some among them were closer than hired staff.

"He has someone I want, too. I want to show you something. I'm going to reach into my pocket, okay?"

The nod.

I took the picture of Krista Morales from my pocket. He studied it for a long moment, then looked up.

"Is this your woman?"

I put away the picture without answering.

"The Syrian has her and a boy. I'm going to get them back."

"Not pay?"

"Not pay. There is no paying. I'm going to take them."

"Where are they?"

"With the Syrian. He has them in what we call a drop house. Prisoners. How many people were you bringing in?"

He thought for a moment, probably figuring out how to say it in English.

"Twenty-six."

"Your people will be there, too."

"Where is this house?"

"Don't know, but I will."

"How you do this?"

"With your help, the Syrian will take me to your people, and mine, and you and I will have what we want. I can do this, but I need your help."

"Why?"

"I have a way to contact the Syrian, but he doesn't know me. He's not

going to take me to see a house filled with kidnap victims just because I offer
to buy them. He will check me out. He will need to believe he can trust me,
and I am who I say I am. This is where we need the Sinaloas. If they believe
I am a legitimate buyer, he will believe I'm a legitimate buyer. I need you to
deliver the Sinaloas."

He nodded again, but he wasn't looking at me, and wasn't nodding
at me.

"I will discuss this with my uncle."

"I understand."

"No, you not understand. One of people we bring is my cousin. My
uncle's youngest grandson."

"Now I understand."

"Yes. Now you understand better."

Sang Ki Park took a step back, and spoke softly to the woman. She immediately stood, and moved to the far side of the room. He gestured at the
chair where the woman had been sitting.

"Sit here now. We will talk."

I sat.

We talked.

We worked out an offer for the Syrian and a game plan for the cartel, and
then he made the calls. I was now in business with a Korean gang known
for extortion, brutality, and violence, and about to put my trust into a drug
cartel known for torture and mass murder. I told myself it was worth it. I told
myself I had no choice. I lied to myself, and knew I was lying, but chose to
believe the lies.

23.

Park spoke with his uncle first, then Winston Ramos, who controlled the transportation of drugs and human cargo north across the Sinaloa-controlled portions of the border from Tijuana to the Arizona state line. It was Ramos who had accepted the two hundred thousand dollars from Sang Ki Park to transport his people into the United States, and it was Ramos who would be targeted for death if their money and people were lost. This probably was not lost on the man.

Ramos immediately offered a settlement in the matter of the two hundred thousand, but Park explained that a second inbound group was about to arrive in Acapulco, and asked Ramos to discuss their transport into the United States with the trafficker who was bringing them. If all went well, Park suggested he might be willing to negotiate on the matter of the two hundred K. Winston Ramos agreed. The trafficker in this scenario was me.

Three hours later, the Coachella winds were up, carrying sand from the desert to scratch at the glass like sun-baked shrapnel. Sanchez & Sons tow yard was still. Rudy had sent their employees home, and he and his two brothers had left. Sang Ki Park and I sat in the office, waiting until Ramos and two other men pulled through the gate in a green Chevy Impala bearing a California license plate. We went outside to meet him.

Winston Ramos was short and flabby, with a round head and round body. His tan short-sleeve shirt drooped over his gut like a tent, and his chinos were baggy. First thing he did when he got out of his car was hitch up his belt.

The other two men were about his age. The heavier man wore cowboy boots, and the thinner man looked like a UFC lightweight retired from an unsuccessful career. The cowboy carried a short black wand a little longer and thicker than a TV remote.

Ramos didn't bother with pleasantries. He glanced at me, but spoke to Park.

"This your transporter?"

I put out my hand.

"Harlan Green."

He waved the cowboy toward me without shaking.

"He's going to check you. You know what to do?"

"I know."

I stood with my feet apart and arms out.

The wand looked like the wands used by TSA screeners, but this one did not screen for metal. He passed it over my chest, back, arms, and legs, searching for the RF and IR signals emitted by transmitters, recorders, and listening devices. I must have passed, because the cowboy nodded at Ramos.

"Okay, now this one."

When the cowboy went to Park, Park slapped the wand away with a quick roll of his left hand, and punched him once in the solar plexus and twice in the face with his right fist. The cowboy staggered back and dropped to his knees. By the time he was down, Park was calmly staring at Ramos.

"If you want search me, search me yourself."

The UFC fighter was two seconds behind the curve, then clawed under his shirt and flashed a garish little Llama .380.

Neither Park nor I moved to stop him, but by the time the gun was out, Ramos saw Park's men coming from behind the trucks. A dozen Double Dragon hitters in dark glasses and great suits.

I said, "These guys know how to dress, don't they?"

Ramos glanced at me, then told the UFC fighter to put away his gun and get the cowboy on his feet. He didn't look scared.

"I came to do business, and you're starting this shit?"

Park touched his arm.

"Come. We speak elsewhere."

"Fuck that. I'm not going anywhere."

He shook off Park's hand, but Park gripped him again.

"You are not here to die. I am not here to threaten. Walk here. Away from our men, so no one hear."

Park steered him across the lot to a sleeping flatbed. I followed along with them. Park's men floated into new positions without being told, securing the area and isolating Ramos's thugs to give us privacy. Telepathy. Or maybe they were good at their jobs.

We were in the sun, and hot, but alone between the big trucks with their men out of earshot. Ramos shook off Park's hand again, and squirmed like he thought someone might stab him.

"What the fuck are you doing, bringing your guns? You think you can scare me into returning your money?"

I said, "I can give you the Syrian."

Just like that. In his face.

It caught him off guard, and took him a moment to catch up. He glanced at Park, then looked over both shoulders as if he expected federal agents to climb out of the trucks.

"What are you talking about?"

"Ghazi al-Diri. The *bajadore* you call the Syrian. The guy who's been killing your crews and stealing your *pollos*."

"I know who he is. Who are you?"

"I told you. Harlan Green."

"Bullshit. Are you a cop?"

He glared at Park.

"Did you flip to the Federales?"

"You owe Mr. Park two hundred thousand dollars."

He was still speaking to Park.

"I told you, we'll work out something with the money."

I said, "This guy is stealing your goods and killing your crews, and you haven't been able to stop him."

He finally turned back to me.

"What's this to you?"

Park calmly re-entered the conversation.

"This man has way to Ghazi al-Diri. Will you listen, or will you leave?"

Park held his hand toward Ramos's car as if showing him the way.

"Listen, leave. Choose, but this man offers way all three may benefit."

Ramos pooched his lips. He was suspicious that Park was giving him the option to leave. He was trying to figure the trick, but he wanted the Syrian, so he studied me again.

"Harlan Green."

"I supply unskilled labor to corporations, agribusiness, and small and large businesses here and abroad. I was expecting thirty field workers from Indonesia, but ICE bagged them in San Diego when their boat went down. I'm stuck, my grower is already talking to someone else, and I need a replacement crew as fast as possible."

He studied me a moment longer, then shook his head.

"I don't believe you."

"You don't have to. You just have to convince the Syrian."

I went through the steps, just as I had with Park.

"Mr. Park wants his people. The Syrian has someone I want, too, so Mr. Park and I are in the same boat. You have the two hundred thousand he paid, and you want to keep it, but you probably want the Syrian more than the money. All three of us have these things we want, but the Syrian wants something, too."

"What?"

"Money. He wants money for the people he's taken."

"Park won't pay."

"Not Park. Me. I can make an offer that might interest him."

"Offer to what?"

"To buy them. Park isn't paying. I will offer to take them off his hands. A flat fee. A purchase."

Now Ramos wet his lips. He was listening, and hearing me for the first time.

"How can you reach him?"

"A confirmed connection with someone who works for him. Confirmed. If I float an offer, it will reach the Syrian."

"He ain't gonna talk to you, man. He don't know you, why should he talk? You might be a federal agent. You're nobody."

"Not if Sinaloa tells him I'm somebody."

Park said, "This is why we speak. You make him somebody."

Ramos shook his head, but I could tell he was trying to make it work.

"Long shot."

"Yes. It's a long shot."

"He's not going to let you get close. There's no fucking way. How can I help you with that?"

"I'm an unknown. But if he's tempted by the offer, he will check me out. He'll ask."

"He knows I want his head on a plate. You think he's going to call, ask me what's up with you?"

"He'll ask the people he used to work with before you ran him out of business. He will ask, but they haven't heard of me, either, so they'll check around, and eventually they'll ask someone who's in with Sinaloa."

Ramos studied me carefully.

"Harlan Green."

"Harlan Green."

He looked at Park.

"You will let the money matter go?"

"If I recover my people, your contract is fulfilled."

Ramos nodded, then glanced back at me. His eyes were the hard, bright eyes of a feral desert dog smelling blood.

"Harlan Green."

"Yes."

"All right, Mr. Green. You give me the Syrian, you and I will be friends, I think."

I stared without responding. After a beat, he motioned to his men, and the three of them returned to his car.

Park said, "You have much balls."

I went directly to my car, and left.

24.

Joe Pike

Pike watched Cole with Park and Ramos by the cab of the long flatbed. Jon Stone was beside him, watching Park's soldiers, but Pike kept watch over Cole.

They were across the street in a storage room above the transmission shop next door to the taco stand. Close, in case it went south.

Stone eyeballed the scene from a perch on an old desk with an M4 across his legs. Pike was stretched on the neighboring desk, standing sentry through a Zeiss telescopic sighting system mounted to a Remington 700 mountain rifle chambered in 7mm Magnum. Using this scope and rifle, Pike could hit cantaloupes at eight hundred meters.

Next to him, Stone's voice.

"This is fucked-up shit."

Pike did not move his eye from the sight picture. Cole, Ramos, Park. The Zeiss was fitted with a laser range finder displaying the range in tiny red numerals in the upper right quadrant of the sight picture. Elvis Cole was forty-two meters away. Overkill.

Stone said, "You know I'm right. He's going to hang his ass over the edge with these two shitbirds? If I'm lying, I'm dying. I sure as hell wouldn't."

Ramos walked away.

"Two."

"Got him."

Pike stayed with Cole and Park, letting Stone pick up Ramos. They had designated Park as Target One and Ramos as Target Two. Jon was on Two. If the meet went bad, Jon would drop Ramos and Pike would drop Park. They would then lay down suppressing fire so Cole could escape. If Cole was killed or wounded, they would terminate everyone in the tow yard.

"What I'm saying is, I know time is of the essence an' all that, but trusting these people to get him inside and keep their pieholes shut is what we in the trade call 'dubious.' Two and his boys mounting up. *Hasta luego*, shitbirds."

"Rog."

"Out the gate. Gone."

"Rog."

Park and Cole finished their conversation, and separated. Pike stayed with Park.

"One."

"On it. Cole's going to his car. One's joining up with his men."

Pike saw it as Stone said it. Park met two of his men, spoke briefly, then moved with them to his black Beemer. If Jon gave the word, Pike could and would drop all three in less than two seconds.

"What I'm saying is—are you listening? This Syrian asshole got his inside information about that truck from *somewhere*, which means someone inside Ramos's crew or Park's crew is selling them out. Shit, for all we know, people in both these turds' crews are selling them out. That fuckin' Syrian might be swimming in information. Have you thought of that?"

Park's Beemer drove away. Pike swung his rifle, and picked up Cole getting into his yellow Corvette. It needed a wash.

Pike lowered his rifle, and stood.

"Yes. I don't like this either."

They packed their gear, and hustled down to follow.

JACK AND KRISTA:
six days after
they were taken

25.

Jack was slouched against the wall with his arm around Krista when the man's muffled scream cut through the walls. Krista shut her eyes and covered her ears. Kwan jerked awake, blinking sleep from his eyes as he sat up. Two of the Korean women were crying and a teenage boy from El Salvador was praying, but they heard the man scream, too, high and sharp, until it abruptly chopped off.

Kwan stomped to the door. He was lumpy with purple bruises, but pounded the door in a livid rage. The guards didn't answer.

Rojas and Medina had opened the door only a few minutes earlier. Rojas referred to something in his ledger, then pointed out a middle-aged Korean man huddled with the two women. He was paunchy, with an overbite and broken, wire-rimmed glasses. Medina took him away to make a call. Three minutes later, the man screamed, louder than any of them had screamed, and many had screamed in the recent days.

Jack held Krista into his shoulder as Kwan spent his fury, and felt for the knife beneath the edge of the carpet. Touching it made him feel safer. Jack had been afraid the guards would notice if he carried the knife in his jeans, so he pulled the ratty carpet loose from the baseboard in their spot beneath the window to create a hiding space. Jack had shown the knife to Krista, but not Kwan.

Jack was afraid of Kwan, though they had been friendly since Kwan dumped the bucket. The guards had beaten Kwan badly, but he took their beating as if it were a reward. And after, he did not act cowed or afraid. He met their eyes as if daring them to give him more. Jack decided Kwan was either fearless or crazy, but also insanely tough.

Shirtless, Kwan's hard muscles danced as he pounded the door. Smudged bruises mottled his skin along with snake-bite burn marks left by the shock prods, but Jack wondered most at the man's scars. Kwan's belly and back showed three or four long puckered lines that might have been wounds, and a large knobby dimple Jack believed was left by a gunshot wound. And his broad upper back held an amazing tattoo of two fierce dragons facing each other as if to do battle.

Kwan punched the door a final time, and stalked back to his place against the wall. He locked eyes with Jack only once, then dropped to the floor.

They were scared because their treatment by the guards had changed. Medina had been using the pliers on more and more of them. If money wasn't sent, the calm and reasonable Rojas turned harsh during subsequent calls. He threatened terrible things, and some of the men and women returned in tears, reporting that Rojas or Medina had twisted their fingers or used the shock prod while they were on the phone, so their families would hear them cry out.

Jack wondered what the guards had done to the paunchy man to make him scream so loudly. Everyone in the room was waiting to find out, but when the door finally opened, Rojas came in and made a short speech. One of the young Korean women translated for the Koreans.

"You will all be happy to know Mr. Chun is on his way home. His family was generous today. You should tell your families to be the same. They have transferred the money we needed, and now Mr. Chun is on his way to their loving arms. If your families cooperate as well, you will soon be home, too. If not, then not."

Rojas remained until the girl finished translating, then left. The people in the room buzzed with this news, but Jack noticed Kwan was smirking.

Jack said, "That's good news. One of us got out."

Kwan snorted, and settled against his wall.

"No family. The people he call no pay."

"Rojas lied?"

"No pay."

Jack felt a chill as he realized what Kwan was saying, and felt for the knife again. He kissed Krista's head, and whispered into her hair.

"We're going to do this, Krissy, okay? We'll just go, is all, just do it."

She nodded, her face still in his shoulder.

They sought a chance to escape every day, but either the utility room door would be locked when the guards were away, or too many guards were around when the door was unlocked. There was always something wrong, but they would try again soon. Miguel was going to show up in a few minutes to bring Krista and the other cook to the kitchen. Every time Kris was in the kitchen, she was closer to the door. Jack believed it was only a matter of time before their chance to escape would come.

Jack kissed her soft hair again.

"I want you to promise something."

"What?"

"We gotta get out of here, right? Someone has to get out, even if it's just one of us."

"We're both going."

"I know, yeah, we're both going, but listen, okay? If you get a chance when I'm not around, go. Get out of here, and go. And if we get into the garage together, but the guards come before we get out, I want you to keep going, okay?"

She sat up.

"I don't understand. What do you mean?"

"I'm saying don't wait for me. If you can get out, go, and I'll hold them off."

She stared at him, and finally nodded.

"Is she going to find us?"

"Yeah, she's going to find us, but we're not going to wait. If you get the chance, go."

The door opened again, ending their conversation, and Miguel told her to get her ass into the kitchen.

Two minutes after she left, Rojas returned, and pointed at Jack.

"Come here, piss cleaner. Since we gotta wait for your mommy to get back from her trip, you gotta earn your keep. I have a job for you."

"You want me to empty the bucket?"

"Leave it. I got something else."

Jack locked eyes with Kwan for a moment, then followed Rojas to the bathroom. A can of Comet, a spray bottle of Mr. Clean disinfectant, and a plastic scrub brush were waiting for him on a pile of threadbare cloth towels.

"Clean the tub. Use this stuff, but don't throw away the towels. We're gonna wash'm. Bring the towels to the kitchen when you're finished, and give'm to Miguel. You understand what I'm telling you?"

"Yeah. I understand."

"When's your mommy coming back?"

"I don't know. Ten days, maybe. I've lost track of time."

"You better hope she don't spend all her money."

Rojas explained to the hall guard what Jack was going to do, then left. The hall guard leaned against the wall, already bored.

Jack wondered what Rojas meant by his crack, then stepped over the cleaning supplies to check out the tub. The smell of feces and urine was strong throughout the house, but here it was even stronger.

A thin red splatter streaked the tile wall like paint flicked from a brush. Pale red smears colored the tub's beige enamel, and pink foam thinned by yellow liquid pooled thinly around the drain. A single island of black hair floated near the drain, held together by something the color of liver, while three long smears of something brown and loose smudged the bottom of the tub. Jack didn't understand what he was seeing at first, then he did, and knew Mr. Chun had died here. They had killed him, right here in the tub, while his screams shook through the walls. They had cut his throat or stabbed him, and he had bled to death in the tub. He had died here. He was murdered here.

They're killing us.

They are killing us.

Jack's hands shook, and the shaking spread to his chest. His entire body trembled, like a reed in strong wind.

Jack glanced at the guard, who was watching with sleepy, lizard eyes.

Jack picked up the Mr. Clean, and sprayed the disinfectant into his hand. He smelled it, and drew the strong smell deep, trying to blot out the awful stink trapped in the little bathroom. He pumped the sprayer to fog the tub and the walls and the air, and breathed deep so the chemicals scoured his nose. He wiped everything down with the towels. He sprinkled the Comet like blue snow, and wet it with more Mr. Clean, and sopped up the blood and piss and Mr. Clean to make the towels awful and foul. He wanted them soaked with death, and so disgusting Miguel would refuse to touch them and order Jack to load them into the washer.

In the utility room.

With the door to the garage.

Jack rubbed and wiped until the tub was clean, then scooped up the bloody, piss-soaked, shit-stained towels, and turned to the guard.

"It's clean. Samuel said I should bring the towels to Miguel."

The guard, who had heard Samuel Rojas say that very thing, shrugged toward the kitchen, and let Jack pass.

Jack said, "Gracias."

He carried the last remains of Mr. Chun in his arms like an overfed baby. Each step brought him closer to the kitchen, and Miguel and Kris, but he felt dizzy and separate from his body.

THEY ARE KILLING US.

He suddenly understood the crack Rojas made when he said Jack better hope his mother hadn't spent all her money. They had killed Mr. Chun because his family couldn't or wouldn't pay. This is how all of them would die. One by one, the money would stop, and they would bleed to death in the tub.

Jack and Krista had to leave. Today. Now. Immediately. So Jack had to make it happen. He was frantic for a plan, but if he returned to their room for the knife, the guard might not let him out. He wanted to tell Kwan, and enlist Kwan as an ally, but Kwan was in the room, which led to the same problem. Once Jack returned to the room, he might not be able to get out again while Krista was in the kitchen.

Jack let a few towels fall, buying himself time to think. He had to do this now, alone, without the knife. Okay, fine. Suck it up, and get it done. Think!

Miguel had a key if the door to the garage was locked. Miguel was bigger and tougher, but he was also lazy and stupid, and turned his back to Jack all the time. A heavy frying pan might make a good weapon, or the big cans of tomatoes Krista put in the soup. Those cans had to weigh a couple of pounds.

Jack could get Miguel into the utility room easy enough by pretending something was wrong with the washer. If Jack could grab the pan or one of the big cans, he only needed to get behind Miguel for a second. He would do whatever he needed to do to open the door.

Jack was so scared his eyes watered. He blinked hard, and gathered the sopping towels in his arms, and continued toward the kitchen.

Miguel usually parked his fat ass in a folding chair at the mouth of the kitchen in the entry. This is where he slept, only now the chair was empty.

Jack hoped this meant Miguel was in the utility room or in the garage, which would be the best of all possible worlds, so he quickened his pace.

His heart pounded and his pulse rushed in his ears as he crossed the entry into the kitchen, gearing up for the battle to come—

But Miguel wasn't in the kitchen, and nothing was as Jack expected.

Medina stood over Krissy, and Krissy was on the floor. Her hands were up to protect herself. Blood smeared on her face.

Jack's world shrank to fuzzy red tunnels filled with roaring static. He saw Krista down with Medina above her, then Medina saw Jack, and his lips peeled away to show the horrible jagged teeth.

Jack floated through falling blood-stained towels as he charged forward without doubt or hesitation.

26.

Marisol was in the kitchen when Krista arrived with Miguel. The skinny guard Krista called the Praying Mantis was slouched against the counter, but he slinked into the living room as soon as Miguel arrived.

Miguel toed a cardboard box filled with canned goods and plastic bags on the floor by the fridge.

"Beans and rice. Make the red kidneys. Got two five-pound bags in there. I got bay leaves and chili peppers. See in there? That'll make'm good."

Marisol looked in the box, but Krista didn't care. She took their largest pot from the stove to the sink, and turned on the tap to fill it.

Marisol brought the bags of beans and rice to the counter, then got their second pot and utensils, and waited her turn at the tap. One big pot for the beans, the other to cook the rice.

Miguel went into the entry, plopped into his chair, and unfolded a car magazine.

Krista glanced at him to make sure he wasn't watching. Krista wasn't tall, but she looked down at her small friend as she whispered.

"I didn't think he could read."

"He can't. He sees only the pictures."

They shared a brief smile, then concentrated on filling the pots. Krista liked Marisol. She was a tiny girl from Ecuador, with cousins who lived in Anaheim. She had traveled almost two months up through the length of Mexico to reach the United States. Her dream was to work as a maid for a rich lady in Beverly Hills, and walk the lady's white poodles every day.

Marisol nudged her.

"How you doing on your side?"

Marisol lived in the other room with the other group of prisoners, many of whom were from Central America. Krista checked on Miguel again before she answered.

"Not so good. They're hurting people."

"Our side, too. If they don't get the money, they make people cry. This girl from Chile—"

Marisol glanced at Miguel, and lowered her voice even more.

"The one with the teeth touched her down there. Her mama was on the phone, and he did these things with his fingers. He told her mama what he was doing."

Krista didn't speak again until they had carried the first pot to the stove, and were filling the second pot. The beans had to be washed, so she dumped the beans into the pot and raked her fingers through the water to wash them.

The information Marisol shared made Krista's hair prickle, and she flashed on the pliers and the way Medina had looked at her, and wanted to scream. Instead, she tried to offer something encouraging.

"A man on our side went home today. They made him scream. We all heard him, but his family must have paid. They sent him home."

Marisol's eyes widened to saucers.

"They let him go?"

"A few minutes ago. He's on his way now."

Marisol slowly shook her head.

"No, Krista. No. They don't let us go."

"He's gone. Rojas told us."

Marisol faced her, and the girl's voice was urgent.

"They don't let us go. They just keep taking the money. There is never enough money. If our families don't find us, we must escape. Do you not know this?"

Krista was wondering how to respond when the door in the utility room opened. Miguel immediately jumped to his feet as Medina came in from the garage. His hands and forearms were smeared with something greasy, and his shirt was blotchy and stained.

Miguel simpered like a Chihuahua.

"You need me to do anything?"

Medina ignored him, and slowly unbuttoned his shirt. He looked Marisol up and down, then raked his gaze over Krista. He peeled out of his shirt like a snake sheds a skin, and dropped it to the floor.

He stared at Krista, but spoke to Marisol.

"Wash this. Make the water hot, and use bleach."

Marisol scurried to pick up the shirt, and took it into the utility room.

Krista heard faint voices, a car door, and an engine starting in the garage. Then the garage door rattled as it lifted.

Miguel tried again, like a simpering fool.

"I guess everything's okay, then, huh? You want me to take care of anything?"

Krista turned back to the pot because she hated the weight of Medina's eyes. His body was broad and hairless. He rippled with muscles, but he was not young and wasn't clean. Loose skin stretched and folded in pale ways she found obscene.

Medina finally gave Miguel an order.

"Check the garage. Make sure Orlato didn't drop something on the floor. Use the bleach."

Miguel hurried past Marisol into the garage.

Krista stared into the pot as it filled, and felt Medina approach. She felt his body heat. He stopped directly behind her.

"Move."

He used his body to nudge her aside, then rinsed his hands and forearms under the running water, depositing his filth into the beans.

"Gimme the soap."

He squeezed a blue ribbon up and down his forearms and over his hands, and worked up a thick lather. He rinsed the suds into the beans, shut the tap, and faced her. Water dripped from his arms onto the floor.

"Dry me."

She glanced up for Marisol or the Mantis or Miguel, but they were alone.

"Dry me. You don't see I'm wet?"

He came closer, so she moved farther away, but still couldn't meet his eyes.

"You should be nice to me, girl."

She stepped away, but he grabbed her by the neck so fast she fell into him, and looked up to see his jagged teeth. She slapped at him, and tried to twist free, but he laughed. Then he stopped laughing, and punched her hard in the face.

Krista fell without knowing it. She bounced off the counter, hit the floor, and looked up at him through a sparkling haze. He seemed very tall, with long legs and longer arms, and his voice echoed from far away.

"It's gonna be good, little *puta*."

He reached from the ceiling with a rubber arm, Krista threw up her hands to ward him off, and Jack came out of nowhere. He flew over her and slammed into Medina like a mongrel dog.

Jack's impact knocked Medina backward. They spun through the kitchen, wrapped together, all arms and legs. Jack made grunting sounds, and found her eyes briefly as he spiraled past.

"Garage."

Krista struggled to her feet, but did not run for the garage. She grabbed the pot from the stove and swung at Medina, but the Mantis rushed in, and lifted her off her feet. Then Miguel and the other guards poured in, and crowded the kitchen to watch.

Medina wrestled Jack to the floor and punched him over and over, his fist rising and falling like a piston.

Krista fought to break away, but the Mantis held tight.

"Stop it! You're killing him—!"

She pleaded, and tried to help, but the beating went on.

"Stop!"

Then the garage door opened, and the man with the ponytail entered.

Miguel and the Mantis immediately pulled Medina to his feet. He fought them until he saw the new man, then immediately stopped struggling.

Krista pleaded.

"He's hurt! He needs help! Look at him, please!"

Jack was belly down on the floor. Blood trickled from both ears down the sides of his face.

"He needs a doctor! Can't you see? Please!"

The new man gazed at Jack, then frowned at Medina.

"You are costing me money."

"Discipline problem. You have to keep them in line."

The tall man looked at each guard in turn, then considered Krista. His expression was so thoughtful she felt encouraged he would help, but then he turned to Medina.

"The dead are worth nothing. Do you see? Get rid of him before the others see him, and clean up this mess."

Krista didn't realize what the tall man's order meant until he and Rojas started away. Jack was hurt, they had no doctor, so they were going to kill him and get rid of his body.

Krista blurted out the one thing she prayed would save his life.

"He's rich! They are *rich*! This is how his mother is away so long!"

The tall man glanced at Rojas, who offered what he knew.

"This is the one whose mother is in China. There is no one to call until she returns."

Krista kept pushing.

"She takes these trips always. My mama says they have much money. If he dies, you will get nothing."

The tall man thought for a moment, then nodded at Medina.

"We shall see. Do what you can for him."

The tall man and Rojas disappeared down the hall as Miguel and another guard bent over Jack. The Mantis took Krista's arm, but Medina leaned close with his jack-o'-lantern face.

"As soon as he's gone, you will make the first call. You gonna call Mama. I'm gonna make you scream real good."

He leered even wider, then told the Mantis to take her to her room.

Krista was scared, but relieved. She had told them one secret about Jack, and it had saved him. But she had come dangerously close to telling them who Jack was related to, and about the army of people who were looking for him. Jack and Krista had agreed on the night they were taken they couldn't tell the *bajadores* who Jack was related to. If these men found out, they would kill him. Jack and Krista could only pray she found them quickly.

The Mantis returned Krista to her room.

The tall man with the ponytail left one hour later.

Medina was good at his word.

Krista made the first call.

He used the terrible teeth, and made her scream.

27.

Nancie Stendahl

Stendahl lowered the windows on her rental car to let in the night-blooming jasmine. Nonstop D.C. to L.A., four hours in the air, hit the ground running, forty minutes later, here she was driving up Kenter Canyon in Brentwood, California. Home. Stendahl had come home because of a call she received from the chief of the Coachella Police Department four days earlier.

Nancie loved the drive up Kenter at night, when the smells of jasmine, fennel, and eucalyptus bloomed, and coyotes and deer might be framed by her headlights. The narrow street began on Sunset Boulevard, but climbed steeply through dense trees and affluent homes until star-field views of the city stretched south and east to the horizons. Nancie Stendahl had missed this drive since her transfer two years earlier to the Bureau of Alcohol, Tobacco, and Firearms's Washington headquarters, but she didn't miss the crappy cell reception.

"Gonna lose you, Tone. I'm on my way up to Bonnie's."

"Can you hear me?"

"So far, but not for long."

Assistant Deputy Director Nancie Stendahl represented the ATF on a congressional task force that included the FBI, ICE, DEA, and the state and local law enforcement agencies that lined the U.S.–Mexican border. This task force was charged with containing cartel gang activity on the Mexican side of the border. Tony Nakamura was her liaison officer with the committee. Normally, the Bureau would have provided a car to someone of Nancie's rank, but this trip was personal.

Nakamura went on.

"I said, the senator's chief bitched me out because you left town with the review coming up."

"I'm available to the senator twenty-four/seven by phone."

"Said that."

"Tell them I'm on a fact-finding mission, and it's necessary if they want a full report."

She waited, but Nakamura was gone. Reception would return when she reached the ridge, but losing him was just as well. Her mind was on other things.

Nancie rounded a last curve by Hanley Park, and pulled up outside a sleek clean modern home with a breathtaking view of the Pacific. It had been her baby sister's house, which Nancie inherited in trust when Bonnie and Mel were killed in a traffic accident on PCH. That was four years ago, when Nancie was between husbands, and serving as the Special Agent in Charge of the ATF's Los Angeles Field Division. Now, four years later, with a new husband, a new job, and a new life in D.C., she returned as often as possible, but for reasons other than the house.

Nancie lifted her wheelie from the trunk, shouldered her purse, and went to the front door. The house appeared normal. The outside lights were on and the soft glow behind frosted sidelights told her the inside lights were also on, but these lights were on timers.

The alarm went crazy when she let herself in, blaring she had sixty seconds to turn it off before LAPD's finest rolled out in force. Nancie keyed in the four-digit code (her nephew's birth year) to shut off the alarm.

"Hey, buddy! You home? It's Nancie!"

She followed the entry to the great room, which looked out on the glowing pool (also on timers) so still and clean it appeared to be filled with air, and called out again.

"Hey, dude!"

The house was neat, orderly, and clean. She was on her way to the bedrooms when her phone rang. She assumed it was Tony calling back, but saw the 760 area code. 760 was Palm Springs.

"Stendahl."

"Ah, this is Sergeant Conner Hartley with the Palm Springs Police Department. I'm calling for, ah, Ms. Nancie Stendahl."

"This is she."

She didn't recognize the voice, but this didn't matter. She had received many calls from the desert during the past four days.

"Ah, Deputy Director Nancie Stendahl? With the ATF out of Washington?"

Like he couldn't get his head around it.

"Assistant Deputy Director, Sergeant, but thanks for the promotion. Have you found my nephew?"

"Ah, no, ma'am, no, I'm sorry. My boss told me to call. He wants you to know we confirmed the Ford Mustang parts found in Coachella came off a vehicle registered to, ah—"

She finished it for him.

"The Arrowhead Trust, Nancie Stendahl and Jack Berman, trustees."

"Ah, yes, ma'am. It was never reported stolen, not here, and not in L.A., either. We double-checked with LAPD and the L.A. Sheriffs, just in case it fell through the cracks, but it wasn't reported."

The Coachella Police and the Riverside County Sheriffs had busted a stolen car ring running a chop shop in Coachella, California, not far from Palm Springs. During the subsequent check of Vehicle Identification Numbers and part serial numbers, the investigators discovered the registered owner of a certain Mustang was something called the Arrowhead Trust, whose mailing address was ATF headquarters in Washington, D.C., in care of Assistant Deputy Director Nancie Stendahl. The chief of the Coachella police had immediately contacted her to ask if she still owned the car.

"The people you busted at the chop shop say where they got my car?"

"Ah, well, that would be the Coachella detectives. They made the arrests. I wouldn't know."

"Are they still in Coachella's custody?"

"Ah, well, I'll have to check."

She made her voice cool.

"Would you pass along my number, and ask your chief to phone me directly? I'd appreciate a call back tonight, regardless of the hour."

"Ah, yes, ma'am."

"One more thing. You checked my home in Palm Springs?"

The Arrowhead Trust owned the Kenter house, the Palm Springs house, and the remains of Bonnie and Mel's estate, all held in trust for Jack, with Nancie as the trustee.

"Yes, ma'am. The chief sent a couple investigators. Everything looked all right."

"Thank you, Sergeant. Please ask the chief to call."

"Yes, ma'am."

She ended the call, and stared into the aqua-blue glow of the pool, wondering where Jack was and how his Mustang ended up in a chop shop without him reporting it stolen. She had been wondering these same things since the Coachella chief contacted her, and she liked none of the possible explanations. After the chief's call, Nancie immediately phoned, texted, and emailed Jack, and had been trying him every day, but had heard nothing. A couple of ATF buddies from the L.A. office had driven up to the house, but reported nothing unusual.

Nancie Stendahl said, "Damnit, Jack."

She dropped her purse on the couch, took off her suit coat, then pushed open the glass slider and went out to the pool.

Jack was a minor when Bonnie and Mel were killed. Her sister and brother-in-law had done all right, both being lawyers, having the Kenter house and a second home in Palm Springs. Then, on top of it, the insurance settlement from the drunk who killed them had been enormous. Nancie set up the trust with herself as trustee and Jack as both co-trustee and beneficiary. She had been between husbands and living alone, so she moved into the Kenter house as his guardian until he started USC, then came the promotion and the transfer to D.C. Financially, Jack was set for life, but now Jack was gone.

Nancie scrolled through her contact list, and called the Special Agent in Charge of the Los Angeles Field Division. He answered immediately.

"Hey, JT. Is it too late?"

"Not for you, boss. Not ever. You here?"

"Up at Bonnie's. Walked in five minutes ago."

"No Jack?"

"Nada."

John Taylor had been her A-SAC when Nancie ran the L.A. office. He was a sharp, tough agent with a stellar record and outstanding management skills. When she was promoted to Washington, JT rightfully took the reins.

"How can I help? You name it, you got it."

"Coachella PD, Palm Springs PD, Riverside County Sheriffs. I want everything they have on the chop shop."

"Done."

She turned away from the pool, and moved back into the house.

"Set me up asap tomorrow morning with the investigating officers out there."

"Will do."

"Face time with the assholes they busted. Whoever made bond, I want them picked up."

"Done. What else?"

She stopped in the living room. Clocked the cordless phone on the kitchen counter and the security monitor on the wall.

"I need an agent on my phone numbers. Jack's cell, we have the two hard line numbers here in Brentwood, and the one hard line in Palm Springs. They're in your files."

"They're in my phone. We'll ID the incoming and outgoing calls for the past two weeks, and run off a list."

"We have a video security system up here. It goes twenty-four/seven on a two-week wipe. I need a full two-week replay with stills of anyone entering or leaving the premises."

"Can you access via the Internet?"

"Yeah. I'll look up the codes."

"Done deal. More?"

She turned back to the pool, and thought hard as she watched the aqua shimmer.

"No. No, that should do it for now. Thanks, JT."

"When do you want to get started?"

"As soon as possible."

"I'll have Mo and Roach on your phones in two hours. Get me the access codes for your digital, they'll run it from their laptops. Can't find them, they'll pull the hard drive there at your house. Just tell them when they get there."

"Thanks, man."

"We'll find him, Nance. Trust me."

"Always did. Always will."

She ended the call, then walked through the house. Bonnie's house. Her baby sister.

Nancie had wanted children, but was unable to conceive. She had doted on Jack, and loved him as fully as if he were her own. Maybe more. Nancie stood at the grave when Bonnie and Mel were buried, held Jack tight, and soaked him with her tears. She had silently promised Bonnie she would take care of their baby boy, forever and always, just as Bonnie would have done.

She had, until now.

"I'll find him, Bon. You know I will."

PART 3

28.

Danny Trehorn

Danny stepped out of the shower at 6:21 A.M. that morning, rubbing the towel over his head and across his back and butt like a shoe-shine cloth; moving fast for a seven A.M. tee time, these four lawyers from L.A. who couldn't play for shit, but enjoyed themselves and didn't throw tantrums when they blew a gimme. Drama queens were lousy tippers, but these guys were solid.

Danny tossed the towel over the curtain rail, slammed on the anti-stink juice, and glanced at the time. If he was out the door by 6:30, he could make the clubhouse by 6:45, punch in, pick up the cart, stock his cooler with water and soft drinks, and be ready and waiting for his foursome by seven.

Perfect.

Shorts, club polo, socks. Good to go, and looking sharp.

Danny was tying his shoes when something pounded on his door so effin' loud he damn near crapped his pants—

BOOM BOOM BOOM.

—at exactly the same time his cell phone rang.

BOOM BOOM BOOM.

Danny glanced at the Caller ID, and saw BATF, as a man's voice outside his door shouted.

"Daniel Trehorn! Police! Please open the door."

What the fuck? It sounded like a joke.

One shoe on, holding the other, Danny gimped to the door and peered out the peephole. A scowling man with short red hair was staring directly at him, and holding a badge.

Danny opened the door, and found five people waiting. Two uniformed policemen, and two men and a woman in suits.

The red-haired man lowered his badge.

"Daniel Trehorn?"

Danny was scared.

"Ah, yeah. What did I do?"

The woman said, "My name is Nancie Stendahl, with the Bureau of Alcohol, Tobacco, and Firearms. Let's step inside."

She didn't ask. She ordered.

Danny never thought to let the club know he would be late until well past his tee time when the government agents left, but by then it didn't matter and Danny didn't care. They were looking for Jack. Danny wanted to help.

ELVIS COLE:
forty-two minutes
before he is taken

29.

Wander Lawrence Gomez drove a midnight blue Audi coupe with dark smoky windows and mag wheels, which was what I told Pike and Jon Stone to expect, only he pulled up beside me at the Cathedral City Burger King driving a sun-bleached gray panel van. No plan of action ever survives the first contact with the enemy.

Wander peered over with his terrible rolling eye. A blank smile twisted across his face like a snake crossing a road.

"Les go. Doan want to keep him waitin'."

"What about my car?"

"We ain't gonna be that long."

Pike and Stone were in separate vehicles somewhere nearby, but I did not know where and did not look for them. I had arrived at the Burger King an hour before Wander. Pike and Stone set up an hour before me.

I walked around to the van's passenger side, and got in. The van was a rolling desert tragedy, but the AC worked well.

"What happened to the Audi?"

"The man gimme this. So you can't see where we goin'. You left your phone in your car?"

"Yeah. Like you said."

I wasn't to bring a phone, watch, pager, or anything electronic. He had warned me I would be searched. The man had rules, and there were no exceptions.

"I find somethin', we're gonna toss it or you goin' home."

"I heard you. I paid attention."

"Okay. It's on you if you blow the deal."

Wander Gomez was six feet two, part Salvadoran and part African-American. He was the color of strong latte except where his father had caved in his right cheek with a cinder block when he was twelve years old. The orbital bones circling his right eye had been crushed, which left his cheek sunken and the surrounding skin scaled with black and pink dots. The eye looked like a coddled egg. It had been cast free to go its own way, and wandered endlessly in a permanent glare, sightless and angry. That's where he got the name. Wander. He called it his magic eye. Said it could see the truth.

Two days earlier, Fredo pointed him out leaning against the Audi across from a bar not far from Echo Lake. The bar was a gathering place for undocumented Salvadorans to share news and information from home. It was also frequented by newly arrived coyotes, who drummed up business before heading south by handing out contact info to anyone who had friends or relatives back home. Wander used his Salvadoran background and magic eye to pick up information about inbound *pollos*, which he then sold to the Syrian or other *bajadores*. Feasting on his own.

I approached him, floated my story, and did not mention the Syrian or suggest where Wander might find a ready-made workforce. My only rule was I would not do business with the Sinaloas. By suggesting there was bad blood between me and the cartel, I had given the Syrian something to check. He did, and decided I looked good in the business department.

Two days later, Wander and I met at the Burger King. One and three-quarter miles after I got into his van, we turned off the highway into an undeveloped area near Rancho Mirage and stopped on the service road.

"Get out. Easier than doin' it in here."

"Right here?"

"Sure, here. These people can't see shit."

We were in open view of the passing cars, but Wander passed an RF wand over me. He did a professional job, which suggested he had scanned people before.

"All right. Get back in, and I'll check the shoes."

I climbed into my seat and started to pull off my shoes, but Wander stopped me.

"In back. Climb between the seats here, 'fore you take off your shoes. You gotta ride back there anyway."

I twisted between the seats, pulled off my shoes, and handed them forward.

Panel vans were working vans. There were no windows behind the front seats, and the rear bay was a dirty metal box smelling of pesticide and grease. Angelo Buono and Kenneth Bianchi had used an identical van as a place to torture and murder their victims, and record their screams.

Wander checked my shoes as thoroughly as he scanned me—searched inside, removed the insoles, and examined the soles and laces. He checked each shoe by hand, and also inserted the wand. Then he handed them back, and held out a black pillowcase.

"Put this on."

When he called that morning, Wander told me I would have to wear a bag so I couldn't see where we were going. I had agreed, but now I was in a dark van that smelled of pesticide and reminded me of the Hillside Stranglers.

"How about we forgo the bag? I can't see anything from back here."

"You kiddin' me, startin' this shit now?"

The angry eye glared at me, then drifted away, then returned before rolling up into his head. The eye looked furious as it came and went, and I wondered what it saw through its rage.

Wander shook the pillowcase.

"Put on the bag. I warned you, an' you said you was cool. Put on the bag or we goin' back to the Burger King."

I took the pillowcase and pulled it over my head. It smelled clean, and might have been Egyptian cotton.

"How does it look?"

"Learn to love it, 'cause you gonna wear it a couple of times today."

"What couple of times?"

"There's never a straight line to the man. That's how he stays safe. You got a couple of rides 'fore you get where you goin'."

Wander started the engine, and guided us back to the highway. Even with the bag over my head, I felt his eye on me, angry and glaring. His magic eye.

I felt trapped in the bag, and easy to kill, and hoped Joe and Jon Stone were close.

JOE PIKE:
the day Elvis Cole
is taken

30.

Joe Pike

Pike watched Elvis Cole's Corvette from a Shell station on the opposite side of the highway a quarter-mile from the Burger King. Jon Stone's black Rover was on Cole's side of the highway a quarter-mile beyond the Burger King. Whichever direction Cole left, either Pike or Stone would be on the correct side to keep him in sight.

Stone's voice came in Pike's ear.

"Movement."

They were on cell phones, each with a Bluetooth bud in his ear. They had satellite phones, but the regular cells were easier so long as they had a signal and military-grade GPS units.

"No joy."

Meaning Pike didn't see the vehicles. Stone had a better view, and was using binos.

"Van's backing out—"

The dingy van crept into Pike's sight line as Stone said it. Pike started the Jeep, and nosed toward the street.

"Got'm. Cole on board?"

"Affirm. Man, you gotta check the driver. This is one ugly fucker."

The van left the Burger King and turned onto the highway, heading away from Pike.

Pike said, "Coming your way."

Pike gunned his Jeep out of the Shell station, and turned onto the highway at the first intersection. He lost sight of the van when he slowed for oncoming cars, but slalomed between traffic and quickly caught up.

"Eight lengths back. I'm by a yellow eighteen-wheeler."

"Looking."

Pike was still settling into a groove when the van's right-turn indicator flashed. They had gone less than a mile.

"Blinker."

"Shit, I don't have you."

"Las Palmas. West side."

"I'm looking."

Pike slowed to put distance between himself and the van. A horn blew behind him, then another, but Pike braked even harder, hanging back as the van turned onto a street between large, undeveloped lots. It stopped in plain sight of the highway.

Pike left the highway, but turned in the opposite direction, watching the van in his sideview mirror. A hundred yards later he turned into a parking lot surrounding a home furnishings outlet.

"They stopped at an empty lot."

"I see'm. They're out of the van. Dude's checking him. Shit, right out in the open."

"I'm north. Set up south."

"Rog. Doing it."

Pike knew the search wouldn't take long and it didn't. Cole and Wander climbed back into the van, and once more rolled south on the highway, then east, leaving the monied areas of Rancho Mirage and Palm Desert behind for the working-class neighborhoods of Indio.

Pike and Stone changed positions frequently so Wander would not notice a single vehicle lingering in his mirror. Pike had fallen back when Jon Stone's voice came in his ear.

"Blinker."

Pike was seven lengths behind Stone's Rover. Five sedans, two pickup trucks, and a biker on a chopped Harley were scattered between them. Stone's left-turn indicator blinked on, and Stone spoke again.

"Turning left at the Taco Bell."

"Yes."

"I gotta slow. Tighten up."

Pike nudged the Jeep closer.

The van turned past the Taco Bell into a mixed area of small residential homes and light-business properties. This made following more difficult because there was less traffic, so Stone dropped farther back. Pike followed two blocks behind Stone, noting parallel streets on his GPS in case he had to maneuver.

Stone said, "Blinker. He's stopping. Three blocks up. I'm stopping, too."

Pike made an immediate right, jumped on the accelerator, and screamed left onto the parallel street, watching for kids and oncoming cars. Five blocks up, he jammed the brakes, turned left twice, and finished on the original street, slow-rolling in the opposite direction. The gray van sat in a driveway three houses ahead on his left, waiting as the garage opened.

Pike said, "Yellow stucco on your right side. Address three-six-two."

The houses along the street all sported light-colored composite roofs over stucco, with attic vents on the gables, two-car attached garages, and weathered chain-link fences. Most of the houses showed trees and some kind of vegetation, but the yellow's yard was parched sand and rocks.

Stone rolled forward as Pike crept past the house. The garage door was open, but a large green SUV filled the garage, leaving no room for the van. Pike glimpsed Cole climbing from the passenger side as he passed.

"Garage open. They're getting out."

"Got'm. Wander and Elvis. They are in the garage. The door's coming down. Stand by—"

Pike turned right at the first cross street, and made a fast K-turn. He stopped short of the intersection with a view of the house. Stone would have done the same at the next cross street.

Pike's view allowed him to see the garage door, the front door, two front windows, and two side windows. The windows were closed, and the shades were down. All the shades in every window, none showing even an inch or two gap at the bottom.

Pike rolled down his window, and recalled the Masai hunters he knew in Africa. He wondered if they could hear the house speaking. He stared at the house, and listened.

Pike was in position for less than five minutes when the garage door jerked into motion.

"Jon."

"Yep."

The door was still climbing when Wander ducked under and returned to the van.

Stone said, "You see that fuckin' eye?"

"See Elvis?"

"Just the geep."

The door rumbled down.

"Was anyone in the garage?"

"Negative. Just the geep."

Wander backed out of the drive and departed past Pike, leaving the way he arrived.

Stone said, "What the fuck?"

They waited. One minute. Two minutes.

"You think they have hostages in there?"

Pike didn't answer.

"Think al-Diri's in there?"

"Shh."

Three minutes after Wander departed, the garage door jerked to life again, and once more climbed its rails. When the door was open, a dark green Ford Explorer carefully backed out. The windows were so dark they looked black.

Stone said, "Field trip. What do we do now, follow or stay?"

The garage door closed. The garage was now empty, but this didn't mean the house was empty.

The Explorer backed to the street, then departed past Jon.

Pike said, "See anyone?"

"No, man. Not through that glass. You think he's in there?"

Elvis.

"Don't know."

"Say again, what do we do?"

Pike stared at the house. There was no way to know if Elvis was inside or gone.

"Take the Explorer. I'll sit on the house."

"On it."

Pike watched the house, and strained to hear voices no one could hear.

31.

Jon Stone

The Explorer dropped south out of Indio down through Coachella and into the desert. It stayed in the right-hand lane, never varied its speed from the normal flow of traffic, and did nothing out of the ordinary. Jon found this suspicious.

Stone dropped so far back he cruised along with the Zeiss binos between his legs. Every few minutes he took a quick peek to make sure the Explorer was where it was supposed to be, and, yep, there it was.

They passed Thermal, California, which has the coolest name ever for a desert town, and Jon thought they might be rolling all the way down to Mexico, but not far past the Thermal airport, the Explorer turned east.

Jon tightened it up easy enough, his big black Rover having a supercharged mill, and followed the Explorer along the top of the Salton Sea into a small residential neighborhood surrounded by farms. He called Pike.

"Looks like we're going to another house. I'm in a little town called Mecca, at the north end of the Salton."

Pike didn't respond, which was pretty much like Pike.

"You get any movement up there?"

"No."

"The geep come back?"

"No."

No. One word answers. Typical Joe Pike non-conversation.

"Okay. I'll keep you advised."

"Jon."

"Yeah?"

"I three-sixtied the house."

This meant Pike had circled the house, checking it out. Jon knew this also meant Pike was worried. Pike was the best recon man Stone had ever known, but circling a house surrounded by nothing but sand and dirt was asking to be seen. Pike would know this, too, and understood the risk.

"The shades aren't just pulled. They're tacked in place. The house is locked down."

"You hear anything?"

"No."

"AC running?"

"Yes."

"You want to go in, I'll come back. We'll bust that fucker wide open."

"No. Stay on the Explorer."

"Rog."

Stone dropped farther back when the Explorer's blinker came on. He had to be even more careful now in the confined residential streets. His eighty-thousand-dollar Rover stood out in the shabby area like a gleaming black diamond, not that this bothered him. It was another challenge, and Stone loved challenges. They made life interesting.

He checked his GPS, and saw the surrounding neighborhood laid out in a rectangular grid. Easy-peasy.

Three blocks ahead, the Explorer turned right. Stone gave it two heartbeats to let them disappear, then pulled a hard right and stood on the supercharged mill. The Rover bucked like an F18 catapulting off a carrier. When he reached the first cross street, Stone jumped on the brakes, nosed forward, and saw the Explorer crossing the parallel intersection three blocks away.

Stone leapfrogged the Explorer another three blocks, but the Explorer didn't appear at the fourth intersection. Jon banked left to the Explorer's street, then left again, then smiled.

"Dead man, you bitch."

Right side, four houses away, the Explorer nosed into an open garage. Another vehicle was in the garage, but Jon couldn't tell the make or model. He waited until the garage door closed, then cruised past the house.

The Explorer disappeared into a faded pink house with a red composition roof. Stone drove past, turned around, then backed into a spot across the street and three houses down. He parked between a Dodge pickup and a Toyota Cruiser, hoping the truck and the SUV would help the Rover blend in.

Jon studied the house, and paid particular attention to the windows. The shades were down and tight as at the Indio house, and no sound or sign of movement came from the property. The attic vents under the gables were framed to look like small doors, and one was ajar as if it was off its hinges. Unlike the earlier house with its barren yard, this house had two ragged oaks in the front yard, a broken line of cedars along the side, a white basketball backboard mounted on the roof above the garage. The backboard was peeling and the net was long gone.

Stone was wondering how long it had been since someone sank a ball through the hoop when the garage door jerked to life, revealing the dark green Explorer and a black Escalade. Jon slumped behind the wheel.

The Escalade backed out and drove away directly in front of the Rover. Jon glimpsed the driver and saw a shape in the passenger seat, but the passenger was only a shadow.

Stone was torn between following the Escalade and staying with the Explorer, but decided to stay. You danced with the girl you brought to the party.

Stone crawled into the back seat and unzipped a green nylon duffel. He dug through it until he found a hard plastic Pelican case, and considered its contents.

Jon's security work often required him to use various bugs and monitoring devices to acquire intelligence. Jon was thinking about taking a look inside the house. He would do this by drilling a hole two-point-five millimeters in diameter through the wall, and inserting a camera and microphone on a wire the size of a #2 pencil lead.

Jon was deciding which drill bit to use when the garage door once more opened, and he closed the case.

Jon was watching the Explorer back out of the garage when he noticed the clutter people accumulate in their garages was missing. No boxes, bicycles, lawn equipment, or Christmas decorations crowded the walls or hung from the rafters. Jon dialed back through his memory file, and realized the garage at the Indio house was also free of clutter.

The Explorer led him north past the Thermal airport into Coachella. Jon thought they were returning to the Indio house, but they turned west through La Quinta and Indian Wells, then south into the desert.

Jon checked his GPS, and saw the highway would track away from the desert communities and into the deep nowhere of the Anza-Borrego Desert, west of the Salton Sea. Traffic thinned, so he dropped farther back until he needed the binos to see the Explorer. They held fast to a steady seventy miles per hour for almost twenty minutes before their brake lights flared. Jon immediately slowed, and glanced at the GPS, expecting to see a road, but saw nothing. He changed from the map to a satellite view, and zoomed the image until he saw a thin filament angled away from the highway. This would be an unpaved county or ranch road.

The Explorer turned off the highway, and immediately kicked up a plume of dust Jon saw without the binos.

He said, "Shit."

Jon let the gap between them widen. He wasn't worried about losing the Explorer because its dust trail was so obvious, but following it would be a problem. If he could see the Explorer, the Explorer could see him.

When he reached the turn, he pulled off the highway, and compared the receding dust trail with the image on his GPS. The few unpaved roads showed as thin gray lines that ran for miles before intersecting another thin line. The Explorer was now on a road that angled away from the highway and would soon join another road that paralleled the highway for miles. This second road then crossed a third road that swept back to the highway. Jon smiled when he saw this, kicked the Rover back onto the highway, and pressed hard on the gas.

Four-point-six miles later, at one hundred nine miles per hour, Jon turned off the highway onto the third road, far ahead of the Explorer. The dust was well behind him, and angling away. Jon checked his GPS again, and trailed after them slowly. He followed them into the desert for two-point-three miles until their plume vanished, which meant they had stopped.

Jon stopped the Rover, and searched the tip of the fading plume with his binos until he spotted a glint in the wavery heat. He returned to the nylon bag for a 60x Zeiss spotting scope mounted to a small tripod. The Zeiss had proven ideal for locating shitbirds on the rocky slopes of Afghanistan. He set it on the Rover's hood, adjusted the focus, and saw the Explorer.

It was parked on a rise near what appeared to be a low stone wall. Two small figures carried something large into the brush. A few moments later, they returned to the Explorer, and carried another large thing away. Jon got a cold feeling one of these things might be Elvis Cole's body.

They made two more trips beyond the walls, then climbed into the Explorer, and left. Jon was torn between following the Explorer or checking for Cole, but there was really only one decision.

Jon watched until their dust plume faded, then adjusted the Rover's suspension for uneven terrain and made his way across the desert. He stopped sixty yards from the crumbling walls, got out with his M4, and offed the safety. His scalp prickled like ants were under his skin, and jacked him into full-on combat mode, ready to bust out thirty rounds of 5.56.

Jon picked his way through the brush until he found the Explorer's tracks, then followed footprints past the wall to a low wash. Jon knew what he would find even before he reached the erosion cut at the edge of the wash. The angry buzz of fat desert flies and meat-eating hornets told him. The stink of rotten shrimp and organ meat told him the rest.

The bodies had been dumped into the cut atop each other in a jumble of plastic-wrapped flesh. White powder was liberally sprinkled over the bodies, but did little to help the smell or discourage the flies. They swirled in an angry cloud, and crawled beneath the plastic.

Jon counted eight, then decided there were nine bodies, both men and women, but could not see them well enough through the plastic to know if Elvis Cole was among them.

Jon slung the M4, photographed the bodies with his iPhone, then returned to his Rover. He pulled off his sunglasses, rubbed his face, and shouted at the horizon.

"They're people, you bastards. Jesus Christ on a jumpstick, they are fuckin' PEOPLE!"

He stared toward the cut, stowed the M4, then took off his shirt and tied it over his nose and mouth to keep out the flies.

Jon returned to the cut, and climbed down among the dead. He peeled back the plastic, looking for Elvis Cole.

He knew Pike would ask.

32.

Joe Pike

Wander had not returned, and neither had the Explorer. Young moms and dads passed with kids strapped into car seats, and three boys rumbled past on skateboards. Pike wondered if Cole was inside with Ghazi al-Diri, and if everything was going according to plan.

A woman wearing black utility pants and a black tank top came out of the house next door with a large German shepherd. She had broad shoulders for a small woman, and fit arms, and looked like a commando in all the black, but she didn't look happy.

The woman and dog walked past the Jeep like they had done this same walk a thousand times and it held nothing new. The dog pulled at the leash, and the woman told it to stop. She seemed angry, but Pike thought she probably wasn't. They had walked together a thousand times, and each time the dog pulled, the woman complained, and her arms and face showed the strain. Pike wondered why she didn't change the pattern. Change one element, and everything changes. All she had to do was talk to the dog.

Pike's phone vibrated. He glanced at the incoming number and recognized Stone.

"Go."

"They're dumping bodies. I followed the Explorer into the desert and saw them. They're killing people in those houses."

Pike studied the house, and wondered if someone was inside dying.

"Elvis?"

"No. No, man, I checked. They dumped four today, but I counted nine. It is fuckin' grotesque."

Pike figured they would be Park's people.

"Koreans?"

"That's what I expected, but no. They're Indians or Pakistanis. How many fuckin' people has this guy kidnapped?"

This surprised Pike. He wondered if they had been held at the house he was watching, or the Mecca house, or another, and how many more were still prisoners.

"How long have they been dead?"

"The four today, no more than five or six hours. The others have been there for days."

"Where are you?"

"Inbound now, but the bodies are twenty south of Palm Desert. I fixed a waypoint. What's happening up there?"

"Nothing."

Stone didn't comment, which meant Stone didn't like it. Pike didn't like it either. Cole was supposed to be in the house, but Wander had not returned to take him back to his car, and no one else had arrived. If they had taken Cole in the Explorer, he now had no backup, and Pike liked that even less.

Stone read his mind.

"Y'know, we have no reason to believe he was in that Explorer."

"Uh."

"But if the Syrian was in Mecca, maybe they dropped off Cole on their way to dump the bodies."

Pike thought Stone might be right about the meeting at a secondary location, but there was only one way to find out.

"I'm going in."

"Wait. I'm fifteen out. I'll make it in twelve."

"Not going to wait."

Pike put away his phone, then went to the rear bay. He stripped off
his sweatshirt, strapped on a ballistic vest, then pulled the sweatshirt over it.
He clipped a Kimber .45 semi-auto at the small of his back, and was about
to clip his .357 Python when the dog ran past trailing its leash. Pike stepped
to the far side of the Jeep to cover his guns.

The dog ran directly to its door, and scratched to get in. Pike guessed the
woman had grown tired of being pulled. She came along the street a few
seconds later, scowling, and shouting at the dog to stop. The dog didn't stop.
Pike turned away when she glanced at the Jeep.

When the woman and the dog were inside their home, Pike clipped
the .357 to his waist, then drove to the house. He got out with a fifteen-pound
sledge, and did not bother to knock.

Pike hit the door square on the deadbolt. The lock crunched into the
wood, but the door did not give. Pike swung again, and shattered more wood,
but something was blocking the door.

Pike stood to the side. He listened at the hole, but heard nothing. There
were no voices, or movement, or men scrambling for guns.

Pike ran back to the Jeep, and drove forward until the brush guard
pressed the garage door, and the cheap door crumpled into the garage.

The laundry room door went down to the sledge.

Pike cleared the house fast, leading with the gun, locked out and good
to go. The house was now empty. Pike found no bodies, possessions, food, or
clothes. The only remaining evidence that something terrible had happened
here were the heavy sheets of plywood covering the windows and doors. This
house had been a prison.

Pike finished, and stood in the living room, breathing. He tried to listen
to what the house knew, but heard only the low steady thud of his heart.

Pike had stood sentry since the gray van delivered Cole to this house, but Cole was now missing.

His friend had been taken.

Pike ran back to his Jeep, backed from the garage, and told Jon Stone to meet him in Mecca.

33.

Joe Pike

The house in Mecca contained even less. The plywood had been removed, and the screw holes filled with painter's putty. No sign remained of Cole or anyone else.

Stone said, "Now what?"

"His car."

"What?"

"Can't leave his car at the Burger King."

"I meant where do we go from here?"

"I know what you meant."

They left Pike's Jeep at the Palm Springs airport. Stone drove them to the Burger King, where Pike picked up Cole's Corvette. He had a key. They would take the Corvette home, get some sleep, and Stone would drive them back in the morning. They would pick up Pike's Jeep, and sit on the bodies. If nine bodies had been dumped, there might be a tenth.

Two hours and forty-six minutes later, Pike rounded the last curve to Elvis Cole's A-frame, and guided the old Corvette into the carport.

The house was dark, but Pike knew Cole's house as well as his own. He turned on the kitchen light, then a table lamp in the living room, then pushed open the glass sliders to Cole's deck.

The canyon below was dotted with lights. Some of the houses were so close Pike saw the flickering color of televisions, while others held the sky blue shimmer of pools. Pike liked Cole's deck. He had helped Cole rebuild it when termites attacked the framing, and helped stain the wood every three years. The night air was chill, and smelled of wild fennel.

Pike said, "I hear you."

The snick-snick-snick of approaching claws, then Cole's cat bumped against his legs.

Pike looked down at the cat, and the cat looked up. It was a ragged animal, with pale scars lacing its black face and shredded ears.

Pike squatted, and ran the flat of his palm from the cat's lumpy head along the peak of its spine. The cat enjoyed this for a moment, then stepped away. The fur along his spine rippled. His ears folded, then straightened, and his warrior face grew angry.

Pike said, "He isn't here."

Pike went inside. He found an open can of cat food and a bottle of Abita beer in the fridge. He forked the remains of the can into a clean dish, then put out fresh water, the food, and a saucer of beer.

The cat stood by the food, but did not eat.

Pike drank most of the remaining beer, turned on the carport light, and stared at Cole's car. Filthy. Pike washed his Jeep every day, and waxed it every two months. Cole's home was neat and orderly, and Cole was fastidiously clean when he cooked, but his car was a mess. Pike did not understand it, though he often wondered if it revealed some truth Pike was unable to understand.

Pike found a mop bucket and towels in the laundry room, squirted dish soap into the bucket, and took the bucket and towels out to the car. An armada of bugs swirled and spiraled around the carport ceiling light.

Pike pulled the hose from the side of the house, filled the bucket with sudsy water, then rinsed the car. He began at the nose, rubbing the car with his hand to slough away the dirt. The cat came out to watch. The water splashed his fur with liquid shrapnel, but the cat did not move.

Pike worked the dirt loose from the hood and sides and tail, then soaked a towel in the soapy water and went over the car again. He rubbed hard, and when the body was clean, he worked on the tires and wheels, then rinsed the body again. He dried the car with the remaining towels, then wiped down the interior.

When Pike finished, he tried to remember when he had last seen Cole's car this clean. He couldn't, and didn't care. It was clean now. When Cole came back, his car was good to go.

Pike dumped the bucket and went inside. He stripped off his clothes, put them in the wash with the towels, then showered in the guest room bath. The cat followed him through the house, and back again when he put his clothes in the dryer.

While the clothes were drying, Pike went upstairs for Cole's gun-cleaning supplies, and brought them down to the dining table. Cleaning lubricant, cotton patches, a bore brush and cleaning rod, a soft cotton cloth.

Pike unloaded the pistols, and broke down the Kimber. He could take the Kimber apart and reassemble it blindfolded, in the dark, and under any conditions. He did not have to think about what he was doing. His hands knew the way.

The cat watched from the far end of the table. Pike pushed cotton patches wet with cleaning lubricant through the barrel and over the frame and slide and the recoil spring assembly and breech face. Pike glanced at the cat as he worked, and noticed the cat wasn't looking at Pike; it watched the parts as they were brushed and wiped.

Pike set the recoil spring assembly into the Kimber's frame, replaced the slide, and fitted the slide lock pin into place. When the Kimber was reassembled, Pike set it aside and worked on the Python. He glanced at the cat again. Its eyes had narrowed into smoldering cuts and its tail flicked like a dangerous snake.

Pike swabbed lubricant through the Python's cylinder chambers and barrel, then over the recoil plate and under the cylinder star. He ran the brush through the barrel and chambers, then swabbed the steel clean, but did not look at the gun while he cleaned it. He watched the cat.

The cat paced at the far end of the table, stalking from one side to the other, its tail snapping violent strikes that stung the air as the fur on its spine rippled.

Pike reloaded the Kimber. He pushed one fat, golden .45 ACP hollow point after another into the Kimber's magazine until it was full, then seated it. He rocked the slide to chamber a round, and set the safety.

The cat came toward him, paced away, then returned. Its dark face was as fierce as a Maori. The fur on its spine was spiked like a Mohawk warrior.

Pike put the Kimber aside and loaded the Python. He opened the cylinder and slid a long .357 magnum cartridge into a cylinder chamber.

The cat came closer.

Pike dropped in a second cartridge, then a third, and now the cat stood only inches away, but it no longer looked at the gun. It stared at Pike, and its molten black face was furious.

Pike finished loading the Python. Six chambers, six cartridges. He closed the cylinder, but held tight to the pistol, and stared at Cole's cat. Elvis Cole's cat.

The cat licked its feral lips, and made a low growl.

Pike nodded.

"Yes. I'm going to get him."

He put the guns in their holsters, drank a bottle of water, then called Jon Stone.

"Come get me. I'm not waiting until morning."

Stone picked him up a few minutes later.

JACK AND KRISTA:
seven days after
they were taken

34.

One day after the beating, Jack opened his eyes, blinked, and looked at her. His pupils were dilated.

"Whush on TV?"

"Can you see me? I'm here."

His eyes rolled, and came back to her.

"Nancie. Mommy ish home."

Krista touched his lips. A stab of fear arced through her every time he mentioned his aunt.

"Shh, baby. Don't talk about Nancie."

His eyes rolled again, widened, then closed.

Jack was stretched out along the wall in their spot beneath their window. The guards had brought Jack back to the room, and placed him by the piss bucket. They had given her ice wrapped in a towel for his head. That was the extent of their aid. Kwan dragged him to their rightful spot under the window. The ice had melted, so she folded the damp towel, and placed it under Jack's head as a cushion.

Kwan sat nearby. No one else in the room had approached. As if they feared the guards would give them the same.

"Talks more. Good."

Jack was mostly unconscious yesterday after the beating, and Krista

thought he would die. His skin grew pale and clammy, and he would trem-
ble violently between periods of calm. He began mumbling earlier that
morning. Krista thought this was a good sign, but didn't know. Jack was hurt
badly. She hoped it was only a concussion, but her head swirled with thoughts
of cranial hemorrhages, brain damage, and flat-lined monitors.

Kwan said, "How you?"

When she glanced up, he pointed to her shoulder. They had called
her mother yesterday. Medina held her while Rojas placed the call. When
her mother was on the line, Medina bit her shoulder to make her scream.
He bit hard, and grinded against her.

She answered quickly, and pushed the memory away.

"I'm fine. It's nothing."

Kwan grunted, as if he approved of her bravery.

"I kill."

She glanced at him, and Kwan smiled, but it was dark and shadowed.

"Soon."

He settled against the wall and closed his eyes, but the smile remained.

Two more Koreans had been released in the hours following Jack's beating. Rojas made the same speech, claiming they were released to their loving
and generous families, but Kwan had once again smirked.

"No pay."

Krista said, "You think they were killed?"

"No pay, you die."

"You're still alive. Who's paying for you?"

Kwan had only smiled, and said nothing more.

Twenty minutes later, Rojas and Medina had forced her to speak to her
mother, and Medina had made her scream.

She touched Jack's head now, and concentrated on him to distract herself
from the memory. She focused on Jack. It was all about keeping Jack alive
until they were saved.

She was totally focused on what she might do to help him when the door
opened, and Medina, Rojas, and Miguel strode in. She thought Medina was

coming for her again, but the three men began kicking the people who were lying in the middle of the room, driving them to the sides. The tall man with the ponytail waited in the door until the floor was clear, then came directly to Krista. She was sure they had come to take Jack away, and shoved to her feet.

"Don't hurt him! He needs a doctor!"

The tall man pushed her aside, and squatted by Jack. He examined one eye, then the other, and felt Jack's forehead. Then he stood, and turned to Krista. He spoke excellent Spanish.

"He is strong. How long until his mother returns?"

Krista steadied herself. She was so scared she wanted to throw up, but her panic eased. If the man was asking questions, he could still be convinced.

"He tell me a week, but I am not sure. He does not speak good Spanish, and I do not have the English."

"You are from Sonora?"

"Si. Hermosillo."

"How do you know he has money?"

"My mama, she tell me. She worked in their home."

"She says they are rich?"

Krista tried to answer the way a village girl would answer.

"They have many houses and cars. His mother, she takes trips to wonderful places. The boy, he does not work. None of them work. This is why she ask him to bring me to her."

Krista did her best to look shy, and a little embarrassed.

"She hopes he will like me."

The tall man made a tiny smile, and Krista felt a rush of power.

"What kind of cars? Mercedes? Porsches? Bentleys?"

She stared as if he spoke a foreign language, and shook her head.

"I do not know what these are."

He smiled again, but this time at how stupid she was. This encouraged her even more.

"But she says they are rich."

Krista knew he was buying her lies because he wanted to believe, so she had to give him something believable without sounding outlandish.

"She told me his father was killed in an accident. They got much money from the insurance. So much they are now rich."

The tall man grunted as if this made perfect sense, then glanced at Jack, and grunted again.

"He is strong. He will live."

"He needs a doctor."

The tall man smiled, but now it was cruel.

"You are his doctor. Save him, and perhaps you can marry his money. I will give you more ice."

The tall man turned, and Krista watched him go. When the door closed, she sat beside Jack, and touched his head. He was alive. They had survived another day. People were searching.

She leaned against the wall, and considered the tall man's greed.

She thought, *I am smarter than you. I will beat you.*

Then Kwan murmured something she did not understand.

"I didn't hear you."

He stared at her.

"They die soon. They die very soon."

"How do you know?"

"My people will come."

Krista touched Jack's head, and tried to hold on to her hope.

"Mine will come, too. They are on their way now."

Jack Berman moaned, and shivered from a cold no one else felt.

ELVIS COLE:
taken

35.

Wander Lawrence Gomez told me we were about to stop, but to leave on the pillowcase. We slowed, turned, crunched over gravel, then braked again.

A door rattled as it lifted, the van eased forward, and the door rattled again. Wander pulled away the pillowcase as the van's front passenger door and side door opened. A black man was pointing a shotgun at me. A Latin guy in the passenger seat had a pistol locked out in a two-hand combat grip.

I blinked at the black man.

"Are you the Syrian?"

"Boy, I'm from Compton. The man ain't here. We gonna search you again, and get you back on the road."

"Why do you have to search me again?"

"Coz that's the way we do things. Get your ass out of there."

Wander gave me the ugly smile, which he probably took to be encouraging.

"You checked out fine, bro. Everything's copacetic."

The black guy stepped back so I could get out in the tight space between the van and a dark green Ford Explorer. They brought me into an empty house to search me, but Wander stayed with the van. It was the last time I saw him.

A few minutes later they loaded me into the Explorer's back seat, bagged my head, and brought me to another house. The man from Compton drove. This time when the hood came off, we were wedged into a garage with a black Cadillac Escalade.

Two Latin men stood by an open door at the head of the garage, looking at us. One of the Latin guys was built burly and strong, and the other had a badly fixed cleft lip. I tried to sound jaded, as if I was so familiar with the world of human trafficking, this kind of thing was yesterday's news.

"Those people aren't Syrian. Is the man here or not? If we're not going to do business, fuckit."

"He's here. You're gonna meet him now."

The two men stepped aside to let us pass, then continued into the garage. They hooked up with the man who rode shotgun in the Explorer.

My driver led me through a utility room and a kitchen, and then to a living room. The house smelled like a cross between sour cabbage and a bus station men's room. Two guards eyed me from a hall, and another from a futon in the living room. Two futons, a couple of folding chairs, and three table lamps were the only furniture. One of the hall guards went down the hall.

I said, "Nice digs."

Heavy plywood had been screwed over every window and outside door like armor plate. Even the front door and the sliders. So far as I could see, the only way in or out was through the garage. The house had been converted to a bunker.

Ghazi al-Diri and another man emerged from the back of the house. Al-Diri was a tall, muscular man with dark skin, black eyes, and a frown line between his eyebrows. His black hair was pulled into a tight ponytail. He wore stonewashed jeans, a lime-colored knit shirt, and three narrow gold rings on his left hand. The other man was shorter, with tiny eyes and a pocked face.

Al-Diri smiled cordially, and offered his hand.

"Welcome, Mr. Green. I am Ghazi. This is my associate, Vasco Medina."

Medina showed teeth that looked like a horror-film prop.

"Harlan. I understand you may be able to help me out."

"This is true. Forgive me, I would offer a seat, but there are no seats to offer."

"No worries. Is the labor here for me to inspect?"

My heart rate was up, but I tried to appear calm. If the Koreans were here, it was likely the people captured with them would also be here, but there was no certainty.

I was all business and ready to get to it, but al-Diri wasn't so anxious. He hooked his thumbs in his pockets, and ignored my question.

"I am told you supply labor. Your interest is agribusiness?"

I gave him the same bullshit I fed Winston Ramos.

"I offer career opportunities to people from emerging nations by supplying low-cost labor to firms open to a workers with untested credentials."

Al-Diri frowned at me as if he didn't know whether I was joking, so I pressed ahead.

"Agribusiness. Yes. This is why I have to inspect these people. Age and health are important. Gender, not so much. Are we talking young studs or frail old men? I have to see them before I can give you a price."

Al-Diri finally nodded as if this made perfect sense, and gestured toward the hall.

"The workers you wish to see are here."

"Perfect."

We made cordial conversation as if we weren't in a drop house reeking of urine where people were tortured and murdered.

He said, "I understand you will not work with the Sinaloas."

"We had a misunderstanding."

"They have misunderstandings with many people."

"Yourself?"

He clapped me on the back.

"The enemy of my enemy is my friend. Here, see what I have for you."

A guard standing post by a locked door unlocked it as we approached. Al-Diri opened the door, but Medina went inside first. The smell of urine, feces, and unwashed people rolled out of the room like an acid fog. My eyes watered, but al-Diri and Medina didn't seem to notice.

"We have twenty-three workers I wish to sell. Fourteen men, and nine are women. Three of the men are older, but healthy and still strong. Three speak Spanish, four have some English, but are not fluent. Most have only Korean. You want to touch them? Feel their strength. Some of the women are attractive."

The room was crowded with people sitting or lying on the floor, but none were Krista Morales or Jack Berman. Most were Asian, but several were Latin, and all of them watched me with sorrowful eyes. They were unwashed, soiled, and the men were unshaven. I tried not to breathe.

I said, "We are speaking of the Koreans?"

"Yes. Only the Koreans."

"There aren't twenty-three."

"There are more in another room. I show you."

"I was told you had twenty-six."

Medina flashed the picket-fence teeth.

"You always lose some. Shit happens."

When Medina opened the second door, Krista Morales and Jack Berman were the first people I saw. They were on the floor against the far wall, and Berman appeared to be sleeping. I saw them, and ignored them. I gave the room a cursory glance, then turned to Ghazi al-Diri.

"I need thirty."

Al-Diri shook his head.

"Only twenty-three are for sale."

"I understand, but I need thirty. I lost thirty farmers in San Diego. My buyer needs and expects thirty. These other *pollos* will do."

I drifted through the room as if I were assessing their suitability. I glanced at Krista and Jack, and realized Berman wasn't sleeping. His eyes flagged, opened, rolled, and closed. A dark crust had built up around his ear.

"What's wrong with him?"

"Are you American? Can you help him? He's hurt."

She was scared. She was so scared she sounded completely different than she had on the phone.

I squatted as if I was looking more closely at Berman, but I looked at her instead and lowered my voice.

"Don't forget your accent. You're playing a Mexican."

She stared as if I had slapped her, but I stood before she could respond and turned to al-Diri.

"What the hell? Are these people injured and sick?"

Medina said, "He ain't sick. I kicked his ass. You have to do that sometime."

I stared at Medina, and smiled.

"Yeah. Some people need their ass kicked."

I turned to al-Diri.

"I deal with injuries all the time. You want me to take a look?"

Al-Diri stepped into the hall, and motioned me to join him.

"This is not important. We have business. Come."

I glanced back at Krista, and found her still staring at me. I wanted to tell her she was only minutes away from being out of this hell, but I joined al-Diri in the hall.

The burly man from the garage and an Anglo with large hands were in the kitchen when we reached the entry. The burly man motioned Medina over. Al-Diri told me to wait in the living room, and joined their conversation. The four men spoke quietly, which left me feeling alone.

After a while, Medina came over and stood nearby with his arms crossed.

I said, "What's going on?"

"Fuckin' Orlato always has some bullshit."

Orlato was the man with the stomach.

Al-Diri followed Orlato into the kitchen, and the Anglo came over and stood behind me. I tried to watch him and ignore him at the same time.

Thirty seconds later, al-Diri returned from the kitchen, and now a gun dangled alongside his leg.

I said, "What's the problem?"

Al-Diri raised the gun.

"You."

Then the Anglo took one step away, and he pointed a gun at me, too.

Orlato came back from the kitchen with a smaller man who looked like a UFC fighter with a loser's face. He was Winston Ramos's bodyguard, and had been with us in Rudy Sanchez's tow.

The Syrian glanced at him, then waved his gun.

"Is this the man?"

"Thas him. He ain't who he say he is. He's friends with Ramos."

Vasco Medina showed me the teeth, then punched me in the face.

36.

The Anglo shouted across the top of his pistol.

"*Down*. Get on the fuckin' floor *now*."

Medina strapped my wrists with a plasticuff when I was down. He punched me in the back twice and once on the side of my neck, then the two men pulled me up until I was on my knees.

Al-Diri walked over and put away his gun.

"Who are you?"

"Harlan Green. Jesus, what are you doing?"

"I am thinking you are a federal agent."

I glared at the UFC fighter.

"Are you crazy, listening to this turd? You checked me out. Why did you bring me here, if you didn't check me out?"

Al-Diri glanced at the UFC fighter, and said something in Spanish. Orlato took the UFC fighter's arm and led him out through the kitchen. I wondered if Pike had seen him arrive, or would see him leave, and would realize something was wrong.

Al-Diri turned back to me.

"I know what I hear, but now I am told you are friends with my enemies by someone who should know. This makes me think I have not heard right things."

"You got ripped off. That guy doesn't know what he's talking about."

"He has never been wrong before."

"He's sure as hell wrong now, and he's costing you money."

I made my voice calm. Krista Morales and Jack Berman were twenty feet away, and needed me. Calm is good when you're trying to appear as if you have more control than you do.

"Your snitch saw me with Winston Ramos and Sang Ki Park of the Double Dragon gang. Winston Ramos is the prick who wants me dead. The Dragons came as my security, or did your snitch not mention Park knocked his buddy on his ass, and humiliated him in front of his boss?"

The Syrian arched his eyebrows, surprised at my admission.

"You met with a man who wishes you dead?"

"Bet your ass. I don't want a price on my head. I put together that tête-à-tête to patch up our differences. The Dragons signed on because they don't like Ramos, either, thanks to you. These Koreans you have are Park's people. Listening to Park and Ramos go on is where I got the idea to buy them from you. You're not making any money off them. You let me have them cheap, we both make money."

Ghazi al-Diri stared at me. If he had spoken with people inside Sinaloa who knew why Ramos had met with Park, what he learned would give my version of events credibility.

I said, "Do your homework. Find someone who knows what Ramos and I discussed at our meeting."

The Syrian ran his hand over his head and along the length of his ponytail. It revealed his anxiety, which meant he believed me enough to weigh his desire for profit against the quality of his informant.

He said, "You would buy these workers if I sell?"

"Thirty. I need thirty to keep my buyer happy. But after this bullshit, I'm only going to pay you half as much as I would have."

His eyes narrowed.

"I have many buyers."

"So sell your *pollos* to them, and turn me the hell loose. I have to find thirty stiffs to lay off on my buyer."

The frown line between his eyes deepened, but then Orlato hurried back from the kitchen. Orlato was holding a phone, and looked even more frantic than before. They had a brief conversation in Spanish, but no one was speaking softly. Al-Diri spun around, and barked orders to Medina and his other men. They hurried away in different directions, shouting to each other.

Al-Diri abruptly turned back to me.

"I will look into this further, and decide whether you can be trusted. Now, we must leave. The *pollos* have to be moved."

"Fine. Call when you figure out what you want to do, but don't wait too long."

The Syrian made a lizard's smile.

"There will be no call. You will be my guest until these matters are settled."

He snapped out a harsh string of commands to Medina, then swirled away. Medina and the big Anglo pulled me to my feet, shoved me toward the garage, and bagged my head again.

Twenty-five minutes later, the bag came off, and they led me from a different garage into a different kitchen where a nervous Indian woman with a red *bindi* on her forehead stirred a pot of soup. It smelled of turnips.

They put me on the floor in the living room, and Medina told a man with a badly fixed cleft lip the Syrian would come for me later. He told the man to take special care of me. He said the Syrian was looking forward to killing me.

Then he showed the rancid teeth, and he and the Anglo left.

The guards went about their business. None of them bothered me. Fifteen or twenty minutes later, the Indian woman brought a paper cup of water, and held it to my lips. Her eyes were large, and wet, and frightened.

She whispered as I drank.

"Only four of us are left. They are killing us."

"I know. I'm sorry."

"Can you help me?"

"I'm sorry."

She let me finish the water, then returned to the kitchen. Tears ran down my face, and I felt as if my heart was broken. I wanted to help her. I wanted to help all of them. I wanted to help myself, but feared all help was lost.

PART 4

Riverside County Jail
Indio, California
Hermano Pinetta

37.

Two Riverside County Deputies led Hermano Pinetta from his cell to a small interview room in the Riverside County Jail. Hermano, who currently wore a blue Riverside County jumpsuit, was a forty-four-year-old two-strike felon looking at serious time if convicted of charges stemming from his most recent arrest.

Hermano's attorney was in the hall outside the door. Oscar Castaneda was a nervous middle-aged man with long hair he constantly pushed from his face, and eyes that flitted like nervous moths.

Oscar glanced at the lead deputy as if he was embarrassed to make eye contact.

"One second, please?"

The guards stopped to let Oscar have his second, so Oscar stepped close and lowered his voice.

"They gonna ask you about a car. You gonna get one chance here. You wanna go home in this life, you answer this lady's questions."

"What lady? What you talkin' about?"

The deputy tugged Hermano's arm before Oscar could answer, and pulled Hermano into the room. Hermano had been in this same interview room three times since his arrest, but never with more than a couple of local detectives he knew by their first names. Now, the little room was

crowded with humorless men in suits who watched him with hungry eyes.
The lone woman sat at the interview table with the men surrounding her like
a chorus of angels. Her hands rested on a manila envelope, with her fingers
laced.

The deputies pushed Hermano down onto a chair opposite the woman,
then hooked his handcuffs to a steel rod bolted to the table.

She said, "Hermano Pinetta."

"Yes, ma'am."

"You were arrested and booked for running a chop shop and receiving
stolen property, to wit, twenty-seven counts re various stolen autos and auto
parts. These are state crimes. You are not currently charged with any federal
crimes. Do you understand the difference?"

Oscar leaned down, and whispered in Hermano's ear.

"Say yes."

Hermano said, "Yes, ma'am."

"The charges against you will be prosecuted by the Riverside County
prosecutor's office. These charges are what we call 'wobblers,' meaning Riverside has discretion to prosecute them as felonies, misdemeanors, or not at
all. Do you understand what this means?"

Oscar whispered again.

"They ding you for a felony, that's your third strike, and you on the farm
the rest of your life. Tell her you understand."

"Yes, ma'am."

"My name is Nancie Stendahl. I'm an Assistant Deputy Director of the
Bureau of Alcohol, Tobacco, and Firearms. From Washington. Would you
like my help with Riverside?"

Hermano felt sick. He glanced at Oscar, whose eyes danced and spiraled
like dying fireflies.

"Yes, ma'am. We would definitely appreciate your help."

The woman opened the envelope, took out a picture, and put it on the
table so Hermano could see it. The picture showed a couple of skinny white
kids standing beside a silver Mustang.

"Parts of this vehicle were found at your place of business. Do you recognize this car?"

"No."

The woman and everyone else in the room simply waited, and Oscar once more appeared in his ear.

"Tell the truth, you stupid motherfucker."

Hermano cleared his throat.

"Yeah, I seen that car. Sure."

The woman leaned forward.

"Where did you get it?"

Hermano hesitated, but Oscar's voice floated in his ear again.

"You give this lady a name, or there ain't no one on this earth gonna help your sorrowful ass."

Hermano said, "My cousin, Luis. Luis Pinetta."

The woman smiled for the first time, but it was not a pleasant smile.

JOE PIKE:
one day after
Elvis Cole is taken

38.

When Pike realized Washington and Pinetta would return for their personal belongings, he shoved Haddad toward the door.

"Move. Out now, Jon. Move."

They pulled out of the house where the Indians were murdered as fast as they entered, Stone pushing Haddad face-first into the Jeep's back seat, Pike gunning the Jeep out and away, clearing the scene before Washington and Pinetta returned. The garage door was still lowering when they parked behind a Dodge pickup less than one block away, the Jeep's engine ticking.

Pike edged down behind the wheel, but saw neither Stone nor Haddad in the mirror.

"Is he down?"

Behind him, Stone's voice came from the darkness.

"He's so down the next stop is a fuckin' grave."

Everything changed when they left Orlato and Ruiz in the desert. Orlato, Haddad, and Ruiz had been sent to dump bodies, but had not returned or called. The Syrian might send someone to see if the Escalade had broken down in the desert, but Pike thought it more likely the Syrian would assume his men had been arrested, and everything they knew would be shared with the police. He would send Washington and Pinetta to clean the house of evidence as quickly as possible.

Stone said, "We're not grabbing these guys, right? We're going to follow them?"

"Yes."

"Groovy."

Jon Stone said nothing more, and neither did Pike.

Pike's cell phone buzzed eighteen minutes later. He glanced at the call screen, and saw the caller was a man who managed a gun shop Pike owned.

"Yes?"

Ronnie said, "Hey, man. Thought you should know. The ATF came around today."

"Okay."

Pike thought nothing of it. His gun shop was licensed by the government to sell firearms. An agent from the Bureau of Alcohol, Tobacco, and Firearms dropped by once a year to check their paperwork and ask questions. *Pro forma.*

"They weren't here about the shop. Said they've been trying to reach Elvis, and thought you might know where he is. Asked you to call, and left a card."

"Why are they looking for Elvis?"

"They want to ask him about an old client or something."

Ronnie was still speaking when Jon Stone touched Pike's shoulder, and Pike cut Ronnie off.

"Gotta go."

Pike put away his phone as a dark Toyota SUV approached the murder house from the far end of the street.

Stone pulled Haddad upright. When the Toyota turned into the drive, the passenger window was down, revealing an African-American male with jerry-curl hair.

Haddad said, "This is Washington. Pinetta is driving."

The garage swallowed the Toyota, then closed.

Pike said, "These two always break down the houses?"

"Yes. They prepare the houses before, and clean the houses after. Every-one has their job."

Pike remembered the heavy plywood screwed over the windows, and how the screw holes left in the Mecca house had been filled with putty.

"They take down the plywood, too?"

"Yes."

Stone said, "What's your job?"

"Pardon?"

"Everyone has a job. What's yours?"

"To speak with people from my part of the world. We take *pollos* who have no other language."

Stone said, "So your job is to fuck over your own people."

Haddad was silent.

Pike glanced at the rearview, but saw neither man. He was thinking about the houses.

"You use a different house for each group of *pollos*?"

"Yes. Sometimes more than one if we have to change."

Stone said, "That's a lot of fucking houses. Where do you get them?"

"I do not know. Orlato, he gives us the address, we go."

They were still talking when the garage opened, and the Toyota backed out. Pike checked the time. Washington and Pinetta had been inside the house for only sixteen minutes.

Stone said, "Look at this shit. They sure as hell didn't clean very much."

Haddad shrugged, and appeared confused.

"I cannot know. They may need something. They may be going to the desert to look for us. Orlato would have spoken with the Syrian by now. The Syrian must know something is not right."

Pike waited until the Toyota turned the corner, then followed them south through the late-night traffic of Coachella to Mecca, and on to the empty darkness of the irrigated farmland west of the Salton Sea. Traffic thinned until Pike realized his headlights were the only headlights in the Toyota's mirror, so he dropped farther back and turned off the Jeep's lights.

They reached a small area of feed stores, gas stations, and local businesses, and then the Toyota's brakes flared, and it pulled into a small parking lot surrounding a bar.

Pike shot past the bar, turned hard, and wheeled around to park on the opposite side. Pike was out before the Jeep stopped rocking.

"You drive. Be ready to go."

"Always."

Pike entered through a side door, and went to a pay phone.

The bar was brightly lit, with maybe ten people spread between the bar and a few shabby tables. Pinetta was at the bar, but Washington had stayed in their car. Pinetta and the bartender were talking like they knew each other. The bartender slipped a bottle of Crown Royal into a brown bag, put it on the bar, and Pinetta paid. Then Pinetta tucked the bag under his arm like a football, and smiled his way out the front door.

Pike hurried out the side, where Stone picked him up on the roll. The Toyota cruised past five seconds later. Stone gave it another five, and nosed out onto the road.

"What happened?"

"He bought booze."

"Booze?"

"Crown Royal."

The Toyota led them into a mixed residential area of small homes and apartments, where Stone was forced to turn off the lights.

Haddad said, "This may be where Pinetta lives. I hear him say he has a woman on the west shore of the lake."

Stone glanced in the mirror.

"Are you fucking kidding me?"

"Why would I kid about such thing?"

The Toyota was four long blocks ahead when its brake lights flashed again, and it turned into the poorly lit parking lot of a small, two-story apartment building. Stone immediately pulled off the street into a building's shadow.

The Toyota parked at the base of the stairs. The interior light came on as Pinetta got out, then went off when he closed the door. Washington remained in the vehicle.

Jon groaned.

"Are you kidding me? We're following this asshole all over the desert for a fuckin' conjugal visit?"

Pinetta and his Crown Royal were halfway up the stairs when blue flashers exploded from behind a building one block ahead of them. The radio car jumped out of nowhere, and roared toward the Toyota as more blue flashers converged from every possible direction. Pike knew this was a major tactical event, and they were in trouble.

"Back out, Jon. Slow. No lights."

"I'm backing."

The units screeched into the parking lot and blocked the Toyota as an amplified voice identified them as the police.

Pinetta was caught on the stairs. He dropped the bottle and froze, hands open and away from his body, but something bright flashed twice inside the Toyota, and Stone muttered a single word.

"Loser."

Flashes and loud cracks erupted from the surrounding radio cars, speckling the Toyota's windows and fenders like furious hammers. Washington's pistol flashed twice more, then three fast times—flashflashflash—but the officers' fire pocked the Toyota until the amplified voice ordered a cease-fire.

As the firing stopped, Pike saw an oversized white SUV on the far side of the parking lot, only this SUV wasn't an ordinary police vehicle. The blue lettering and insignia on the side were difficult to see in the dim light, but visible. ATF. SPECIAL RESPONSE TEAM. The Special Response Team was the ATF version of SWAT.

"Jon. See the van?"

"I did. The big boys came to play."

They were creeping backward across the dark yards and had almost reached the cross street when the rear of the Jeep was suddenly splashed with white light. A siren whooped, and more flashing radio cars cut off the street behind them.

They were trapped. When the officers saw Haddad and Stone's M4, their search for Cole would end.

Pike said, "On foot. We gotta jam it on foot."

"I hear you."

Stone cut a hard tight turn going backward, then dropped the tranny into drive, and hit the gas hard, digging with all four tires toward the narrow space between the two nearest houses.

Pike braced.

"Too narrow."

Stone said, "Just right."

Jon Stone jerked the emergency brake to lock the back wheels, and spun the Jeep broadside between the two houses, blocking the way with Pike's door toward the darkness.

Stone said, "Get him. I got this covered. Go!"

Jon Stone did not look back. He popped the driver's side door and stepped out with his hands high to face the oncoming police, shouting for them not to shoot, giving himself to them to cover Pike's escape.

Pike slipped out the door and ran into the darkness between the houses.

39.

Pike hurdled rattling chain-link fences between inky backyards and vaulted cinder-block walls in the deep black shadows between houses. Twice he cleared fences with dogs at his heels, and once a free-roaming pit bull chased him across an empty street. Pike turned into its charge, and slapped the pit hard on its snout with his .357. The dog broke off its chase, and Pike ran on, pumping fast toward the lake and away from the highway.

He stopped twice to listen, but heard no pursuit. The police sounds were lost. No shots had been fired, so Jon was okay.

Pike turned south at the lake, and ran another half mile before looping back to the highway. A truck driver wired on Ritalin gave him a lift north, and thirty-eight minutes after the police raid exploded around him, Pike reached the Palm Springs airport, used the valet key he carried, and climbed into Stone's Rover.

Breathe.

Pike closed his eyes, and filled his lungs, then pushed with his diaphragm. He breathed deep again. Pranayamic breathing from the hatha yoga. Pike lost himself in a cool forest glade, dappled by sunlight filtered through lime green leaves. When he breathed, he smelled moss and sumac. His pulse slowed. He grew calm. He centered.

Pike started the Rover, then realized he didn't know what to do, so he shut down the engine. His instincts told him to push forward, but Haddad, Washington, and Pinetta were gone. Jon was now gone. Cole and the two kids were still missing, the police were involved, and when Ghazi al-Diri learned Pinetta was arrested he would be off balance and fearful.

This was good. The Syrian would be flooded with incoming information, but never enough to answer his questions. He would freeze in place, scramble for answers, and work himself into a panic. Panic was good when the other guy panicked.

Pike focused on what he knew. The ATF visited his gun shop looking for Elvis Cole, and now a major tactical event involving the ATF had taken out Pinetta and Washington. Pike had no idea how the two events were connected, but the ATF was a small, elite agency. They didn't have the manpower to flood an area with agents, so Pike believed this was not a coincidence. He took out his phone, and called Ronnie back.

"When did the ATF come in?"

"This morning. A little before eleven."

"What did they say?"

"Just the stuff about asking Elvis about an old client. Was that bullshit?"

"Yes."

"They told me he wasn't in trouble. They told me to pass it on in case that's why he hasn't returned their calls."

Pike found this interesting, and wondered how many times they had called, and how long they had been trying to reach Cole.

"And me?"

"They were hoping you could tell them where he was. That's all they said about you."

"One agent or two?"

"Two."

"They left a card."

"I got it right here. Special Agent Jason Kaufman, L.A. Field Division over in Glendale."

"Number."

Pike copied the name and number, then phoned his own home in Culver City. Pike had an unlisted number, but found a message from an ATF agent who identified himself as Special Agent Kim Stanley Robinson. Robinson floated a story similar to Kaufman's, but not identical. Robinson wanted to speak with Cole regarding allegations made by a former client who was now in federal custody, and hoped Pike could help them reach Cole. Robinson left a number, too, but his number was in Washington. The time marker on the recording showed the message had been left sixteen minutes before Kaufman visited Pike's shop.

Pike phoned Elvis Cole's office next. He had no way to check Cole's home voice mail, but he knew the replay code for their office, and found two more ATF messages. The most recent was left yesterday morning by Agent Kaufman. The older message was left the day before by a woman who identified herself as Nancie Stendahl, with the ATF, and asked Mr. Cole to phone her as soon as possible. She left a D.C. number, but no other information.

Pike copied her contact info as he had the others, then put away his phone. The ATF wanted Cole badly enough to work from both Washington and L.A., and Pike was convinced it had to do with the Syrian, but he didn't see how knowing this helped him find Cole.

Pike focused on the three drop houses, including the house where the Indians were murdered. The number of houses the Syrian had access to bothered him, and so did the plywood. Pike understood sending men to remove DNA and forensic evidence, but taking the time to remove the plywood seemed needlessly risky. The longer a criminal stayed at a crime scene, the greater the odds he or she would be caught. The Syrian obviously felt the risk was necessary. Pike wondered if this had to do with the source of his houses.

Pike started the Rover and drove south to the Indio house.

The neighborhood was quiet with the lateness of the hour, and the house was dark. Its garage was a gaping black cavern with the door pushed down, but if anyone had come to gawk at the damage, they were no longer present.

Pike cruised past to see if someone was watching, then parked one street over and approached the house on foot from the rear. He checked the neighboring houses, yards, roofs, and vehicles. When he was confident no one was watching the house, he returned to the Rover, rounded the block again, and parked in front of the dog lady's home.

Her windows were lit, so Pike went to the door. This late, he knew she would be reluctant to open the door, so he took off his sunglasses to make himself less threatening, and brushed the dust from his jeans and sweatshirt.

The big German shepherd barked when Pike was halfway up the drive, and kept barking when the woman shouted at it to shut up. A pattern, like the tug-of-war when they walked.

Pike rang the bell, and the barking grew frenzied.

"Shut up! Would you please shut up! Jesus! What am I going to do with you?"

The location of her voice told him she was looking through the peephole.

"It's late. What do you want?"

"My name is Pike. I'd like to ask about the house next door."

"What? Jesus, would you shut the fuck up, I can't hear the man! I'm sorry, what about the house?"

Pike stepped away from the door, and waited. A few seconds later, the door cracked open, and the dog barked even louder.

The woman peered through the crack, hunched over because she held the dog's collar. The woman's eye was dark brown. The dog's eye was golden.

"I couldn't hear you. I'm sorry. She's very protective."

Pike studied the golden eye.

"She's scared. She'll quiet if you open the door."

"I'm not kidding. She bites."

"She's fine."

The woman opened the door enough for the shepherd's head to push through, but she didn't stop barking. She was a good-looking dog, with a black mask that lightened to gold between dark golden eyes. The woman now blocked the door with her hip so the dog couldn't escape, and shouted at her to shut up.

Pike said, "Good dog."

The dog lowered her ears and stopped barking.

Pike held his knuckles to her nose. She sniffed, then whined at him through the crack.

The woman said, "OhmiGod, I've never seen her like this."

"She's a good dog."

The woman opened the door, and came out holding the dog by its collar. The dog strained to get closer to Pike, and thumped its tail on the porch. The woman introduced herself.

"Joanie Fryman. Are you the police?"

"No, ma'am. I want to ask about this house."

"That's why I thought you were the cops. I called about that place."

"Today?"

"Four or five days ago. There's something going on over there. These cars come and go, but you never see anyone, and I thought I heard someone moaning."

She frowned at the house as if it was the most disgusting place on earth, then noticed the garage.

"Jesus, what happened to their garage?"

Pike said, "It looked deserted, so I knocked. You know the people who live there?"

"Just cars going in and out. It's a rental. Jesus, I hope they're gone."

"How long have they had it?"

"Only a couple of weeks. A family named Simmons lived there before. They were nice."

Joanie Fryman suddenly looked at him.

"Are you interested in renting it?"

"Maybe."

She flashed a bright smile.

"Maybe renters aren't so bad."

"Know the owner?"

"That's Mr. Castro, but he lives in Idaho. He uses a rental agent. I met her. I have her card in here—"

Joanie turned to go for the card, but the German shepherd dug in to stay with Pike.

"Jesus, dog, would you come?"

"Leave her with me."

Joanie Fryman rolled her eyes, and released the dog's collar. The dog scrambled to Pike, ears back, tail wagging as she licked and nuzzled his hands.

"OhmiGod, this is insane."

Joanie Fryman rolled her eyes even wider, and hurried into her home.

Pike squatted in front of the dog. He ran his fingers through the thick fur on her shoulders and neck, and scratched the sides of her head. She was a strong, powerful dog with all the right instincts, but no rules to guide her. A good dog needed rules, same as a man.

Pike studied the golden eyes. He had known K-9 handlers, when he was a Marine and an LAPD officer, who had killed men to protect their dogs, and he had seen those same tough men resign when they lost a dog, as if they had failed their partners and could not live with their grief.

Pike said, "Take care of her. Do your job."

Pike scratched the dog's ears until Joanie Fryman returned with a beige business card.

"This is her."

Pike looked at the card. Desert Gold Realty. Residential and Commercial Rentals. The realtor was Megan Orlato.

The corner of Pike's mouth twitched when he saw the name. Orlato. She would be Dennis Orlato's sister or wife or maybe his mother. Orlato supplied the Syrian's houses.

"I hope it's available. You'd make a nice addition to the neighborhood."

Pike thanked her, but wasn't sure what else to say. He let the dog lick his hand, then patted her head.

"They're war dogs. She would die for you."

Pike left Joanie Fryman with her dog and returned to the Rover. Desert Gold's office was in Palm Desert, not far away. Pike entered the address into the Rover's GPS, put on his sunglasses, and arrived ten minutes later.

40.

Jon Stone

Jon Stone sat quietly in a clean, bright interview room at the Riverside County Sheriff's Station in Indio. He was handcuffed to the table, but the detectives who hooked him up left without explanation, and also without asking questions. Stone found this interesting, and wondered if they had been directed to do so, and by whom.

Jon sat there alone for almost an hour before a businesslike woman with short brown hair came in. He smiled when he saw her. She wore a wrinkled black suit, and Jon thought she looked tired.

"How're you doing in here, Mr. Stone?"

"Fine, ma'am. How about you?"

Jon stood as best he could with the handcuffs, and she waved him down.

"Please sit. I've had better days, but I suspect you can say the same."

"Some better, some worse. It goes with the job."

She took the seat opposite him.

"And what would that job be?"

Jon gave her one of his brightest smiles.

"I'm a military consultant under contract to the United States government and certain multinational corporations approved by the United States to employ someone such as myself."

She smiled back, and arched her eyebrows as if he was a moron.

"For real?"

"Doesn't get realer."

She laced her fingers, and introduced herself. Nancie Stendahl. ATF. Assistant Deputy Director, out of Washington. Jon was impressed. She was obviously behind the Pinetta arrest, and now here she was in the interview room. Alone. This was interesting.

She cleared her throat, and made it even more interesting.

"Do you know of and are you associated with a man named Elvis Cole?"

That one caught him out of left field, but he answered without hesitation.

"Rings a bell. He sing?"

"I'm trying to find him."

"Wish I could help."

"Mr. Haddad says you're trying to find him, too."

"I don't know a Mr. Haddad."

"Do you know a man named Joe Pike?"

Jon gave her the smile that made him look like a cruising tiger shark.

"I'd like my attorney if we're going to talk. I asked the detectives to call him, but they said something rude."

Her face tightened with irritation for the first time.

"You gave them a Washington phone number and told them to call the Deputy Director of the National Security Agency."

"Yes, ma'am. He'll take your call if you use my name. Boy has me on speed-dial."

She completely ignored him, which impressed Jon even more. All that "right to an attorney" business went straight out the window.

"Mr. Haddad claims you and Mr. Pike murdered a man named Dennis Orlato and a Colombian citizen named Pedro Ruiz not far from here in the desert."

Jon made the shark smile grow wider.

"Sounds far-fetched. Live Scan kick back anything on my prints?"

Jon's fingerprints were digitally scanned when he was booked, and automatically submitted to the Department of Justice for a criminal history and identification check. Jon knew what his record would kick, and waited for her reaction.

"It did. You have no criminal history, and an interesting military record."

"Did it say 'interesting'?"

"It was blank except for a note instructing us to contact the Department of Defense for additional details."

"Huh. They do that sometimes. For people with special jobs, if you catch my drift."

Jon arched his eyebrows and smiled again.

"I know why they do it, Mr. Stone. Mr. Haddad also claims Mr. Pike shot Orlato in the head at point-blank range."

"Another far-fetched lie. See those green teeth? Drug addict."

"Where is Mr. Pike now?"

"No idea."

"Mr. Haddad says Mr. Pike was with you in the Jeep, and fled only seconds before you were arrested."

"I don't know what to tell you. You believe one lie, you'll believe them all."

She glanced down at her laced fingers, and Jon realized her fingers were laced because she was holding herself together. She looked up, and wet her lips.

"This isn't a lie. A woman named Nita Morales hired Mr. Cole to find her daughter, a girl named Krista Morales. She hired Mr. Cole because she thought Krista was eloping with a boy named Jack Berman. Jack Berman is my nephew."

Jon nodded one time, and it took all his training and discipline not to show more.

"Mr. Pike and Mr. Cole work together, and now we find you driving

Mr. Pike's Jeep with a bound man and a fully automatic M4 battle rifle. Do you see how these things link together?"

Jon Stone smiled, but this time he didn't look like a shark.

"Funny how lies can start to look like the truth, isn't it?"

"So you understand, I've been trying to find Mr. Cole to offer my help, but he hasn't returned my calls, and now he appears to be missing."

Stone nodded, and wondered how much she knew about her nephew's situation.

"It may be he can't return your calls."

"So you and Mr. Pike were trying to find him?"

"One of us still is."

"Okay, now here's something I need you to understand. My interest is in saving my nephew and any other people who have been abducted. I have the full force and authority of the United States government behind me. Help me use that power, Mr. Stone. Let me help you."

"I'm in jail."

"This is where you're going to stay. I'm going to find my nephew, but I can't have civilians riding around with illegal weapons, killing people."

"I understand."

"Will you help me?"

Stone knew she wouldn't like his answer, but he believed it with all his heart.

"Your nephew's best bet is already on the hunt. Let Mr. Pike do his thing."

"I can't do that."

"Ms. Stendahl, you can't stop him."

Stone gave her his very best killer smile.

"Now do your nephew a favor, and please call my attorney. I'm trying to make your life easier."

She left without a word. Jon watched her go, and knew she would be back.

41.

Joe Pike

Desert Gold Realty was a narrow storefront closer to Cathedral City than Palm Desert, wedged between a gift shop and a women's clothing store. The shops and offices were closed, which suited Pike because the surrounding streets were deserted.

The realty office had a glass front with color flyers of available properties taped to the glass. The flyers suggested Megan Orlato's primary business was vacation rentals for weekenders and snowbirds. The interior was dark. The only light came from a computer on a desk at the rear. A small round table with chairs for customers was up front, but there was only the one desk in back with posters above it, and a low filing cabinet behind it. Pike looked for the telltale red light from an alarm touch pad by the back door, but saw nothing.

Pike drove around to the parking area behind the office. The back door was the typical fireproof commercial door found everywhere, with a single commercial-grade deadbolt. He studied the lock, then drove to a Chevron station three blocks away to look through Stone's gear. He found an electric pick gun and tension wrenches. State-of-the-art lock-picking equipment.

When the Rover was gassed, Pike drove back to the office, cracked the lock, and opened the door. He expected an alarm, but when nothing happened he assumed the alarm was silent.

Pike had at least four minutes inside if the breach registered at a top private security firm. The duty monitor would run a system diagnostic to make sure the alarm hadn't been triggered by a malfunction, then phone the subscriber. If the subscriber could not be reached, the monitor would alert a mobile unit or the police, who would respond only after finishing their current call. Four minutes was the best-case response time, but Pike knew the real-world response times were much longer.

Pike turned on the lights. The posters he saw from the street were promotions for Desert Gold Realty. *Serving the Desert Communities for 13 GOLDen Years!*

Pike went directly to the file cabinets, and ignored the computer. Searching unfamiliar computer files could take forever, but the file cabinet contained only three drawers. The first drawer contained files with labels like *Visa, Amex, License & Fees, Utilities, Autos,* and *Medical.* Pike decided these were personal files, so he moved to the next drawer. The second drawer contained files alphabetized by street names and addresses. Pike quickly checked for the three addresses the Syrian used, but they were not among the files. He pulled two random folders to check the contents, and discovered signed leases. The files in the second drawer were of properties currently being rented.

The third drawer held a yellow box file labeled *Available Properties.* The three addresses the Syrian used were here. Each of the three folders contained a listing agreement between the property owners and Desert Gold Realty. Pike checked to see if the properties were owned by the same person, but saw the owners were different. All three also lived out of state, which meant they probably had no idea how their property was being used. Since the owners lived out of state, Desert Gold Realty was specified as the property manager. This meant Desert Gold oversaw maintenance, gardening, and repair for the absentee owners. This allowed the Orlatos to keep unwanted visitors away for the two or three weeks a property was used by the Syrian.

There were thirty or forty folders in the yellow file, including the three. This meant Cole was almost certainly in one of the remaining locations, and it would be a location with an absentee owner. Pike took the files, closed the drawer, and was turning to leave when he saw the picture.

A framed photograph stood on the desk showing a woman with Dennis Orlato. He wore a blue suit and she wore a tight, flowery dress. They were smiling, and posed with an array of white roses beneath a neon sign saying WEDDED BLISS CHAPEL LAS VEGAS. Megan Orlato wasn't his sister or mother. She was his wife.

Pike checked the time. He had been in the office four minutes and twenty seconds.

He looked at the picture. They weren't kids. Megan Orlato was younger than Dennis, but he appeared only a few years younger than he had when Pike shot him. The picture was taken no more than six or eight years ago, which meant the marriage was recent.

Megan Orlato was an attractive woman. She was taller than her husband, and slim, with high cheekbones, a long nose, and almond-shaped eyes. Looking at her now, Pike remembered something Orlato said before he died.

The Syrian will trade for me. I'm married to his sister.

Pike checked his watch again. Four minutes fifty seconds.

Pike hadn't believed it at the time, but now he wondered if it was true.

He glanced at the posters. Desert Gold Realty. Serving the Desert Communities for 13 GOLDen Years! Longer than her marriage to Dennis Orlato.

Pike turned to the first drawer, and took out the file labeled License & Fees. Copies of her real estate license and business license were the first two items in the file. The licenses dated from long before Dennis Orlato, and so did her name. Both had been issued to Maysan al-Diri.

Pike took out the files labeled Autos and Medical. The auto file contained receipts for repairs, two of which had been mailed to Megan Orlato at 2717 Croydon Avenue in Indio. The medical file contained insurance forms mailed to Megan Orlato at the same address. Megan Orlato's home.

The corner of Pike's mouth twitched for the second time that day. He had something better than a list of locations.

He had Ghazi al-Diri's sister.

THE DATE FARM

42.

Elvis Cole

Two men carried a body wrapped in thick plastic and duct tape to the garage. I watched from the floor with my wrists plasticuffed behind my back.

When they passed with the second body, I pushed to my feet and charged with my head down like a bull. Their faces were bright with surprise when they dropped the body. I hit the first man with a front kick to the center of his chest, then spun low into the second man with a come-around round-house sweep that cut off his legs, but by then the dude with the bad cleft lip shoulder-cocked me from behind.

I woke up back in my spot by the lamp, dreaming that Krista Morales was watching me through a peephole and laughing it up with the Syrian because I was such a lousy detective. I had found her for all of five minutes, and lost her in record time. Now I didn't know where she was or I was, or even if she was still alive. I tried to get up, but someone had cuffed my ankles.

The third body went out. The third body was small. The woman with the *bindi*. I tried to remember if I thanked her for the water. I couldn't re-member. Had I thanked her? Was her last memory of me one of rudeness?

Tears dripped off my nose. I looked down, and the tears were blood. I worked the Jiminy Nita Morales gave me out of my pocket, and wedged it under the lamp.

I said, "Bread crumbs."

Somewhere between Burger King and now, the Syrian's sleight-of-hand security system worked. Pike wasn't here. I never doubted, not once, he would find me. My task was to stay alive until it happened or I could escape on my own. The United States Army sent me to something called Ranger School. The Ranger motto was *sua sponte*. It meant *you're on your own, asshole.*

Okay.

Bring it.

We do not quit.

Four hours later, Washington and Pinetta clipped the ankle strap, bagged my head, and took me for another ride. Pavement changed to gravel, we slowed, entered another garage, and stopped. Only this time when Washington pulled off the hood, we were in a large, dirty room the size of six garages. A sliding door half the width of the wall had been pushed open so we could drive inside. Three SUVs and five off-road pickups with knobby tires were parked around us. Trucks like these had left skid marks and tracks at the crash site where they hunted down Sanchez.

I said, "What is this place?"

"Old date farm. This building here is where they used to box up the shit and load it onto trucks."

Rows of long-dead date palms were visible through the big door. The trunks were thick and tall, and plated with diamond-shaped scales. The sun was setting, and cast the trunks with coppery light. They would have been beautiful when they were topped with green fronds, but now the dead, topless trunks looked like forlorn totem poles. I wondered if Krista and Jack Berman were here, or if they had been taken somewhere else.

"Are these the new digs?"

"For you."

We passed from the packing shed into a building split between offices and a small commissary. Three guards were hooking up a gas range while two more rigged a power cable, and four others carried sheets of thick plywood. There were more guards here than in the earlier two houses, and none I recognized.

Washington and Pinetta guided me to a small office with a reinforced door. A bottle of water and yellow bucket were on the concrete floor, but nothing else.

Washington said, "Sleep tight. Don't let the snakebugs bite."

Pinetta laughed, and I turned to show my wrists.

"You want to cut these off so I can pee?"

"No."

They left and locked the door. I heard screw guns, saws, and hammers throughout the night, and sat on the dirty concrete but did not sleep. I managed to rub my pants down so I could pee, then rub them up again.

Late the next day, a hunched Latin guard with a big Adam's apple and an overweight Anglo skinhead with a Texas drawl opened the door.

I said, "Where's Washington and Pinetta? They were bringing Starbucks."

The skinhead said, "On your feet, dickhead."

Glib.

Ghazi al-Diri was waiting when they pulled me from the room, and didn't look happy.

I said, "How long does it take to check me out? This is getting ridiculous."

"The girl tells me this boy is worse. You have medical training?"

Everything shifted with his question. Ten seconds earlier, I had not known if I would see Krista Morales and Jack Berman again. Now they were here.

"I've handled injuries and health problems with my crews. You want me to look at the kid, I'll look at him. I can probably help."

They led me across the commissary and along a short hall into the next building. The skinhead was named Royce, and Royce liked to bitch. He and most of the other guards had arrived yesterday, and didn't like busting their asses all night to put up the plywood. He went on about it until the Syrian told him to shut up. Then he shut, and we passed more guards. Most carried shock prods and clubs, but some had short black shotguns and one had a Chinese Kalashnikov. They looked tense and anxious, and their silence and weapons made me wonder what the Syrian was expecting.

The next building was split down the center by a single long hall running the length of the building. Two doors were on each side of the hall with another door at the end, but the door at the end and the two far doors were now blocked with plywood. More guards lingered in the hall.

The gawky guard unlocked the door to our left, and let us into a long room that ran the length of the building. It had probably been used as a storage room or lunch room, but was now stripped to bare concrete, and its windows were covered with plywood. Men and women were seated along the walls and huddled in small groups across the floor. There were more prisoners now than at the earlier house. More Latins. More black people and Anglos. A handful who could have been Middle Eastern. Berman was lying against the wall, with Krista and a muscular young Asian man at either end of him. Krista stood when she saw us.

Al-Diri said, "Here. See what you believe. Is he close to death?"

I shrugged my shoulders to point out my wrists.

"The cuffs. I need my hands."

The Syrian motioned to Royce, who clipped off the plastic.

I went over, smiled at Krista, and knelt by Berman's head. Krista stared at me as if she was trying to figure me out.

I smiled like the friendly family doctor because al-Diri and his men were watching, and spoke loud enough for them to hear.

"How's he doing?"

This time when she spoke she remembered her accent.

"Not too well, I think, but maybe the same? His eyes, they move but do not see. He says the crazy things."

Berman looked better. He was less pale, and his skin wasn't clammy. When I touched his head, he looked at me. His eyes seemed vacant, but more or less focused, and the pupils matched in size. I'd seen baseball players, army buddies, and guys at the gym look worse. I had looked worse myself more than once. I held Krista's eye for a moment.

"Yeah. I see what you mean."

I checked for a fever, peeled up his eyelids, and felt his head for injuries. He had three large contusions behind his right ear, and winced when I touched them.

I got up, and went to al-Diri as if I didn't want to speak in front of the girl.

"He has a bad concussion for sure, but I've seen worse. I didn't find a break, but the one thing I can't tell is whether he's bleeding. If the pressure is building on his brain, he's screwed. If not, he should be okay in a few days if you keep him iced."

The frown line notched his forehead.

"Iced?"

"Yeah. Ice his head. Reduces the swelling, and might even stop the bleeding. You have ice here?"

"Yes. We have power."

I'd seen his men working on the commissary power when they'd brought me here.

"Get some towels and ice, and I'll show you. We also have to get some water in him. You let him dehydrate, he's gone. He'll be fine if you make him drink."

Al-Diri told the gawky guard with the Adam's apple to get what I asked for, and the guard hurried away.

Something buzzed, and al-Diri pulled a phone from his pocket and moved away. He cupped the phone, and gestured to Royce.

"Find Medina."

When Royce left, I squatted by Berman and whispered to Krista.

"Don't react to anything I say. My name is Elvis Cole. I'm working for your mother. I'm going to get you out of here."

She showed no reaction except to wet her lips. She glanced past me to check the guards before she spoke.

"Now?"

"Soon. Someone on the outside is coming to help, but we'll go whenever we get a chance."

I looked at the Asian kid.

"Kwan Min Park. Your grandfather and cousin are helping me."

A tiny smile cracked his features. Kwan Min Park was being smuggled into the United States because he was wanted for seven murders in South Korea.

"We leave. Soon."

I glanced back at Krista, then Jack.

"He's hurt, but he's coming around. What happened?"

Kwan said, "Teeth."

He bared his teeth in a horrible grimace.

Krista said, "Medina. The guard with broken teeth. He was hurting me."

She stopped, and stared at me as if that was all she wanted to say.

"I understand. Are you okay?"

"So far. He keeps looking at me."

I glanced across the crowded room. Medina wasn't with us, but the large room was thick with nervous prisoners and roving guards. A group of Koreans huddled in a far corner, but no more than a dozen. I looked at Kwan.

"Where's the rest of your group?"

"Some here, some other room. Like before."

Krista said, "There's another room like this across the hall. They split us, half on this side, half on the other."

"There must be a hundred people in here. That's two hundred people."

"They brought us last night, our group and two others. I overheard this guard, he said one of the groups is from Russia. They have almost thirty Russian people across the hall."

It was insane. Two hundred people of little or no means who had been kidnapped, imprisoned, and were now being ransomed to their equally poor families and miserly employers for as little as a few hundred dollars each to maybe a few thousand. Locano was right. The Syrian's ugly business was based on quantity. If he collected one to two thousand each for two hundred *pollos*, he would see two hundred to four hundred thousand dollars for the people around me. If he stole two hundred people ten times a year, he saw two million to four million dollars.

I wondered why al-Diri brought the three groups to a single location, and why all three at once.

"Did the guard say why they brought you here?"

"Some guards disappeared. They just vanished or something, and now everyone thinks they were arrested. I guess they're worried their friends will tell the police where we were, so they moved us."

"A crew of guards? Like the men guarding you?"

"Yeah. Gone."

Pike. Something or someone was putting pressure on the Syrian, and I knew that someone was Pike.

I checked the Syrian again. He was still on the phone, but now Medina and Royce were with him, and the Syrian looked angry.

Kwan said, "You have gun?"

I tapped my head.

"My mind is my weapon, Jedi."

Kwan studied me for a moment, then turned away.

Krista leaned close to whisper.

"I have a knife. Jack found it at the other house."

She reached toward her waist as if to show me, but I stopped her.

"Keep it. If you need it, use it. I'm going to get you out of here."

"What if your friend can't find us?"

"He will. There are people who won't let you down."

The gawky guard with the Adam's apple returned with a pot of ice and a threadbare towel. Krista warned me he was coming, and told me he looked like a praying mantis. The name made me smile.

When he gave me the ice, the sharp-cornered outline of a pistol bulged in his right front pocket. This made me smile even more.

I wrapped ice in the towel and wedged it against Berman's head. The Syrian shouted at someone in the hall. I liked it that he was angry. I thought about Pike again, and knew he was hunting.

Royce and the Praying Mantis came back a few minutes later, cuffed my wrists, and took me back to my room. I bumped Royce several times to check his pockets, and decided he carried no gun. I didn't mind. The Mantis's gun was with us, and would be easy to take.

They did not let me leave my room again until my third day at the date farm. I did not see Ghazi al-Diri again until that third day. I did not see Royce and the Praying Mantis again until the third day, which was the day I took the Mantis's gun and killed them.

Joe Pike was hunting.

I would hunt, too.

43.

Joe Pike

He was parked on the sand a mile north of Coachella, watching distant headlights slide along an invisible freeway across an invisible horizon when Megan Orlato woke. Took a second for her head to clear, then she felt the tape and binds, and stiffened as if she were being electrocuted. She fought and twisted against the binds and tried to scream through the tape. Her eyes were crazy-wide with fear, and should have been. Fear was right and proper. Fear was correct.

Megan Orlato was laid across the back seat. Her wrists, arms, ankles, and knees were secured with plasticuffs. Duct tape sealed her mouth. Pike was behind the wheel, turned to see her, his right arm hooked around the headrest, calm and relaxed. They were alone. Nothing moved except for the distant headlights.

Pike tried to recall how long since he last slept, but couldn't. Didn't matter. You sacrificed what needed to be sacrificed.

Pike stared at her until she quieted. He watched her watch him, and listened to her breathe. Her breathing was loud and ragged, but finally slowed.

"Your name is Maysan al-Diri. You are Ghazi al-Diri's sister. You and Dennis Orlato supply drop houses to your brother."

He moved for the first time to lift the yellow file box he took from her office.

"The houses where people were tortured and murdered are your listings. Properties for sale or rent, with out-of-state owners."

He leaned across the seat, and gently peeled off the tape.

She shouted for help, screamed and shrieked, and thrashed again. He simply watched until she was winded. Then she finally spoke.

"I was in the kitchen—"

"Now you're not."

She was stirring honey into hot tea. She had not heard him enter. Did not hear him approach. She never knew he compressed her carotid artery, cut off the oxygen to her brain, and put her to sleep. She had not seen him until this moment when she opened her eyes, there in the moonlit desert.

"Dennis is dead. I shot him here."

Pike touched the center of his right eyebrow.

"Ruiz and Washington are dead. Pinetta and Khalil Haddad are with the police."

She was breathing hard again.

"Who are you?"

"Where is Ghazi?"

She breathed harder, so Pike touched the files.

"Twenty-two have out-of-state owners, so Ghazi will be at one of them. The time you save me is worth your life."

She didn't respond.

"If not, I'll leave you with Dennis. Ghazi is mine either way."

"Why do you want my brother?"

"He has my friend."

"Will you kill him?"

"If I have to, yes. And you. Where is he?"

She wet her lips, a secret gesture in the back seat shadows, betrayed by a glint of blue light on her tongue.

"The date farm. A commercial listing."

"Where?"

She told him. It wasn't far.

"Don't lie. If you're lying, you won't get a second chance."

"I'm not lying. He wanted a bigger place. I had the farm."

He followed her directions back to Coachella, then south and east into the desert again, well outside the city. The date farm was laid out in a perfect rectangle between paved streets, fifteen hundred feet on the long sides, seven hundred fifty on the width, split down the center by a road of crushed gravel, and crowded with rows of trees. The trees were dead and had long ago dropped their fronds. They reminded Pike of Marines frozen in permanent ranks. A large painted sign stood at the entrance: FOR SALE—READY FOR DEVELOPMENT—DESERT GOLD REALTY. He saw the outline of a building set well back on the gravel road, but nothing more. He saw no lights.

"He's here now?"

"I guess. I don't know. He asked for a bigger place, and this is what I had. I don't help him move."

Pike studied the building, and realized he was seeing two buildings. He wondered if Elvis Cole was inside one of them, and if Cole was still alive.

"How many buildings?"

"The property is twenty-eight acres, with five buildings, metal-and-wood construction covering fourteen thousand square feet of usable floor space. You have three septic tanks, and it's fully plumbed with county water."

Pike looked at her.

"I don't want to buy it."

"It was a farm. The buildings were used for processing and packaging dates. Two of the buildings were used for maintenance and equipment storage. One of the buildings has offices and a commissary for the staff."

"How many ways in?"

"Just the main entrance here. There was a gate on the west side, but the owners put in more trees."

Pike wondered at the size of the place. The three other addresses had all been small, single-family homes.

"Why bigger?"

"He thought Dennis and the others had been arrested. He wanted to get his crews out of the places Dennis and the others knew about."

"How many crews?"

"Three, I think. He was using three houses."

"Everyone came here?"

"This is the only new property I gave him."

Pike found a spot to park on an unpaved road north of the farm, put fresh tape over Megan Orlato's mouth, and slipped between the trees. The five buildings were grouped together in the center of the orchard almost five hundred feet from the street. Three were on the east side of the drive, and faced the two on the west. Glints of light showed from the east buildings, but not the west. Pike moved to the lights. He searched for sentries as he approached, but found none.

Pike studied the fronts of the buildings for several minutes, noting the doors and windows, then crept along the rear. Snoring and the occasional low voice came from the first building. A man spoke too loudly in the middle building, and two other men laughed. When Pike reached the end of the south building, he found several pickup trucks outfitted for off-road use parked outside a long sliding door, along with a large box truck. Pike wondered if this was the truck Sanchez used on the night Krista Morales was taken. Pike decided the prisoners were in the north building, the guards were housed in the center building, and the south building was being used as a garage. The garage was likely the only way in or out of the buildings.

Pike stood between the trucks and looked down the length of the gravel drive to the entrance. It was almost two football fields away. Only way in, only way out. Two football fields was a long way.

Pike worked his way back to the Rover, checked that Megan Orlato was secure, and considered his options. He could not see the building through the trees, but he knew where it was and stared at that place in the moonlit shadows. Three crews meant about eighteen armed men and an unknown but large number of innocents. The doors and windows would be reinforced. Pike would have to enter through the garage, fight his way through guard country to the last building, locate Cole and the kids, then fight through the guards a second time on the way out. He wondered again if Elvis Cole was inside.

He said, "I'm coming."

The odds didn't scare him, but better odds meant a better chance at success, and Pike believed he had a way to improve the odds. He glanced at Megan Orlato, then phoned to see if Jon Stone was still in jail.

44.

Jon Stone

Jon Stone walked out of the Riverside County Sheriff's Station beneath an overhead full moon at the beginning of its lazy slide to the west. Everything in Jon's possession at the time of his arrest had been returned with the exception of Khalil Haddad, who would remain a guest of the United States government. No loss.

Jon was miffed when Nancie Stendahl stomped out of the room because the folks in D.C. cut him free. At least the two young deps who processed him out had the good grace to be impressed he got to keep the M4. They asked if he was a spy.

Jon burst out laughing. Spy. Jesus.

Nancie Stendahl said, "You always laugh at yourself?"

"If you heard the crap in my head, you'd laugh, too."

Stendahl was leaning against Pike's Jeep, which had been released along with everything else. The parking lot was near empty, though he saw the big white ATF van on the far side.

Stone was pleased to see her. He sympathized with her personal involvement, and respected the all-in effort she was making to find her kid. Jon was big on all-in effort. He hoped she wouldn't ruin the moment by lecturing him about the rule of law. If she started with that crap, he was going to re-cite Dostoyevsky's *Crime and Punishment* in the original Russian to freak her out.

She didn't. She looked beat to hell, strained, and frayed at the edges. He wanted to buy her a cup of coffee, but he had things to do.

"Do you know where my boy is?"

"Nope. Know who has him, though. So does Haddad."

She perked up.

"Who?"

"Dude named Ghazi al-Diri. Haddad's boss. You have a pad, something to write with?"

He stowed the M4 in the back seat while she searched herself for paper, and put his pistols, ammo, GPS, and phones on the driver's seat. When he turned back, she was poised with a pen and a napkin. He rattled off a longi-tude and latitude, then checked her napkin to make sure she had it right.

"These coordinates bring you to a body dump. You'll find eleven or twelve people wrapped in plastic. Haddad probably murdered half of them. You'll find two stiffs who aren't in plastic. They murdered the rest."

"Who killed the stiffs?"

Jon ignored her question.

"Don't be misled by Haddad's agreeable manner. These are evil fucking people. You wanna walk while we talk? I want to look over this Jeep."

"Why are you telling me this?"

"You want to shut these guys down at the border. The more Haddad gives you on the Syrian, the more intelligence you'll have on how the cartels do their thing. Good intel is everything. I know that firsthand."

Stone gave the Jeep a quick walk-around with Stendahl for company. It had picked up a few dings. Pike wouldn't be happy.

"Ghazi al-Diri is the Syrian?"

"The Mexicans call him the Syrian. For all I know, he's from Bakersfield. You know what a *bajadore* is?"

She shook her head.

"He works the border, stealing whatever the cartels send up. Mostly, that's people trying to sneak in without documents."

"On the U.S. side?"

"Most of these guys work south, but a few are beginning to work north. It's easier to dodge the police up here than the cartels down there."

"Does he live here? Have family?"

"Maybe Haddad can tell you."

Stone checked the time. He wanted to call Pike.

"Good luck, Stendahl. I gotta go."

"Ghazi al-Diri has Elvis Cole. He has my nephew. We both want someone he has, so we should work together on this."

"Uh-uh. Won't happen your way."

"Jack is the closest thing I have to a child. He is my only living blood relative. You expect me to kick back, hoping someone else finds him?"

"Work your case. You might find him before us."

She put herself directly in front of him, and jabbed Stone in the chest.

"He's my blood. I promised my sister I'd find him. I swore at her grave I'd keep him safe."

"You're a sworn officer. It won't happen your way."

"Help me find him, goddamnit."

She jabbed him harder, and Stone stepped away.

"Listen—"

Stone looked at the silver-blue moon, then shook his head.

"When we find these people, if Cole's dead, they aren't walking out. There will be no court of law. No judge and jury. You're an Assistant Deputy Director of the ATF. This will not go down in any way you can live with."

"You don't have to do it like that."

Stone checked his watch. *Tempus fugit.*

"Gotta go. Wherever Jack is, you want him somewhere else. I have to go."

She looked like she was going to say something more, and she did, but only the one thing.

"Good luck."

Jon watched her cross the lot to a midsize sedan, then climbed into the Jeep and started the engine. He booted the sat phone and GPS. It took a moment for the phone to load and lock on a good satellite, but a light flashed green, and Jon was in business.

A message instantly loaded.

Jon hit the playback, and heard Pike's voice.

"Call."

Pike answered on the first ring, and Jon reported his status.

"I'm clear. You good?"

"I have Ghazi al-Diri's sister."

Stone laughed. He laughed so hard his eyes burned. Pike was a riot. Absolutely the best.

"I love it. That is so *perfect*, bro. What are you thinking, a head-up trade, the sister for Cole?"

"No trade. We offer a trade, we'll put al-Diri's focus on Cole, and he'll be harder to reach."

"Does she know where they are?"

"A date farm outside Coachella. I'm looking at it."

Pike described the farm and the intel he learned from the sister. Al-Diri had pulled three crews and three groups of *pollos* to a date farm when he learned Haddad and the two turds Stone and Pike dropped in the desert were missing. The farm amounted to a fortress crowded with the Syrian's soldiers.

"Is Elvis there?"

"Won't know until we get inside."

Stone considered the farm as Pike had described it. Delta was all about hostage rescue and snatching bad guys. Jon knew this stuff inside out.

"Fifteen to eighteen gunned-up guards jammed up with a hundred fifty–plus friendlies is asking for collateral damage. It also ups our time on target."

Time on target meant the time it would take to locate Cole and the kids once they entered the buildings, and get themselves out. The longer the time on target, the greater the risk. If you hung around long enough, you became part of the scenery.

Pike said, "How would you play it, no trade for Cole?"

"Trade for someone else. We have the sister, we use her. Give her to Sang Ki Park."

"When?"

"Now. Drive the play. Push it so fast this prick doesn't have time to think."

"I'm listening."

Jon Stone wheeled away, loving his plan so much he grinned from ear to ear. He was the best shit-hot troop at this stuff to ever grace the earth; none finer, none more deadly, *ever*! A man among men.

Nancie Stendahl

Stendahl sat in her rental until Jon Stone drove away, then walked briskly to the SRT van. She entered a world of muted red light through the rear door, and made her way past hanging gear to the electronics bay.

Mo Heedles said, "Hey, boss. Good work. We're looking good."

Mo was a large woman with short red hair, who hunched over a laptop computer. The computer was wired to the van's onboard cell booster to ensure a strong signal.

Stendahl stood behind her to see the laptop's screen, and watched a flashing black dot move away from the Sheriff's Station on a street map.

"What's our range on this?"

"Infinite? We bounce off cell towers. We can follow your boy no matter where he goes."

Nancie Stendahl took out her cell, and phoned Tony Nakamura in Washington. Late there, but he was used to it.

"Tone, Nancie. I need two SRT teams and a helicopter staged by oh-seven-hundred tomorrow. Anywhere in the Palm Springs–Coachella area."

"Got it."

"I'll advise when and where as I know."

"Rog."

Nancie put away her phone and watched the black dot. She didn't care where it was going; only that she was present when it arrived.

45.

Sang Ki Park
Wayward Palms Motel

Sang Ki Park followed the blond mercenary's directions that morning, and found himself at a faded roadside motel between Indio and Coachella. The two-and-a-half-hour drive went quickly, and was ripe with the promise of salvation and vengeance. A successful recovery of their kidnapped workers would go far in restoring his uncle's confidence. The recovery of the old man's grandson would ensure his redemption.

The mercenary's room was drab and dingy, but the surrounding desert was crisp with a lingering chill, and beautiful with a first kiss from the morning sun. Sang Ki Park felt honored to share in this moment. Especially with such a beautiful woman at his mercy.

"Are you comfortable?"

Megan Orlato said nothing until the blond man spoke Arabic.

"I'm fine, for Christ's sake. Let's get this the fuck over with."

The mouth of a whore. She was sister, wife, and participant with the men who had stolen, tortured, and murdered Park's workers.

Park, the woman, the crazy blond mercenary, and two Double Dragon soldiers were in the room. An additional twelve Double Dragon soldiers waited nearby in their cars. Park's uncle, Young Min Park, who was Kwan

Min Park's grandfather, was driving out now, but would likely not arrive until after Kwan was recovered. This was as it should be. As the revered leader of Ssang Yong Pa, Young Min Park must be shielded from physical danger and legal prosecution. But the old man, like all old men, was weak in his feelings and hungry for the sight of his grandson.

The blond man with the spiky hair checked his watch.

"You good to go?"

Park kept his eyes on the woman, seated in a tattered chair with his men near at hand. The two mercenaries who worked with Mr. Cole had captured the *bajadore*'s sister, and now wished to trade her for Park's stolen workers. The blond mercenary had explained this plan earlier that morning.

"Yes. I am good."

"You remember what to say, or you want to go over it again?"

"I am good."

"No negotiations. No delays."

"I am good."

The blond man turned to the woman, and spoke Arabic until she interrupted.

"Speak English. Jesus."

"I don't care what you say, but you have to say something. If you clam up, I'll make you."

"Fuck you."

The blond man dialed the phone. It was her cell taken from her home and delivered by Mr. Pike. It contained her brother's direct number, stored in the memory under "Bobby." Using this phone was important, for Ghazi al-Diri would only answer if he recognized her incoming number.

The blond man listened for the ring, then passed the phone to the woman.

She closed her eyes as if steeling herself, then spoke.

"It's me. I'm sorry, baby, they got me. No, this Korean dude. Some guy pulled me out of the house last night and gave me to this Korean. They killed Dennis. Dennis is dead—"

The blond man twisted the phone from her hand, and passed it to Park.

"Your sister is the property of Ssang Yong Pa. You have twenty-six of our people. We will have them back in this way."

Park told Ghazi al-Diri where the trade would take place, when, and how it would happen, exactly as the mercenary instructed. There was no room for discussion.

"Say yes, she will live. Say no, you will hear her die now on this phone. You will then kill my people, but this is a loss we can accept. We will hunt you forever."

Park listened for several moments, then repeated the instructions.

"You must say yes now."

He listened a moment longer.

"Very well. You must reimburse ten thousand American dollars for each of the three dead. Do not deviate from these instructions. Do not be late."

Park pressed the power button to terminate the call, and returned the phone to the mercenary.

"He has agreed."

The woman closed her eyes when she heard this and wilted in relief.

The mercenary went to the door.

"Do you need anything else?"

"No."

"If they don't show, don't kill her. We might have to use her again."

"They will come. I could hear much love in his voice."

The mercenary stared for a moment, then laughed very big as he left.

Sang Ki Park thought his joke funny, too, but masked his joy with a scowl. The mercenary had insisted Park carry out the plan as instructed, but the mercenary served his own goals, and Park served the goals of Ssang Yong Pa.

The plan would change as Ssang Yong Pa required.

46.

Joe Pike

Pike met Jon Stone to hand off Megan Orlato and swap vehicles. They circled the date farm once on foot to fine-tune their plan, then parted. The Koreans had reached Banning Pass by then, and Jon had to meet them.

Pike drove to a feed store that opened at four A.M. He used their restroom, bought a bottle of water, two bags of trail mix, and a bag of dried mango, then returned to the farm. He parked behind an abandoned irrigation truck in a field across from the mouth of the gravel drive, and ate the food as the sky slowly brightened.

He thought about Elvis Cole, and their friendship, and hoped Cole was inside and alive. He told himself Cole was alive. Pike took the Jiminy Cricket from his pocket. He looked at it. A toy cricket. Pike put it back in his pocket.

If Cole was dead, there would be hell to pay.

The day grew full-on light. Nothing stirred at the farm.

Pike's phone rang at 9:32 A.M. on a beautiful day in the desert.

Stone said, "He agreed. Go."

Pike left the Jeep, ran hard for the date farm, and disappeared into the trees.

Ghazi al-Diri

Ghazi al-Diri's life ended with the Korean's call. He was in the commissary when his phone buzzed, letting his coffee steep in a French press he brought from São Paulo. Now, he slipped the phone into his pocket, and poured the coffee. Several of his men were near, eating burritos of eggs and beans they had made for themselves. Ghazi moved away from them to think. He was angry, but might yet survive if he remained calm.

Maysan changed everything. The Korean gangsters had somehow learned she was his sister, and now held her like a *pollo*. Ghazi had no choice but to assume the gangsters now knew everything Maysan knew—his phone numbers, his home in Ensenada, how he had operated north of the border these past two years, and even his current location. This frightened him the most as they might even now be watching the farm.

Ghazi acted quickly. The trade for his sister required the box truck and many men, but much more needed to be done if he was to survive, and these things were unpleasant.

"Rojas! Where is Medina?"

"With the *pollos*. You want him?"

"Yes, both of you. In the garage."

Ghazi had more of the coffee as Rojas hurried away, then strolled to the garage. Ghazi had agreed to the exchange, but he would not make the trip. He would do everything possible to save his sister, and prayed the Korean gangster was good at his word, but Ghazi al-Diri did not believe he would see her again, and felt certain the exchange was a death sentence.

Rojas and Medina appeared almost at once. He straightened like the commander he was, and faced them.

"We are returning the Koreans. We need eight guards for the move, two for the big truck and the rest in the smaller trucks. They should be armed. Rojas, I want you on the big truck. You will be in charge."

Rojas looked surprised, but made no objection. They had been together a long time. Ghazi would hate to lose Rojas, but Samuel was the smarter and more capable. If recovering Maysan was possible, Rojas was more likely to succeed.

Rojas said, "Someone has bought them?"

"The gangsters have my sister. You will be exchanging the *pollos* for her. I have made the arrangements."

Al-Diri quickly outlined where and how the exchange would take place, told Rojas to pick his men, and move out as quickly as possible.

Rojas and Medina turned to leave, but al-Diri called after Medina.

"Medina, stay. I have something else."

Medina turned back and waited. Al-Diri took a moment to be clear his thinking was right. He was not losing only the Koreans. He had decided to abandon the date farm, and without his sister's access to properties, he had no place to keep them. He could not let them walk away, as they were witness to heinous crimes, so something had to be done.

Ghazi al-Diri was clear. He had made the only right and true decision.

"We will need another big truck. When Rojas is gone, we will leave this place. We have to get rid of the *pollos*."

Medina studied him for several seconds, then shrugged.

"There are always more *pollos*."

Vasco Medina was the right man for this job.

"You sure you don't want to wait for Rojas? It will save us the cost of a truck."

"We have no time to wait. We will meet Rojas elsewhere."

Medina grunted thoughtfully, then slowly smiled to show the ruined crocodile teeth. Medina understood. They would not wait for Rojas because Rojas and the truck would probably not return.

"Okay. I can get us a truck, no problem. Bigger, maybe. We're gonna have what, a hundred twenty, a hundred thirty?"

"Yes, something like that."

Medina grunted again.

"We could leave them here. That would be fastest."

Ghazi had considered this, but immediately discounted it. The date farm was connected to Maysan. Were so many bodies found here, the resulting investigation would eventually link her to Ghazi, and lead to his eventual identification.

"No, we cannot leave them."

"Okay. I know a place we can reach with the truck. I'll take care of it."

He started away, but stopped.

"What about the rich boy? Him, too?"

Ghazi had soured on the uncertain chance a widowed mother would pay. Rich people could be trouble, so al-Diri wanted to get rid of the boy with the others.

"Him, too. We have no time to waste."

"What about the asshole who's in with the Sinaloas? I hate that fuckin' asshole."

"Everyone. Get the truck and get them loaded. I want to get out of here."

"Can I take care of this how I want?"

Ghazi al-Diri cringed. Medina meant the killing. He was a man who would enjoy the killing. In Mexico, they did it with hammers.

"However you want, but not here. Wait till you get wherever you are going. Then you don't have to carry them."

Medina made the crocodile smile again, and Ghazi wondered why the man never fixed his teeth.

Ghazi al-Diri watched Medina walk away, then went to his car. He was driving a charcoal gray Lexus SUV Pinetta got cheap from one of his thieves. Pinetta would be difficult to replace; far more difficult than Ghazi's brother-in-law, whose only talent had been Maysan's love.

Ghazi lifted a short, black shotgun from behind the front seat. He did not trust these gangsters, and felt sure they would attack. He could feel them. Someone was hunting him.

Ghazi made sure the shotgun was loaded, then followed Medina inside. There was still much to be done before the killing began.

Kwan Min Park

Kwan was seated with Jack and Krista when Samuel Rojas and the other guards entered and went to his people. One of the guards lashed a man with his club to clear a path, and Rojas went to a girl named Sun Hee. Rojas used her as a translator because she spoke the best English.

Sun Hee jumped to her feet, listened to her master, then translated his words. Had she been male, Kwan would have hated her for cooperating and likely broken her neck. As a submissive female, he expected no less than her humiliating subservient behavior, but had sought to use it. He had instructed her to offer her sex to the guards so that she might steal a weapon, but so far she had failed.

As she spoke, the group traded glances, some smiling, and rose to their feet.

Jack said, "What's going on?"

Kwan looked at his friend.

"Not know. How you?"

Jack Berman closed his eyes and touched the back of his neck.

"Hurts like a sonofabitch. You know headache? I have a monster headache."

Kwan wasn't certain what "monster" meant, but knew it must be bad.

"You better. See good. Talk."

Krista smiled.

"Much better."

Sun Hee interrupted. She begged Kwan's forgiveness for daring to speak, and quickly explained as he watched his group straggle to the door. Kwan was surprised, but such a thing was expected.

Krista spoke as soon as Sun Hee hurried away.

Krista said, "Where are they going?"

"We go. Ssang Yong Pa make us free."

He saw the confusion in Krista's face.

"Family. Clan. Ssang Yong Pa my family."

Kwan studied his new friends, and felt mixed about leaving them. He gripped Jack Berman's arm.

"First night, guards beat, you try help. Kwan Min Park remember. Now, forever, we friends. My clan, much power. Kwan Min Park, much power. Great warrior. I kill many men."

Kwan read the fear in Krista's eyes before she interrupted.

"Kwan—"

The club crossed his back with a sharp explosion of pain. Kwan turned in time to see the club falling again, parried it to the inside, and stopped himself from punching the guard Krista called the Praying Mantis in the neck. Sun Hee was with him, as was the belligerent guard with the teeth, Medina.

Sun Hee was frantic.

"You must come. We go now. You must come."

Medina pushed the Mantis and Sun Hee aside, and grabbed Kwan's arm. Kwan let the man pull him to his feet, then shrugged off his hand. Kwan stood very close, nose to nose, eyes close. Medina grimaced almost as if growling and pushed his shock prod into Kwan's side. The sharp pop when it discharged was like being kicked, but Kwan did not react. The prod tortured his flesh, but Kwan smiled to show his defiance.

The Mantis and Sun Hee both pushed him toward the door, ending the moment, and Kwan glanced back at his friend Jack Berman.

"Kwan not forget. I help you, Jack Berman, as you try help me."

Kwan turned away, and allowed himself to be herded into line with the others. Outside in the hall, the remaining half of their group was being herded from the other room, and Medina disappeared.

Sun Hee, beside him, twittered like a wearisome bird.

"You should not antagonize them. He is very angry."

"His anger does not interest me. Be quiet."

"We are not yet free. You should be careful."

"He should be careful. When we are free, he will meet the true me."

Kwan pushed her ahead so he wouldn't have to listen.

They passed through the kitchen and into the garage. The big truck had been backed to the door, and was waiting for them. Kwan noted the guards here in the garage carried shotguns or military weapons, and appeared nervous. He wondered why.

The end of the line slowed as those in front climbed into the truck. Kwan Min Park was near the end. He was happy that he would soon see his grandfather and cousin, and wondered if they would be on hand to greet him. He would miss Korea, but taking his rightful place among Ssang Yong Pa in the great city of Los Angeles had long been a dream. He shuffled forward, moving closer to the truck and to his destiny.

Kwan wondered if he would see his friend Jack Berman again. He hoped so. He was imagining them drinking *soju* and singing at one of his grandfather's *Noraebang* studios, when some hard thing slammed into the back of his head.

The world sparkled.

Kwan felt himself fall, but had no power to stop. He opened his eyes almost at once, and realized he was on his back.

Medina grinned down at him.

Kwan felt a surge of fear, and tried to rise, but men held his arms and legs.

Medina raised a steel hammer high above his head, and brought the hammer down.

Kwan Min Park tried to turn away, but couldn't.

Joe Pike

Pike watched the six men slip past the box truck as they left the garage for the pickups. Two had AKs, and the rest had shotguns. They mounted up, two men each in three of the smaller trucks. Two more men came from the garage and climbed into the larger truck's cab.

Pike was pressed into the sandy soil at the base of a date palm forty yards away. He keyed his sat phone, and gave Jon Stone the description and license plate of each of the four vehicles.

Stone said, "Copy. Eight men out?"

"Eight."

"Helps."

Three minutes later a bronze Dodge pickup pulled away, followed by a silver Ford. The box truck rumbled after the Ford, and the last pickup fell in behind the box truck.

Pike whispered again.

"Leaving now."

As the trucks rolled toward him, Pike stared at the garage. Two men watched from the door, then moved back into the garage and disappeared into the shadows.

Pike didn't move as the trucks passed. He held his position until they reached the street, glanced back to see them turn, then spoke again.

"Going in."

Jon Stone said, "Other side, bro."

Pike moved deeper into the trees, and watched the garage as he ran from trunk to trunk to the building. He came out of the grove behind the garage, drew his pistol, and made his way to the door. He heard nothing, so he eased to the ground and peeked. Three SUVs and a pickup were parked inside, but he saw no one.

There was a door at the far end of the giant garage past the SUVs. Pike knew this would be the way in. He was making his way toward it when he saw a three-foot smear of fresh blood on the concrete as if something had been dragged. Then the smear stopped, and fresh drops and a line of blood as thin as a string trailed out of the garage. The drops were bright and filled with the color of fading life. Someone had died as they boarded the truck.

Pike jogged directly to the door, and checked the knob. Locked. He was reaching for his pick gun when the door suddenly opened.

An Anglo with large hands blinked at Pike, and an African-American man beside him frowned.

"Who are you?"

Pike shot the man with the large hands, and reset on his friend.

Pike spoke two words.

"Elvis Cole."

He stepped inside, and closed the door.

Elvis Cole

The guards were different that morning. They moved faster than usual past my little office-cell, and their voices were strained and clipped. Sometimes they argued. I heard muffled shouting and what might have been women screaming, and an engine revving, but I wasn't sure about any of it.

Royce and the Praying Mantis opened my door, and Royce told me to get on my feet. Even Royce looked different. Closed off, and grim.

"Get up, asshole. Let's go."

I turned sideways to show the cuffs when I stood.

"Cut these things. I have to pee."

"So piss yourself. C'mon."

He took my arm and pulled me past the commissary. The hall was crowded with guards and prisoners, who were being moved from one room to the other. Someone shouted in Spanish, and the guards pushed people more roughly than usual, and used their shock prods.

The Mantis pushed me into the room with Krista and Jack, which was now much more crowded.

"What's going on?"

Royce said, "You'll find out. Shut up and sit down."

They turned away, moving to other parts of the room. I saw Krista and Jack in their usual spot, and picked my way to them. Jack was awake and focused, and sitting upright.

I said, "Remember me?"

"Sure. Kinda."

"You look a lot better."

Krista leaned close as two guards moved past.

"Kwan and his group got to leave. They're going home."

I realized Kwan and the other Korean victims were missing.

"This morning?"

"Yeah, and now they're putting everyone from the other room into ours."

I thought about Sang Ki Park's adamant refusal to pay, and wondered why his people had been released. The guards who were shoving people into our room moved like men who were running out of time, and feeling the pressure. Pike was big on pressure, and might be working with Park. If Pike was close, everything could and would change in a heartbeat.

I edged closer to Krista, checked the area for guards, and turned so my back was to her.

"You have the knife?"

"Yes, like you said."

"Cut. They're tough, so cut hard."

She went to work with the knife. When she slowed, Jack edged closer to help, and a minute later the plastic gave. I kept my hands behind my back, and sat with my back to the wall.

The prisoners from the other room were soon in ours, and Ghazi al-Diri made an appearance. He stepped through the door with several guards, spoke briefly to Medina, and left. Even al-Diri carried a shotgun.

Medina then spoke with the guards, who spread through the crowd near the door, pulling people to their feet and pushing them into the hall. When people farther from the door began getting up, other guards rushed to push them down, but the closer people kept being pushed out.

Krista whispered.

"What are they doing?"

I suspected I knew, and hoped I was wrong. Al-Diri might be moving us to a more secure hiding place, but I flashed on Thomas Locano, telling me about mass graves in Mexico.

I nudged Jack.

"Can you walk?"

"Yeah. Sure."

Krista said, "He can't walk."

"I can walk."

We were watching the people closer to the door drain from the room when Medina, Royce, and the Mantis left the other guards, and came over. Royce had a shotgun slung over his shoulder, and the Mantis and Medina carried shock prods. The pistol was still in the Mantis's right front pocket.

Medina stopped so he was standing over Krista, and leered at her with the awful smile.

"We all goin' for a little ride, but you'll be more comfortable if you ride with me."

He bent to take her arm, and I saw his shirt was spattered with blood. Streaks and drips of blood marked his shirt with slaughterhouse designs, and more blood speckled his face.

I saw the blood as he pulled Krista to her feet. I saw the blood, and it didn't matter if Joe was here or help was at hand.

He pulled Krista to her feet, and I stood with her, and in that moment the sharp unmistakable sound of a gunshot echoed from the next building.

The room froze in that instant except for me and Medina. He pushed Krista away, and swung the shock prod down like a club. I stepped outside, rolled his arm between us, and hit him in the mouth with the first two knuckles of my right hand. He staggered back, but I had his arm, so I punched him again as Royce unslung the shotgun. I drove Medina backward into Royce, then stepped into the Mantis, hooked my elbow into his throat, and tore at his pocket for the gun. I was still in his pocket when Royce pushed Medina away, came up with the shotgun, and Krista Morales stabbed him in the shoulder. He squealed and swatted at the knife as if swatting a bee. The pocket tore away, I shot him twice in the chest, then shot the Mantis.

Medina was gone. Many of the guards had run to see what was happening, and now the sound of gunfire popped and pounded through the buildings. Some prisoners ran, others dropped to the floor, and still others curled into balls.

I grabbed Royce's shotgun, pulled Krista and Jack close, and shouted over the screaming.

"We'll be trapped if we stay. Can you walk?"

"I'll run."

I shot two guards, and we pushed our way into the crowd.

Sang Ki Park

Sang Ki Park felt benevolent toward the defeated foe before him. The man nodded respectfully, and introduced himself.

"My name is Samuel Rojas. We have your people here."

They were making the exchange at an abandoned quarry a few miles north of the Salton Sea. The man called Rojas gestured to the large truck behind him, from which people were already emerging. The men from the three smaller pickups were helping Park's people from the truck.

Park would inspect his people once they unloaded, then keep the truck to transport them.

Rojas said, "You have a lady for us?"

Sang Ki Park raised his hand. The woman stepped from the back seat of his BMW, but came no farther. She was not allowed to come farther.

Park appeared patient as the people he brought from Korea gathered in a small group, but he was not. In truth, he was looking for his cousin, and anxious to be done with this. His uncle was now waiting at the motel, and he did not wish his uncle to wait long. His uncle was not a patient man.

It did not take long to unload twenty-three people. Less than two minutes. Certainly no more than three.

Park frowned. Twenty-two people now milled in a group before him, and none were his cousin.

He was about to say something when two men carried a body from the truck, and placed it on the ground a few feet away.

Sang Ki Park stared at the crushed head of his cousin, Kwan Min Park.

He felt very tired, but at the same time filled with a rage so fierce it might drive the heart of a dragon.

Samuel Rojas said, "May we have the lady now?"

Park glanced at Samuel Rojas, then turned and walked to Megan Orlato. When he reached her, he drew a Sig Sauer pistol from beneath his jacket, and shot her in the head.

Fourteen Ssang Yong Pa soldiers then emerged from their hiding spots and opened up with automatic weapons, killing Samuel Rojas and the seven men who had come with him.

When the killing was done, Park had his twenty-two employees put back aboard the truck along with his cousin's body, and all of them drove away.

Nancie Stendahl

Eighteen hundred feet above the desert, and homing on Jon Stone's black dot, Nancie Stendahl adjusted the headset.

"Say again."

Mo said, "Fly heading two-zero-zero."

The pilot nudged the helicopter a few degrees to the west, bringing them farther out in the desert on a south by southwest course.

Nancie had four people along on the flight: the pilot and Mo with her

magic laptop in the front seats; Nancie, JT, and an SRT coordinator named
Stan Uhlman. The two SRT teams were staged twenty miles apart and await-
ing direction.

Mo's voice came through the headsets.

"Six miles."

Stan Uhlman said, "There's no roads down there. What's he driving?"

Nancie said, "Jeep. It's red."

Uhlman sounded doubtful.

"I don't know."

"Four miles. We should see him soon if he's here. He's stopped."

Mo grinned over her shoulder.

"What's your bet, boss? We got your boy?"

Nancie said, "You still have a read on the second signal?"

"Yes, ma'am, I do."

Nancie grinned back.

"Then if Mr. Stone found the bait transmitter and got cute with it, I'm
betting he didn't find the second, and that's where we'll find him."

JT pointed past the pilot.

"There's a road. I got a road."

Mo said, "One mile. Less than a mile."

Nancie peered over Mo's shoulder to see the little black dot on her laptop, then looked out the window. Out here in the middle of nowhere, the
map graphic provided no landmark to help orient the dot. All Nancie saw
was the dot.

Stan Uhlman said, "There. What's that, trucks?"

The pilot tipped the nose over, dropped down to four hundred feet, and
picked up speed.

JT said, "Oh my God."

Nancie said, "Closer."

The pilot tipped the chopper on its side, sank to two hundred feet, and
orbited the scene.

Uhlman said, "I make three pickup trucks and multiple bodies."

JT said, "Nine. I see eight adult male, one adult female. No Jeep. No red Jeep. Boss?"

"Roll the SRTs. Notify the sheriff's to secure the scene."

"What about us? You want to set down?"

Nancie peered at the bodies through her binoculars. None were Jack, and none were Jon Stone. None were moving, or showed signs of sustainable life.

Nancie said, "What's the heading for the second signal?"

"One-one-zero."

"Fly one-one-zero."

The pilot banked north, and flew toward Coachella.

Elvis Cole

The hall and the commissary were a chaos of running, hiding, crying people. The immigrant prisoners didn't understand what was happening or where to go, but the guards shared this same confusion, which likely saved us. They didn't know who was shooting, or why, and most assumed they were being invaded by the feds. At that point, they panicked like the prisoners and thought only of getting away. Only two guards tried to stop us, and both times I pulled the trigger first.

Jack tried hard, but was wobbly and slow. It was clear we needed a vehicle, so we pushed through the commissary toward the garage.

We crossed the commissary past the offices, and had turned toward the garage when Jack Berman fell. I bent to lift him, when Medina lurched from an adjoining hall with a shotgun. He smiled, but now his teeth were gone and his shredded mouth bloody.

He jerked the shotgun to his shoulder, and that's when Joe Pike stepped around the corner and shot him.

Medina dropped as limp as a string, but Pike shot him again, then dumped his empties, fed in a speed-loader, and finally looked at me.

Pike said, "Got you."

He wasn't talking to Medina.

I fought down the smile, and half-carried Jack toward the garage.

"Garage. Only way out."

Krista said, "Is this your friend?"

"Yes."

Pike led us past the last few offices into the garage. The guards had taken the cars, and the garage was empty.

"Wheels? This kid can't walk."

"Straight ahead and across the street."

Random gunfire came from the trees. I heard automatic-weapons fire behind us, and wondered if it was Jon Stone.

Pike and I carried Jack Berman between us. We jogged straight down the gravel drive as the gunfire lessened behind us, crossed the street, and made our way to Pike's Jeep where it was parked beside an old irrigation truck.

Jack said, "I can walk. I'm fine."

We ignored him.

Pike unlocked the Jeep. Krista opened the back door, and we pushed Jack inside.

"We have to get this kid to a hospital. Krista, you okay?"

"I'm fine."

I nodded at Pike.

"Let's get out of here before we get hung up with the police."

Pike closed the door, and Ghazi al-Diri stepped from behind the old truck. He carried a short black shotgun, and his ponytail had come untied. His hair hung loose at his shoulders.

I said, "Joe, this is Ghazi al-Diri, the Syrian."

He raised the shotgun.

"Put down the keys and walk away. I want the vehicle."

His men must have taken his car and left him with nothing.

Krista said, "Fuck you. We have to take my boyfriend to the hospital."

The Syrian jerked the gun to his shoulder, and shouted.

"Move or I kill you!"

A loud roar of automatic fire kicked up debris from the ground at his feet, and the shotgun spun lazily away.

Then the roar stopped, and Jon Stone ran up, put al-Diri facedown in the dirt, and parked a knee on his neck.

Stone nodded at me.

"You good?"

"I'm good."

"Where's the boy?"

"Jeep. We have to get him to a doctor."

Stone touched the M4's muzzle to the back of al-Diri's head.

"Go. This one's mine. See after Mr. Berman."

We did.

Nancie Stendahl

The black dot did not move. Nancie hoped this was a good sign. Stone was probably parked, and if Stone was close to Jack, this meant she was close to Jack.

Mo said, "Two miles, heading zero-eight-zero."

The five people on the helicopter looked in the same direction at the same time. Farms. Rectangles of green painted on the gray desert sand.

"One mile. Right in front of us."

The pilot tipped the nose and dropped to three hundred feet.

Stan Uhlman said, "Anyone sees a red Jeep, please raise your hand."

"Quarter mile. Three, two, one, we're on top of it."

JT said, "What is that, palm trees?"

Mo said, "It's a date farm. It looks deserted."

Nancie said, "Lower."

The pilot dropped to two hundred feet and made a slow pass. They saw no people or movement or life. They saw no bodies.

Mo said, "We're right on top of it. You see that building? It's parked in that building."

Nancie said, "I see five buildings. Which one?"

"On the end. First one in from the entrance."

Nancie said, "Land."

The pilot touched down on a flat area to the west of the orchard, and safely away from the trees. Nancie, Mo, JT, and Stan walked back together as the rotor spun down. The pilot stayed with her ship.

They were thirty yards from the building when Nancie's cell phone buzzed. She answered automatically.

"Nancie Stendahl."

"Keep walking."

"Who is this?"

"You know who! I'm too cute to forget."

She couldn't help herself.

"Jon Stone."

"Jack's safe."

Nancie stopped, causing Mo and Stan Uhlman to bump into her.

"Talk to me. Where is he?"

"He was delivered to the Coachella Regional Medical Center about an hour ago. Emergency room. Go see him when you finish here. Take him home."

Nancie looked at the building.

"What do you mean, finish here? What's here?"

"Present. You find my first present?"

"Did you kill those people?"

"No, ma'am, I did not. Keep walkin'."

"What the fuck do you think you're doing? Who killed those people?"

"Walk. I'll call back in a bit, fill in some blanks."

"How'd you get this number? This is my personal number."

"Go see. From me to you."

She lowered her phone and walked to the building, picking up speed, but stopped cold when she reached the door. A bound man was on the floor. His hands, arms, legs, and ankles were bound, and a strip of duct tape covered his mouth. He had long black hair bunched around his face, and he stared at her with angry eyes. She stared back, then slowly walked over.

"Are you Ghazi al-Diri?"

She pinched the corner of the tape and ripped it off.

"Are you Ghazi al-Diri?"

"Who are you?"

She smiled, and showed him her badge.

"I'm the person who's looking forward to speaking with you."

She pressed the tape back over his mouth, then went back to the others and phoned in additional SRT teams.

47.

Elvis Cole

The ER staff let Krista stay with Jack while they evaluated him. They told me it shouldn't take long, so I phoned Nita Morales from the waiting room while Pike looked on. I used his phone. The only person there besides us was an elderly woman who held rosary beads and stared into space.

I said, "She's safe. I'm bringing her home."

Nita was silent. I let her have those moments because they are personal and precious, and after a few seconds I heard the soft whispers of her crying.

"Thank you. I knew you—I knew you were—"

"Shh. It's okay. She's with me, and I'm bringing her home."

"I want to talk to her."

"I'll put her on, but I want to tell you where she's been and what she's been through. She's with Jack now, so I can speak freely."

A touch of frost brittled her voice. I could feel it from a hundred miles away.

"Did he get her into this?"

I softened my voice, and made it caring. I truly did understand where she was coming from.

"No, Nita, he didn't. She's with him now because we brought him to the

Coachella hospital. He's going to be okay, but he got hurt pretty bad trying to take care of her."

I told her everything I knew about what happened while Krista was held by Dennis Orlato's crew. I felt, and still do, that giving Nita the time to work through her fears would help later when she and Krista spoke.

Pike and I were still waiting twenty minutes later, so I asked a male nurse if Jack was still waiting to be seen. When the nurse told me the evaluation had finished fifteen minutes ago, I asked him to send Krista out.

She fidgeted when she saw me.

"They want him to see a doctor closer to home, but he's going to be fine. He called his aunt. I want to wait with him until she gets here."

"He can wait for his aunt by himself. I'm taking you home."

"I'm going to stay. He doesn't have anyone here. I think I should stay."

"We're going home. This isn't over until you're home."

I would have carried her if she refused, but she didn't. She didn't like leaving Jack, but she also wanted her mother.

The three of us said almost nothing as we drove back to L.A., but it was a clear and pretty day, and the traffic was light. Krista rode in back. She spoke quietly to her mother for a few minutes, but most of what I heard were yes or no answers. She had lived it, and was burned out now, and didn't have more to give. Sometimes it takes a few days. Sometimes, longer. She gave back Pike's phone and said nothing more until we entered the Banning Pass. The desert was behind us, and falling farther behind.

She said, "I just wanted to see."

"This wasn't your fault. The Syrian, Orlato, the people who did these horrible things—it was their fault. They did it. Not you."

A little while later, I heard her sniffle. I reached back, and held her hand.

When we reached the city, I phoned Nita to tell her we were five minutes away. Nita and twenty-five or thirty people were waiting outside when we arrived, and they were all wearing the T-shirt. *Elvis Cole Detective Agency. World's Greatest Detective.* They had spent the past two hours making the shirts.

Nita enveloped Krista and wouldn't let go, and cried so hard she shook. Farther back in the crowd, the big kid with the big shoulders I'd met on the first day called out.

"Magazine guy!"

He gave me a thumbs-up, beaming.

Nita grabbed onto me next, and wept even harder.

"God bless you. God bless you for this. I owe you everything. I owe you my life."

I hugged her back, as tight as I have ever hugged anyone, and then Pike drove me home. We took the Hollywood Freeway north to the Cahuenga Pass, then Mulholland along the crest to Laurel. I don't think we spoke ten words, which was normal for Pike but not for me. As with Krista, sometimes these things take time.

We drifted down Woodrow Wilson to my little street, rounded the last curve, and saw my home. I smiled when I saw it. I usually do.

We parked across the drive, and went through the carport to the kitchen door, which is how I always enter my home, but this time something was different. I studied the car.

"It's clean."

Pike touched the yellow skin.

"Needs wax."

"You washed it?"

"Rinsed it."

He frowned at his Jeep, and turned away. It had picked up some pits and dings in the desert, along with a heavy layer of dust.

I reached the door, and realized I didn't have my keys.

"No key."

Pike let us in.

My keys and cell phone and things were on the counter where he left them.

"You want a beer? Something to eat?"

"Water."

I got two waters from the fridge, and we drank them, leaning against the counters. My cat came in. He purred when he saw me, blinked at Pike, then rubbed against my leg.

I said, "Hey, bud."

He did a figure eight between my ankles, wandered over to Pike, and flopped onto the floor.

I took a breath. I had some of the water, and took another breath. I looked at Pike.

"Thank you."

He dug something from his pocket, and held it out.

"You dropped this."

I smiled at the little Jiminy, then put it on the counter. Nita told me she would take it back when I found her daughter, and I was going to hold her to it. Dreams really can come true.

I wanted to shower. I wanted to brush my teeth, and floss, and shave, and get out of clothes that smelled of blood and torture and death. I wanted to put the desert behind me, but some things are more important.

I gathered up the plastic mop bucket I keep in the laundry room, some dish soap and towels, and took them outside. Pike and the cat followed me.

I filled the bucket with soapy water, soaked a towel, and went to work washing Pike's Jeep. I rubbed hard to get rid of the desert. Pike picked up a towel and joined me. The cat crouched under my car and watched.

We washed away the dirt and dust, but the desert had put dings and pits in the paint that were part of the Jeep now, but that's as it should be. They would fill with wax over time, and eventually be lost in the shine.

That day would come with enough work and patience. Pike knew it, and I knew it, too.

We washed his old Jeep, and buffed its bright skin. We made the Jeep as right as we could, and everything with it.

ACKNOWLEDGMENTS

The Putnam production team went above and beyond to make this book happen. The author apologizes for jamming their time line, and thanks them for their herculean efforts on his behalf, most notably Meredith Dros.

Copyediting is an often thankless job done under difficult circumstances. Patricia Crais worked with a constantly changing manuscript, requiring her to revisit and revise her own work for far too many last-minute, sleepless nights. Thank you.

Neil Nyren and Ivan Held are the Thor and Odin of publishing. No publishers could have shown more courage, faith, and support. They are war dogs.

English-to-Arabic translations were provided by David Coronel. English-to-Korean translations were provided by Ashley An and Jae-Jin Kim. Thank you, all.

Thanks to Aaron Priest, as always, for having my back, and pushing me forward.